Praise for *Every Stolen Breath*

"A thrilling page turner, engaging and beautifully written, *Every Stolen Breath* will leave readers breathless until the end."

BRENDA DRAKE, *NEW YORK TIMES*
BESTSELLING AUTHOR OF *THIEF OF LIES*

"Brisk pace, unexpected twists, and touching romance—*Every Stolen Breath* checks all the boxes! Do not miss this highly entertaining tale!"

PINTIP DUNN, *NEW YORK TIMES* BESTSELLING AUTHOR
OF YA FICTION, 2018 RITA' WINNER BEST YOUNG ADULT
ROMANCE, 2016 RITA WINNER BEST FIRST BOOK

"In this impressive debut, Gabriel balances a high-adrenaline, high-stakes storyline with meaningful meditations on power and corruption, ego and greed, grief and guilt. Lia Finch is a complex, compelling hero whose courage and persistence will inspire readers everywhere."

JAMES KLISE, EDGAR AWARD-WINNING
AUTHOR OF *THE ART OF SECRETS*

"Fast-paced and taut, this book grabbed me from the very first scene and then didn't let go. With a fascinating protagonist, and high tension from the start, this was a thrilling read."

AMELIA BRUNSKILL, AUTHOR OF *THE WINDOW*

"A tense, atmospheric thriller that gripped me from page one. Lia's quest to bring her father's killers to justice is harrowing, heartbreaking, and ultimately hopeful. My heart is still racing."

RACHEL LYNN SOLOMON, AUTHOR OF
YOU'LL MISS ME WHEN I'M GONE

"Gabriel has crafted a thrilling narrative with twists and turns that left me gasping. As Lia struggles to maintain her grip on reality, it becomes impossible to know who to trust or anticipate what will happen next. *Every Stolen Breath* is a must-read for fans of YA thrillers."

KARA MCDOWELL, AUTHOR OF *JUST FOR CLICKS*

"In this extraordinary and suspenseful debut, Kimberly Gabriel has created the hero the world needs right now—Lia Finch is unwavering, tough as nails, whip-smart, and honest. Gabriel's fast-paced, tensely plotted novel will have readers holding their breath late into the night."

KURT DINAN, AUTHOR OF *DON'T GET CAUGHT*

"A terrifying premise set against Chicago's stunning backdrop, with a whip-smart protagonist and enough twists and turns to keep your heart racing to the very last page—Kimberly Gabriel's haunting debut will take your breath away."

DAWN IUS, AUTHOR OF *LIZZIE,*
OVERDRIVE, AND *ANNE & HENRY*

EVERY
STOLEN BREATH

KIMBERLY GABRIEL

BLINK®

BLINK

Every Stolen Breath
Copyright © 2019 by Kimberly Gabriel

Requests for information should be addressed to:
Blink, *3900 Sparks Dr. SE, Grand Rapids, Michigan 49546*

Hardcover ISBN 978-0-310-76666-7

Ebook ISBN 978-0-310-76715-2

Interior design: Denise Froehlich

Printed in the United States of America

19 20 21 22 23 / LSC / 10 9 8 7 6 5 4 3 2 1

For Marc
because we always have been
and always will be
better together

One of these tourists is about to die.

They flock to Navy Pier from places like Plainfield, Iowa and Hartville, Ohio, where I'm sure they lead normal lives. But here, they become hoarders of magnets and sweatshirts and shopping bags plastered with Chicago emblems. They eat Dots ice cream, take pictures of the new Lakefront mansions, and ignore the warnings about walking in groups fewer than four.

They're easy targets, all of them.

I pull my sweater sleeves over my palms and narrow in on a pudgy woman wearing pantyhose, tennis shoes, and monochrome blue. She's easily the adult version of Violet Beauregarde from *Willy Wonka* after Violet turned into a giant blueberry. The woman bends over and picks up a coin from the ground. As if it will bring her luck.

A lanky guy with red stubble and a designer trucker hat almost trips over her. He swerves at the last second, stumbling over his own feet before smoothing out his flannel shirt and resuming his jaunty swagger.

They're oblivious. It could be either of them, and they wouldn't see it coming.

Of course, the second I mark them as potential victims, I can't even blink without envisioning their beatings and how they begin. A fist in the back of the neck. An uppercut punch in the gut. The first hit comes out of nowhere—a seemingly random attack from a guy in the crowd. Then within seconds, dozens of teens appear, swarming the victim like a colony of flesh-eating ants—hitting and kicking to the death.

Just like they did to my dad.

A damp chill rustles through my hair as the wind skates off the lake behind me. My chest tightens, and I glance at my purse slumped beside me on the weathered bench slats. As tempted as I am to reach for my inhaler, today is not the day to show that kind of weakness. I pinch the bridge of my nose and remind myself to stay vigilant. Alert.

The day's too gray to see the whole half-mile stretch from where I'm sitting at the end of the pier. Even the lines of the Ferris wheel towering over the middle look blurred as they push through a heavy sky. Still, I don't see any reinforcement—police officers, a SWAT team.

You'd think a tweet with the date and coordinates of the next attack would alert them all. It's not like the code was hard to figure out. But when I called the city's Anonymous Tip Hotline, the operator dismissed me like I was some delusional kid flipping out over a random comment she'd found on the Internet. She assured me she'd pass my note along and reminded me the Death Mob era was behind us. Then she hung up before I could think of an articulate rebuttal, leaving me sitting there, mouth gaping like some taxidermized fish.

Even Detective Irving neglected to call me back—not that he actually proved his competency after my dad's death. Apparently, like all city officials, he'd rather sit behind his desk and adamantly deny that the Death Mob's Swarm has been lying dormant for the last two years, waiting for the right moment to reemerge.

By now, at the very least, this place should be littered with under- cover agents snapping their telephoto lenses at every potential perpetrator—something part of me knew would never happen. CPDs become predictable like that. And with their tendency to botch every- thing, maybe it's better I'm here alone, armed with an iPhone and the perfect opportunity to prove everyone wrong.

It wouldn't be the first time a high schooler had to jolt adults into action.

I check my phone's battery life. According to a witness, the first teen who hit my dad had two silver spikes pierced through his bottom lip. For attackers that operate on anonymity, the lead was rare. Not that Detective Irving thought so. He claimed it was hearsay. Said he needed tangible evidence. Pictures. Videos. Clear shots of their faces.

I scroll through the images I've already taken. Enough to rival any tourist. And while I haven't seen Lip Spikes, that doesn't mean there aren't others already here, blending in with the crowd.

Raising my phone again, I imitate the tourists. I angle and fidget with my screen like I'm capturing something picturesque and click. The walkway ahead. The plaza to my right.

Down the pier, a small group clusters beside the mini cruise ship. A captain and first mate stand at the end of a carpeted ramp, greeting each tourist climbing aboard with a reassuring, artificial smile. I zoom in on the third crewmember, who stands at ease. His eyes shift around, like he's searching for any sign of disturbance. For something about to begin?

I snap a shot and scrutinize it. His age is right—between fifteen and twenty-one. But nothing else fits the Swarm's profile. He isn't alone. He's not masking his identity.

My breath hitches, making the inhale shallow and unsatisfying, as I chuck the phone into my bag. I close my eyes, relax my shoulders, and curse the weather for changing too quickly this year. *Air in. Air out.* Slow. Methodic. My lame attempt at convincing my body that breathing isn't so hard.

A phone chimes next to me.

My attention snaps to a girl approaching from the left. She sits beside me on the bench. Nineteenish. Bronze skin. Copper-colored hair slicked back in a tight ponytail. Her oversized scarf conceals her neck, half her face. Sunglasses. A local—likely hiding her identity.

I jerk my eyes away. Take another deep breath. Pinching the pendant on my necklace, a tiny four-leaf clover imprinted on a silver disk, I twist the chain around my finger. Scan the crowd.

An older group near the hot dog stand cackles at the vendor telling jokes in his fake Italian accent. The popcorn guy next to him takes money from three girls—all too young—and scoops popcorn in one continuous motion. A thirty-something couple takes selfies by the railing.

A half-dozen other couples and families loiter around, but the crowd is still sparse, still filled with tourists. None of them are Swarm material except Copperhead next to me and the teenage boy twenty feet to my right.

Without turning my head, I risk another glimpse. He's still sitting hunched over at the base of some monument. Eighteenish.

Broad-shouldered. He jams his hands inside the pockets of an oversized Chicago hoodie like he wants to be mistaken for a tourist. Headphone wires disappear beneath the hood concealing half his face. He's been sitting like that for over an hour. Even though I've snapped a dozen pictures, I can't stare at him longer than a few seconds at a time without getting a piercing pang in my gut.

"Will you sign a petition to preserve our city's parks?" A short, pixie-like girl holding a clipboard tight against her chest addresses Copperhead, who doesn't look up, like her headphones make her impervious to solicitors. What I wouldn't give for headphones right now.

By the time I grab my book and bury my face in it, Pixie Girl has already turned toward me.

"Do you like our city's green space?"

I keep my head down, cuing her to move along, but Pixie Girl is undeterred. Just my luck.

"We're collecting signatures today to stop the Lakefront Project from selling off the parks along Lake Michigan. We had a city ordinance dating back to 1919, which protected that land..."

I make the mistake of looking up. Pixie Girl has long, narrow ears sticking out of her short blonde hair. She wears shimmery eye shadow. At this point, I have to assume she's embracing the whole elf-image thing.

She misinterprets my glance for interest, and her eyes ignite with fervor.

"...should belong to the city, not wealthy businessmen and bureaucrats with their million-dollar homes..."

"I'm only sixteen," I say, unable to tolerate any more of her rant.

"You can still sign. This is just a statement of support indicating—"

"Not interested."

I'm about to tell Pixie Girl that fairies don't exist when her face flattens. She shoves the clipboard toward me. "I'm out to collect three hundred signatures today."

I look at Copperhead, wondering how she escaped this persecution.

Impatient, I grab the clipboard and sign my name. Pixie Girl smirks, curtseys. "Thank you for your support."

As she skips off to find her next victim, I glance down the pier toward the city. My pulse races as I realize I can no longer see the entrance to Festival Hall or the beer garden fifty yards away. People are milling. The crowd has grown thicker in the last few minutes.

I profile the crowd. Two families—definitely tourists. Three more scattered clusters, all traveling in packs. But this time I see loners. A boy facing the lake, watching the waves. Baseball cap. Head down. I count four others like him leaning against the railing. They stand at least ten feet apart. Two of them talk without looking at each other. One listens to music. The fourth watches his phone as if it might ring. As if something is about to happen.

All these people who fit the Swarm's profile seem to have materialized out of nowhere in the time Pixie Girl forced me to sign her worthless petition.

I grab my phone and steady my hand. With my best attempt at looking both casual and self-absorbed, I hit record. I take a panoramic video of the teeming crowds. I capture the boys at the railing. One of them turns his head, and I zoom in on the left side of his face. I get the kid at the base of the statue again. His exposed nose and chin. At the last second, I flip my phone around and smile as if recording myself commemorating my Labor Day weekend at Navy Pier. In doing so, I capture the girl next to me. Even if they're all disguising themselves, it's enough to incriminate at least some of them.

I jam my book into my bag and throw the strap over my torso, eager to head back toward the city. Get the hell off this pier before the attack breaks out. This has always been the riskiest part. I can't get trapped at the end of the pier. The water is behind me. It's too high to jump.

Clutching my phone, I head toward my escape on the north side of the pier, a narrow walkway by the parking garage that's isolated from the main stretch. But three steps in, a group of guys—five of them—masked by hats, hoods, and sunglasses round the pier's grand ballroom, heading toward the lake and the bench where I'd been sitting moments ago. Each of them looks massive and, worse, *enraged*.

Blood drains my body, leaving me numb and useless when I see the two spikes piercing the lead guy's bottom lip like fangs.

The guy who killed my dad.

They're closing in.

My hands shake. I struggle to hit record. As I do, Lip Spikes lifts his chin, giving me the best shot I'm going to get.

I turn back toward the main stretch and halt. Another cluster converges from the pier's south side, blocking both exits. I scan for the best way out only to find the boy with the oversized hoodie at the base of the monument, staring.

At me.

His eyes are paralyzing. They look colorless—or gray, I can't decide. They are fascinating and strange, eerily bright. For the tiniest of moments, I don't even notice the expression behind them. But when I do, my stomach drops. His glare is sharp and piercing, like he hates me, like he knows what I'm doing, *what I've already done.*

He flips a cell in his hand.

Everything in me tightens.

Buzzing and ringing surround me. Teenagers wearing heavy clothing—hats, sunglasses, scarves, hoods, gloves—circle the pier. My gaze flickers between them. Half of them are tucking their phones away. The other half seem to be checking them, the lights of their screens peppering the fog with little blue orbs. The buzzing is deafening. I want to cover my ears and curl into a ball against the railing. I want to crawl under the bench and hide there.

I dial 911 and hit *send.*

And then I stop breathing. I realize now why the boy is staring at me.

It's not because he knows what I've done. It's much worse than that.

The Swarm isn't after a tourist.

They're after me.

CHAPTER 2

S omeone screams.

The noise is so loud and animalistic, my knees buckle and I collapse. I cover my head with my arms, bracing myself for a hit.

Curled into a ball, I'm vaguely aware of people shrieking and fleeing. I listen for footsteps charging me, but the pounding of my heart echoes in my head and mutes the world around me. This is it. I'm going to die. Petrified. And alone. Knowing in my final thoughts that I failed my dad and everything he stood for.

A low, muffled rumble of jeering and yelling emerges like a balloon. It pops, and the noise is overwhelming and terrifying and coming from someplace else. Dozens of them horde in a riotous circle around their victim forty feet away.

A bubble of air bursts from my mouth. They aren't after me. But the tiny rush of relief is replaced by a new wave of limb-numbing fear.

These are the people who murdered my dad. They beat him beyond recognition. The Swarm's enormity hits me as their thick wall of bodies huddle together, a deadly drove with one primal aim. Pressure coils around me, wringing my insides, strangling my throat though I know, better than anyone, that this is the worst time to panic.

I close my eyes and force myself to breathe, draw air into my lungs. I count down. *Three. Two. One.*

Swiping my phone, I scramble to the back of the bench. I stay low and peer through the wooden slats as dozens of them shove each other to get closer to the attack. Every hoot and scream makes me flinch. More emerge and join the chaos. Where were all these people hiding just moments ago, before the first hit?

I clutch the phone to my ear, the 911 call still active.

"Death Mob." My voice is hoarse. "Navy Pier." It shakes as I recite details to the operator asking me question after question in her stupid, calm voice.

A man screams from inside the pit. It's pleading, terror-ridden, and slices through my core.

I drop the phone and cover my mouth, silencing my own cries. Somewhere in the center of the attack, that man clings to life as dozens of fists pummel him. And there is no one nearby who can help—not a local or tourist or police officer.

The ship with its captain and crew drifts from the dock, its ropes dangling off the sides. The vendors have disappeared with their carts as if they were never here. Everyone's gone. Fled. Escaping the horror at the end of the pier, where a man is being beaten to death.

And I'm trapped on the other side.

One guy with oversized sunglasses and a faded gray jacket laughs—a high-pitched cackle—like he's enjoying it. He shoves a guy in a black knit hat next to him. Black Hat sprawls on the concrete. His sunglasses fall from his face. His jeans rip at the knee. But he doesn't give up. He stands and bounces on his toes like a boxer. Then he charges Gray

Jacket, tackling him around the waist, bringing them both down. They punch and kick. Every couple of hits, one of them smiles as if the whole thing is some kind of sick and twisted game.

I imagine my dad in the center of the attack and press my fingertips against my eyelids, burying the thought that threatens to paralyze me. I refuse to let that happen and make myself an easy target.

Grabbing my phone, I hold it just above the back of the bench, using the wooden slats to steady it and hit record. All around the outer edge of the attack, the Swarm turns on each other, a massive out-of-control brawl. I snap shots. Rapid fire. Ten. Twenty. Until the shake in my arm and the burning in my lungs become too intense.

I dig through my bag for my inhaler and my keys. Wind whips my stringy blonde hair across my face, making it impossible to see. Yanking my black rubber band from my wrist, I throw my hair into a ponytail, frustrated to be wasting time on silly details.

It's only a matter of time before they see me. The Swarm usually takes one victim, but there have been plenty of cases where someone gets attacked for being too close. And I'm too close.

I take a long puff from my inhaler before weaving my keys through my knuckles. I've always been small, so my dad made me take self-defense lessons in middle school. I was good, but any idiot can follow directions in a simulated fight. If my attacker doesn't start with a right hook, I'm not sure what to do next. I've never had to test my ability to improvise. I clutch the strap of my bag with my left hand. If someone charges me, I have at least two swings—my bag and my makeshift weapon.

My nerves buzz with adrenaline. I lean against the iron railing separating the pier from Lake Michigan and glance over my shoulder at the water below. The drop has to be thirty feet, at least. Water slams against the pier. Every time a new wave crashes, a foamy white spray bursts up the side.

An erratic chanting reverberates through the Swarm. I turn, expecting to see a deranged mosh pit full of breakout fights and people pummeling each other. But instead my eyes fix on a girl with choppy jet-black hair standing in the crowd, clutching the bag slung across her body. The tense inward curve of her shoulders throws me. She isn't chanting or cheering like the others. She looks nervous, pained. Agitated.

I fumble for my cell and click one last shot. She stands out, but no one else seems to notice her. I scan the group for anyone like her only to find the boy hiding beneath the navy hood. His colorless eyes lock in on mine.

I press my back into the railing as if it will somehow hide me.

His glare is deliberate. He dips his chin and walks toward me. His cold gaze doesn't break. He weaves his way through the crowd like he has all the time in the world. Without warning, he picks up speed and runs.

My knees seize. I drop my phone and scrabble for my keys, preparing my two hits. But the boy closes the space between us so fast, I don't have time to plan.

Something flashes to my left.

I spin just in time to see another guy lunging at me.

Before I have time to brace myself, the boy in the hood knocks my would-be attacker away with little effort. I'm his for the kill. I swing my bag at his head. He blocks it. I throw my punch, but he grabs my arm and my waist in one fluid motion. His arm is thick, his grip solid. I think of an anaconda squeezing the life out of its prey.

I claw at his wrist with my free hand. He spins me around and pins me against the railing, forcing me to stare at the water below. Taunting me. He wants me to be terrified by the water, by how high up we are. I'm too busy searching for a safe spot to land. If I fall too close to the wall, I won't make it.

He leans in so close his lips brush my ear. Dread washes through me. What if killing me is the least of his plans?

"Can you swim?" His words are low and coarse. At first, I'm not sure I heard him correctly.

"Can you swim?" he says, louder.

I don't understand what he's doing or why he's asking or what he's going to do to me next. I nod once, unable to talk.

"There are concrete blocks against the wall beneath the surface. Jump ten feet out. When you hit the water, swim away from the pier. To the right."

I hesitate.

I can't figure out his angle. Is he telling me this, knowing I don't have a chance, that I won't make the fall? Or is he giving me hope—a cruel joke—because he has every intention of throwing my body toward the concrete?

He scoops my legs from beneath me and flips me over the railing. I clench the rail, squeezing it, while I fight for balance on a ledge too narrow for my toes. He stands on the other side clutching my wrists with a vicelike grip, steadying me.

The Swarm blurs behind him, forty feet away. I search his face for signs of mockery or malice, something that indicates he's going to kill me. His eyes are steady, unreadable. The perfect straight line of his lips gives him an almost clinical expression. Beneath his hood, I can just make out a dark brown hairline. Everything about him is off. So much of his face is exposed.

A gust of wind hits me so hard, my eyes flutter. His hands tighten around my wrists.

"You got this," he says.

I can't tell whether it's a question or encouragement. A weird wave of déjà vu flits through me. *I've seen him before.*

"Why are you doing this?"

His voice grows threatening. "Turn and jump."

I hang over the water. The height appears to have doubled. Ten feet out now seems impossible to reach. My grip becomes sweaty. My pulse thumps erratically. If I don't jump now, I'll slip and have no chance of making it.

"Jump or I throw you," he growls.

Behind him, people begin cheering and jumping with their arms in the air.

"They'll kill you."

I look one last time over my shoulder at the spray, the water crashing against the cement wall. I choose my spot. The countdown begins. *Three. Two . . .*

Just as I kick against the pier, my left foot slips. My grip slides off the railing and I sense the wrongness of it all. I haven't turned around. I don't get the spring I need, and I begin falling too close to the wall, too close to the white foam and the blocks beneath the water's surface.

My body is weightless, helpless, as I freefall.

Everything blurs.

As the world spins away, I swear I see him reach for me and call my name.

"Lia . . ."

smack the water headfirst. Disoriented and confused, I spin and sink like dead weight. I can't breathe. Can't control my body. Can't find the surface.

And I need to find the surface.

There are bubbles and murky gray water. Seaweed. Concrete. And then nothing.

There's nothing after that.

When I was nine, I walked across the frozen lake at our friends' house in the burbs and fell through the ice. As soon as I hit the water, thousands of frigid needles pierced my skin, causing a pain more intense than anything I'd ever known. I lost control of my body and breath until I was sure I would die. It was my dad who pulled me out. His grip was strong and desperate as he lifted me to the surface and ran me inside.

Doctors claimed it was a miracle my crap lungs didn't shut down. They were all impressed by my "will to live"—something I clung to as proof that beneath my weak exterior, I had inner strength, that in a defining moment my subconscious chose to fight rather than sleep.

A distant bell toll pulls me back with each chime, filling in details of "here" and "now." I'm wet. Cold. My clothes cling like shrink-wrap where I lay half passed out against the white slats of a dock, the lake rocking below me.

I blink and squint, adjusting my vision to the dull light, and find myself staring at the giant brass bell ringing at the dock's end. The golden dome swings from its post like an upside-down tulip dangling against an ashen backdrop. As each arc grows smaller and each chime fainter, I can't help but wonder what made it start ringing.

It stops.

I swear I see the very top of the Ferris wheel from Navy Pier. It looks so small. Far away. I struggle to lift my aching body for a better look and realize how badly my lungs burn. I can just make out a soft halo of red and blue emergency lights in the distance, near the tip of the pier, when suddenly a stampede of footsteps thunders toward me.

The Swarm. They've found me.

I shoot up, desperate to be on my feet. But I'm too quick. Clumsy. My head spins. My stomach heaves. I lean over the side of the dock and puke.

Something warm and dry and heavy is thrown over my shoulders.

"Get her inside."

I'm scooped up. I fall back, and everything goes black.

I wake a second time on a couch, cocooned in towels and a thick down quilt. A fire burns beneath a massive wood mantle topped with iridescent vases and a huge abstract painting almost as big as the fireplace itself. The fire casts an eerie glow, bringing warmth to the muted daylight.

Pressure grips my chest, like I'm wrapped in weighted blankets.

I reach for my inhaler on instinct. I *always* have it. My life depends on it too often. And it's gone. Kicked aside on Navy Pier? Lost at the bottom of Lake Michigan? I take two deep breaths, testing the limits of my lungs. Air wheezes as it scrapes against the back of my throat, but breathing isn't as difficult as I'd expected.

I fumble for my silver pendant, the one thing I can't replace. Still there.

But my phone. I can't remember what happened to my phone. An aching lump hardens at the base of my neck. The pictures, the videos—they're protected. They would've uploaded to the cloud. But if the Swarm were to discover them . . .

I lift my head, determined to find my phone before anyone else, but the room tilts and spins. It's too much, and I collapse against the pillow, taking another deep, burning breath.

It's always my body that fails me.

"Turn it up."

The man's voice comes out of nowhere. I think of the dock and the footsteps. I try to dredge up how many sets of steps I heard, but instead I picture Lip Spikes and the Initiators charging that man on Navy Pier, parting the crowd like a missile through water.

My hands start twitching, like some Pavlovian response. I try to steady them, but the twitching spreads up my arms, my elbows.

This is temporary, I try to convince myself. *It will pass.*

But the surge of panic doesn't subside. It's overwhelming and suffocating and threatening to take over every nerve in my body.

I bury the image of the pier and replace it with a favorite memory.

I visualize Pa'iloa Beach in Maui. I squeeze my eyes shut and narrow in on details. The damp black sand beneath my feet. The purple sky filling the horizon. The sun rising against a stormy backdrop as the ocean's white foam swishes along the shore. Mindful of the air coming in and out of my lungs, my spasming heart searching for its rhythm, I focus and breathe and stay in the moment the way I was taught after my dad's death by a shrink whose name I can't remember. The twitching simmers to mild trembling until I've gained control over my limbs and I'm able to think logically.

Without moving too much, I try to glimpse who's talking. Someone behind the couch, on the far side of the room. Out of sight.

The television grows louder, and a woman's pseudo-serious news report fills the room. "We have confirmed that officials received an anonymous tip warning about the attack, which at the time they dismissed. As to the man's identity, that remains unclear. Witnesses say that within seconds, approximately one hundred teens swarmed and mobbed a man in his late twenties or thirties at the east end of Navy Pier."

Keep it together, Finch. I tell myself. *Bury it.* I imagine a black, twisty tunnel spiraling through my head and down my spine to the deep caverns of my gut, where I lodge the sights and sounds and everything that happened on the pier.

"Paramedics rushed him to Northwestern Hospital, where he is reported to be in critical condition. The hospital will not comment on the extent of his injuries; however, sources say he is not expected to survive."

She's emotionless when she says it, like she's reporting traffic. How can she talk like it doesn't matter whether this guy lives or dies?

"We will continue our ongoing coverage as we wait to hear from the mayor ..."

Another guy's voice speaks over the television. "Shouldn't you be with him right now, Richard?"

Richard—I assume—responds. His nasal voice is curt, uptight. "I'd say a girl washing up on the mayor's dock an hour after the attack is fairly important."

Nameless Guy's tone reeks of derision as he says, "I was starting to think you wanted to keep her. I mean, sure, she smells awful, she has seaweed in her hair, she's unconscious and half your age, but whatever does it for you."

I grab the back of the couch and heave myself upright. The room rocks and blurs. Three silhouettes stand against an oversized window flooded with gray light. I push myself up to face them, but my knees buckle. I fall against the couch's arm.

"Take it easy. You hit your head," says a new voice. It's deep and comforting, like he wants me to surrender.

The shadows inch toward me like I'm some rabid, wild animal. I jerk back, maintaining distance, squinting to make out the details of their faces. I stumble over the coffee table and into the side of an armchair.

"You were wheezing pretty heavily, and your O$_2$ levels were low. I gave you a shot of Prednisone to help you breathe. What do you normally take?"

One of the shadows walks closer, arms out, indicating he won't hurt me. "Albuterol?"

My head feels jumbled, like someone poured syrup in it, slowing down my thoughts and senses. It takes a second to remember the name of the medication I depend on to stay alive. I nod, hesitant to say too much.

"My name is Dr. Marshall. You can call me Steve."

I flinch at hearing my dad's name. Dr. Marshall—I cannot call him Steve—doesn't seem to notice.

"May I listen to your lungs?" Dr. Marshall steps away from the window. Deep laugh lines circle his eyes. He holds a stethoscope in one hand as though asking permission to use it, all in a very anti-Swarm kind of way.

The silence stretches out between us as I gauge whether these three are a threat. I don't think they are, but I also don't know if I can trust my instincts right now. I hone in on the doctor, who looks at me with a patient expression as he waits for me to decide he isn't Death Mob affiliated. And I nod again.

Dr. Marshall slides the cold metal disk up and down my back as I breathe, slipping into routine. I imagine the pops and crackles he's hearing. Most doctors overreact the first time they listen to my lungs.

Another man steps closer. Tall. Lanky. Better dressed than I expected. I peg him as Richard, the one with the nasal voice. "How did you end up on the mayor's dock?"

At first, I don't think I've heard him correctly. The mayor's dock? The mayor lives in a Lakefront mansion—I've seen it plenty of times. I try to think of how long it would take to drive from Navy Pier to the mayor's house. Five, six minutes without traffic? The two aren't close.

Richards squats to eye level. His tie falls forward, hitting my knee. He blushes as he fumbles for it, pressing it against his dress shirt. It's a weird reaction for a guy wearing such an expensive tie.

"You go to my school," Nameless Guy says. His tone is critical.

I blink, pushing against the fog governing my head. Nameless Guy wears a collared shirt like it makes him superior. I know him, but from where doesn't register.

"You're friends?" Richard asks.

"God, no," Nameless Guy says to his phone. "She's nuts—as in legitimately crazy. In third grade, she told everyone she had a twin sister who went to another school. Talked about her all the time. Couple months later we all found out she made the whole thing up. Her twin died at birth." His eyes meet mine. "That was you, right?" He snaps his fingers like it's just come to him. "Amelia—that's it."

My stomach churns as his name comes to me too: Cullen Henking, the mayor's smarmy son.

"Don't mind Cullen," Richard says, his long, thin legs jutting out like a frog's. A giant frog with a crooked tie. It'd be funny if Cullen hadn't just mocked my childhood struggle to cope with the dead twin I never knew.

"Your lungs sound better. Any chest pain?" Dr. Marshall asks.

"Chronic." My voice is thick, scratchy.

Dr. Marshall smiles, no doubt overcompensating for Cullen's indiscretion. "You also have a nice-size gash on your temple I stitched up. With any luck you won't have much of a scar." He grabs a pen light out of his pocket and flashes it in my right eye. It's bright and abrupt and knocks me off balance.

Dr. Marshall catches my shoulder and gently pushes me upright. "Steady there. We'll call you an ambulance and get you to a hospital." He pockets his flashlight and wraps the stethoscope around his neck. "You have a mild concussion. You could use oxygen as well."

Richard leans closer. "Shortly." His narrow shoulders hunch over. "How did you end up on the mayor's dock, Amelia?"

"Lia," I say, with a cough.

His eyebrows arch like I've disclosed a secret. "Excuse me?"

"My name is Lia."

Dr. Marshall lifts a glass toward my face. "Water?"

I take a sip and notice Cullen Henking slumped in a leather wing chair, staring at his phone and smirking like I've said something amusing, and I feel myself scowl. Girls at our school usually fawn over this guy.

"Lia, I'm Richard," he says, drawing my attention. Richard's short hair is gelled to one side. Sandy brown—like my dad's, and the thought of him diffuses my irritation. My dad wore his hair the same too, except Richard's sticks up a little in the back. "I'm the mayor's chief of staff." He gestures toward Dr. Marshall. "We called a doctor when we found you on the dock after the attack at Navy Pier. We think you climbed out of the water and rang the dock bell before you passed out. Can you tell us what happened leading up to that?"

The lines on Richard's forehead scrunch as he waits for me to piece it together. But I can't. I don't remember ringing the bell, or climbing out of the water, or swimming to the dock after falling in. The last thing I remember is the guy charging me, grabbing me, yelling at me to jump off the pier. A guy who knew my name.

Richard licks his lips. "Lia, were you involved in the attack?"

His questions skip around, making them hard to follow. Several seconds pass until I realize he's asking if I'm part of the Death Mob. "No." I jerk away.

"Sorry. I had to ask. But you were there?"

A stinging sensation forms behind the bridge of my nose. I think of the man screaming from inside the Swarm. "Yes."

"What can you remember?" Richard says.

Nothing, I want to tell him, but the pain and the images from deep inside begin to snake their way up to the forefront of my thoughts. The crowd so thick that people brushed against each other as they moved. And then the Initiators. Five guys—massive, destructive, led by Lip Spikes—sliced the crowd in two. Scattered blue orbs punctured the mass like firecrackers as dozens of teenagers seemed to emerge out of nowhere. Energized to fight, they pivoted and spun toward the same direction like some choreographed dance. How had I missed them? They all fit the profile. They all wore hats, glasses, scarves, and gloves to conceal their identities. And somehow, they remained camouflaged among the tourists. I didn't see them until the attack broke out.

"They came out of nowhere." The words are tight. I can barely get them out. "I was trapped."

After the first hit, screaming erupted. The pier became frenzied chaos as everyone began running, trying to escape. Except me. My feet didn't work.

"I jumped into the water."

I picture the attackers. I hear them cackle as they beat a man clinging to his life in the middle of their pit.

"There was nothing else I could do," I say, which isn't true. I could have done more to help—caused a diversion, gone in after him. I stood forty feet away while he was beaten to death, and did nothing.

I should've prevented this. I knew about the attack before it happened—I should've tried harder. Tracked down Detective Irving.

Forced him to listen to me. I was so focused on "tangible evidence" indicting my dad's killers. Why didn't I think more about the victim who could be dead already?

"I have to go." Get out. Find a computer. Check the cloud. Everything will be there, and somehow it will redeem every stupid mistake I made today. I stand, but Richard holds out his hand.

"Do you remember any details, Lia? Faces? Anyone you could identify?"

Lip Spikes. Copperhead. The guy with the gray eyes. His face was the only one not covered. His expression was so serious right before I fell.

Dr. Marshall taps Richard on the shoulder. "I'm sure the police will question her thoroughly when she's ready."

"One more." Richard's phone buzzes. He drops it while trying to pull it from his pocket, grabs it, and gives it a quick glance before tucking it away. "Why were you on the pier, Lia?"

I blink several times, stalling for time, knowing it's crucial I get this right. CPD has always been so dismissive of anything I've given them. Detective Irving clearly didn't follow up on today's lead. But this guy is the mayor's assistant. If I told him about the tweet, the pictures, the video, he could use what I captured to isolate the attackers' identities and start building a case. I'm on the edge of sharing it all when somewhere inside of me, a warning light flickers. I have to check out the footage first, before everyone dismisses me as a crazed conspiracy theorist. And I need to lie until I do.

Cullen snickers. "I'm sorry, but I can't handle the suspense. Ask her what her last name is."

Richard and the doctor look at Cullen. Then back at me.

"Finch," I whisper, and wait for them to connect the dots.

Richard's brow pinches together like he's spinning through a Rolodex of names and faces.

Cullen, of course, can't wait that long.

"As in Steven Finch," he says. He scoots to the end of his chair like he's watching a show.

I stare at my water and take another sip, clinging to my father's name like an anchor.

Richard stands. I can feel him studying me as if looking for the family resemblance. He folds his arms across his chest and tucks his palms into his armpits. "Your father was really—"

"The Swarm's last victim," Cullen says, cutting him off. "Well," he adds, "unless you count the one today."

And just like that, my life is reduced to some sick joke.

I consider charging Cullen. Smacking that condescending smile off his face. Screaming at him for mocking the fifteen victims the Swarm has attacked in the last eleven years. And I might, if my head wasn't spinning.

Richard leans over, putting his hands on his knees. His movement is constant, dizzying. "I'm sorry to hear that." He smiles as if to reassure me. It's awkward and draws attention to the gentle slope of his puffy neck. "The mayor and I are committed to doing whatever we can to help you through what must have been a horrifying experience."

"You're a strong young lady," Dr. Marshall says as he helps me stand. "That's a little over a mile you swam after you fell and hit your head. Right now, you need rest and probably a change of clothes." He clutches my bicep, assisting my first few steps. "Should I call your mother and let her know which hospital you'll be at?"

I nod.

"If I may—" Cullen begins.

"That's enough from you," Richard interrupts.

"Someone might want to tell her about the news cameras outside, in case she wants to shower or something. She's about to be the most famous girl in Chicago. A first impression is a lasting one. Just saying."

I wipe my face free of emotion, denying him the reaction he's looking for. Both Cullen and the media can go to hell.

Dr. Marshall leads me away, and I let him. As much as I despise Cullen Henking for deliberately humiliating me, my thoughts are preoccupied. We walk through the foyer, past some weird, ostentatious sculpture, and up a wide staircase, as I fixate on one alarming certainty: I've never been a good swimmer. Even without a head injury, there's no way I could've swum a mile by myself.

CHAPTER 4

My left eye twitches. I press my palm against it. Closing it stops the throbbing tics, but every time I do, I hear the man's screams as the Swarm pummels him. His echoes rip through me, shredding my stability.

I clutch a fistful of blanket from my lap and ground myself in its plush fabric. I concentrate on the steady buzzing of my nebulizer, the cool mist of meds billowing around my face, brushing my cheeks. I inhale deeply and release, over and over and over again, until the sounds of Navy Pier are stifled.

After my dad's attack, nightmares of his death haunted me wherever I went. In the rare, worthwhile moments of therapy, Dr. What's-His-Name showed me how to self-monitor my recurring dreams and catastrophic thinking. He taught me about mindful med-itation and how to rein in my panic attacks, so I could appear like a sane person in public. I got plenty good at it when I was around people. Being alone was harder. That's when my defenses crumbled. Eventually I figured out that if I spent my evenings at the coffee shop down the street, the constant commotion would distract me from imagining every graphic detail of my dad's final moments.

If I survived that, I can survive this too—despite whatever Dr.

What's-His-Name would think. He used to overanalyze triggers. Knowing him, he'd insist that today's attack would set me off and require intense therapeutic intervention. That there'd be no way I could handle this on my own. But he never understood my resolve, and I refuse to be that girl again—unable to function—which of course I vow while sitting on the living room couch, chained to a nebulizer pumping a cocktail of Prednisone and Albuterol mist into my nose.

My mom hovers in the kitchen, cleaning the inside of our refrigerator. She hasn't spoken more than a few barked commands since we left the hospital. Not that I'm surprised. She freaks out over anything that might jeopardize my health—mental or physical. Last year she almost had me homeschooled after I was hospitalized for pneumonia. When she found out it had been going around our class, she interviewed a dozen tutors. She became an expert on state standards and testing and how homeschooling might affect my chances of getting into an Ivy League school.

I can only imagine what she'd do if she knew I went to the pier expecting the attack. I pinch my four-leaf clover pendant and cling to the hope that the footage I got will redeem me for my reckless mistakes. It has to. I captured the Death Mob. Lip Spikes. Copperhead. Parts of their faces were exposed. Enough to incriminate them, I'm sure of it. And I captured the breakout fights along the edge. I got Black Hat when his sunglasses fell off. The girl with cropped hair, the guy with bright gray eyes.

It'll be enough to arrest some of them. They'll rat out their leaders. The Swarm's whole infrastructure will collapse. Whoever has organized the attacks for the past nine years will rot away in prison for the rest of his life. And my dad will be vindicated.

Even if my phone fell into the water, the images will have uploaded to the cloud—something I double-checked before heading to the pier.

I glance across the room at my computer, which can confirm the reason for everything that happened today with just a couple clicks. Any other night, my mom might be heading up to bed by now, and I'd be sifting through everything I'd captured, backing up data, and preparing to call Detective Irving. But until she decides I won't die in our living room, there is nothing I can do but wait her out one excruciating minute at a time. My head falls against the couch cushion as I inhale the medicated mist, forcing my lungs to open and expand like they're supposed to.

My mom sets water and pain pills on the glass table in front of me. She pauses, casting a disapproving look at WGN's investigative reporter, Emi Vega, who's yapping away with the pretense of concern.

I shove pillows over the neb machine to suffocate its insufferable buzzing and crank the volume on the remote. Emi's eyes bore into the camera. She furrows her brow as if to emphasize the seriousness of her words.

"We are standing outside Amelia Finch's home right now, where she lives with her mother, Maggie Finch. Earlier today Amelia witnessed the Death Mob's attack on Navy Pier, and narrowly escaped by jumping into Lake Michigan. As you might remember, Amelia's father, Steven Finch, was the last victim to be brutally attacked and killed a little over two years ago."

My stomach knots. Where is she taking this?

WGN flashes to an overly tan news anchor trying to seduce the camera. "Emi, the Death Mob, which many locals call the Swarm, usually goes after tourists. At the time of Steve Finch's death, didn't sources speculate he could have been targeted?"

"Exactly, Brian. Finch was the lead prosecuting attorney building a case against real estate tycoon Bill Morrell for allegedly organizing the Death Mob murders. Three weeks before the case went to trial, Finch was killed and the case was dropped. Because of it, many people speculated his attack was intentional."

Overly Tan News Anchor leans forward. "Now Finch's daughter is almost mobbed. That seems like an unlikely coincidence. Emi, do we know why she was at Navy Pier?"

Emi blinks twice before responding. "Amelia gave her official statement to police at the hospital earlier this evening. Authorities are not sharing that statement yet." She dips her chin. "Certainly, tonight and the days that follow will be difficult for the Finch family."

My mom walks away without commenting.

If I didn't find the cameras so intolerable, I'd march outside and smack Emi Vega in the middle of her broadcast. Of all Chicago's superficial reporters, I despise her most. After my dad died, she basically said it was his own fault for creating "an enemy list a mile long" with his high-profile cases. She diminished his life's achievements, implying he took cases for name recognition only, including his case against Morrell. Slandering a dead guy unable to defend his legacy is a cheap and dirty gimmick. Which apparently wasn't beneath her, or any other media desperate for airtime.

How convenient of her to omit from her broadcast that Morrell killed himself a week after my dad's murder, proving my dad was onto something.

Light from the news trucks outside seeps through the sides of every drawn curtain in the room. I want to staple the fabric to the wall. The incessant flashing feels like an alien invasion with a giant spacecraft landing in my front yard. Not something I really care to deal with tonight.

WGN shows their ten-second clip of me ducking into a black town car in front of the mayor's house. I'm wearing a brand-new Tory Burch coat. My wet, ratted hair adorned with seaweed looks darker. Sandy instead of whiteish blonde. Following it, they have a clip of Richard outside the mayor's house telling reporters I've requested privacy as my mom and I "deal with these traumatizing events." His shoulders bend forward like he's hiding his height. He claims the mayor found me on the dock and carried me into his home. Sure, I was passed out when it happened, but I didn't see the mayor the entire time I was in his house, making me wonder whether he was there at all.

"The mayor," Richard continues, "is doing everything he can to help Miss Finch deal with what she's experienced."

I pull my hair back, wet from showering, and twist it at the nape of my neck so it falls down my back as one slick ponytail.

A giant thud comes from the kitchen, startling me. My mom stands over the spilled leftovers of tonight's dinner, which neither of us ate. Taco meat, shredded lettuce, diced tomatoes, and cheese fan out across our tile floor while she stares at the mess like it's the worst thing to have happened to her today. My eyes flit back to the TV screen.

Emi Vega flashes a bright, insincere smile. "... our hearts go out to the Finch family and the victim's family tonight."

Outside, the lights dim as WGN cuts their live feed. I turn down the TV volume and shut the nebulizer off, even though my liquid cocktail isn't fully evaporated. I test my freshly pampered lungs with a deep inhale before gathering the neb pieces and walking from our impeccable living room to our impeccable kitchen—aside from the scattered taco fillings.

I try not to stare, but my mom's immobility unnerves me. Setting the neb parts on the counter, I grab the broom from the utility closet, just as clean and organized as the rest of the house. Clutter is inexcusable—even behind closed doors.

It isn't until I start sweeping our ruined meal that my mom turns away and washes her hands in the sink.

This is how it's been since she met me at the hospital. She ran into the ER, frightened and disheveled, in rare Maggie Finch form, to give me the longest, tightest hug we've ever had. Then she excused herself, no doubt to fix misplaced strands of fallen hair and reapply her lipstick. When she returned, she didn't say a word. Didn't even make eye contact. I gave my statement to the questioning officers while she stood in the doorway, lifting her chin away from my bed as if she didn't want to hear anything I had to say.

I dump the first dustpan of food into the trash and resume sweeping.

My mom turns off the water and grips the lip of our sink. "Detective Irving said someone left an anonymous voice mail warning him about the attack."

Two messages. I'm tempted to correct her. "He didn't exactly listen."

She turns and glares. "He said the same girl has left him eighteen messages in the last two years." Tiny strands of hair stick out from her head as if full of static electricity. For a woman who prides herself on perfection, she looks so unkempt, I'm taken aback. "What exactly have you been doing?"

It's practically an admission of her denial. Every night since my dad's death, I've scoured social media. Hunted for any hint that the Swarm still exists. "I read the news," I say, enabling the lies she must have told herself about how I spent that time on my computer.

"I told him you didn't know anything. I begged him to drop it."

Of course she would. Of course she would thwart any contribution I might be able to make.

"CPD is full of corruption. If the wrong people find out you knew anything about this, they'll come after you."

"I was careful."

"Really?" my mom snaps. "You almost got killed. On top of that, your face is plastered all over the news. Reporters are trying to figure out what you were doing there in the first place. How is that being careful?"

I continue sweeping. At least I'm doing something instead of pretending my dad never existed. And cleaning and reorganizing every inch of this house doesn't count. Flaunting a perfect silverware drawer or linen closet doesn't mean she has control of her life. Or what happened to him.

"Whatever you're trying to do, it stops here. I mean it. No phones. No Internet. It doesn't take much for them to run your online activity. If the Swarm notices you've found out more than you should, they will kill you to keep you quiet. Do you understand?"

I can feel her eyes boring into the back of my head.

"If I need to take away every device you have, I will."

I wait for the inevitable *How could you do this to me?* follow-up, but instead her voice breaks as a sob catches in her throat. "Dammit, Lia."

I glance over my shoulder.

Her body wilts, and for the first time I notice how old she looks. My favorite picture of my mother is from her wedding day. Her long, golden hair slightly blown back. Her eyes—narrow and green like mine—shine as she stares at my dad. They're dancing. One hand covers her mouth like she's laughing at something he said. I love the picture because I don't know my mom that way. She never speaks about my sister, Annie, but my dad once admitted that my mom smiled less after Annie died.

When my dad died, it sucked away any remaining happiness. I can't even imagine what she'd do if something happened to me.

"What were you thinking?"

Something in me softens, and I consider giving her an honest response. I'm searching for the right words when she sees the neb cylinder isn't completely drained. "You didn't finish your meds!" she accuses, like she caught me snorting drugs.

Any emotion she'd stirred up inside me flattens. I sweep a pile of lettuce and cheese into the dustpan and brace myself.

"You can't stop a treatment halfway through."

I squeeze the pan's handle, dumping another pile into the trash. "They gave me two at the hospital."

"This isn't something to mess with. If your lungs stop working…"

It's always about my lungs. My breathing. My body that doesn't work right. "I hardly think—"

"Exactly! You never think—that's the problem. You just run around doing whatever pleases you in the moment without thinking about what's going to happen next."

I bite the inside of my cheek and stare at the granite countertop, the broom and dustpan clutched in my hands.

My mom rips off a paper towel and begins frantically wiping the kitchen sink until every drop of excess water has been rubbed away. She balls the paper towel, clenching it in her fist. "Do you have a death wish, Lia?"

"No." She doesn't care that her insinuation hurts.

"Your father was a smart man who planned everything out to the last detail, and he died investigating this."

It isn't the first time she's thrown in my face that I'm not the brainchild she hoped I'd be. Or the first time I've wondered if Annie would have been the prodigy expected from the offspring of the great Margaret and Steven Finch.

She throws the paper towel into the trash. "You're all I have. Remember that."

And there it is—her favorite go-to line. I feel horrible enough that someone's in the ICU because I didn't think it all through and plan it better. But any response would only continue the conversation, and more than anything I need her to leave. I need to study those images from the pier and prove to everyone that I can still salvage something from this: it's not like I did it all for nothing.

She rubs her temples with one hand. Her skin has become translucent. Her eyes flicker toward the neb parts. "Finish that." She walks around the peninsula. "I'm headed to bed." The intensity in her voice deflates. "Don't open the door—for anyone. With any luck, they'll give up within the next couple hours." She glares sideways toward the front of our house on her way toward the stairs.

With my mom finally gone, I stare at my computer, listening for signs that she isn't coming back down. My body, which has ached with a dull throbbing since I woke at the mayor's dock, grows light and jittery as I bide my time. I grab the neb parts on the counter and rinse them in the sink. Water splashes along the sides of the basin my mom just wiped. I set the pieces on a paper towel and wait. Upstairs, her faucet runs while she brushes her teeth. The drawers of her dresser roll out and back in. Then, silence.

A car door slams outside. Aside from the low, white-noise rumbling of news teams doing whatever it is they do when cameras are off and the hushed droning of the TV, my house is quiet and still.

I race on my tiptoes to the living room and flip the laptop open. My fingers are clumsy and slow, and I fumble to type my password and access my online gallery. I scroll through the images. The videos. I don't see anything from the pier, which can't be right. I search *pictures*, then *specialty videos*—I even search under the date. I took dozens of them—hundreds. But according to this, the last time I used my camera was six days ago. Maybe they haven't downloaded yet. They just need more time. But the sinking feeling in my stomach tells me otherwise. Somewhere in the back of my head, a tiny voice confirms that someone has hacked my phone, seen the evidence, and erased it.

I stare blankly at the TV showing a bird's-eye view of Navy Pier.

If someone's found my phone and deleted those images, it can only mean one thing. Someone knows why I was there. And they don't like it.

An image of the gray-eyed attacker flashes in my head. The clinical look on his face as he studied the water. The severity behind his eyes when he ordered me to jump. What was he trying to do? Help me? Kill me?

A chill shudders across my neck. Did he really call my name?

Outside lights flash on—several sets of them. The TV screen switches to Overly Tan News Anchor sobering his expression. Emi Vega's picture, as she stands outside my house, appears in the upper corner. I leap toward the couch for the remote. I toss the blanket and throw pillows looking for it. I drop to my knees, stick my hand beneath the couch, and finally find it. My shirt becomes twisted. I crouch low, listening to Emi spew her thoughts, my wet hair clinging to my face.

"...from Loveland, Ohio. Jeremiah Dopney, age thirty-three, had checked into the Westin by himself..."

WGN shows his picture. He's thin but attractive. Dark hair, blue eyes, dark scruff. He's smiling in a way that lights up his whole face. He looks . . . friendly, sociable. The kind of guy who travels with people, visits people. Not the type to come to a city by himself.

"Please don't die," I whisper.

Emi says something about "critical condition" before my neighbor's dog barks, jolting me.

"Charlie!" I release my breath. "Shut up, you stupid dog." As I say it, I imagine some slum reporter sneaking around the back for a glimpse of what I'm doing, and I'm somewhat relieved to have a guard dog.

I glance toward the stairs, making sure my mom isn't coming down. "Jeremiah Dopney from Loveland, Ohio" is the first real puzzle piece I've had in the last two years. Without the images from the pier, it's all I have to go on.

Dismissing the scrutiny I'm under from reporters, likely the Swarm, and my mom, who's about to become the worst type of helicopter parent, I summon the energy to get up off the couch and head toward my dad's office to figure out how it even possibly connects.

CHAPTER 5

A few months before my dad died, he bought an old six-foot print of Chicago's skyline along Lake Michigan for his office. He was nostalgic like that. The first time I saw it, I didn't get why he wanted it. The city looked stark and bare without the Lakefront mansions.

After he died, I spent hours staring at it, taking consolation in the picture's calming presence. Parks, public beaches, and harbors line the lake. Before its renovations, even Navy Pier's small, rickety appearance had charm. I look at Navy Pier in the picture, imagining it swathed with emergency crews, awash in red and blue flashing lights. I'll never see Navy Pier as charming again.

Locking the office door behind me, I lift the picture off the wall and flip it around. When I don't pass out, I scoff at my discharge papers for listing "lifting heavy objects" as something I shouldn't do with a concussion. I lean the picture against the wall and step back to take it in. Covering the frame's brown paper backing is a five-foot-long timeline with pictures and newspaper articles webbing out in all directions. My own mini crime wall.

I squint, scrutinizing the details I've memorized. Prior to my dad's death, there'd been eleven organized attacks. Thirteen deaths in nine years. When the attacks first began, they occurred every couple months. I barely remember that time, but according to my parents it was the scariest time to live in Chicago.

Kneeling down, I trace my finger across attacks numbers nine through twelve, all separated by five or six months. My finger pauses over the twelfth, my dad's name and date written in bold, black pen.

His absence hurts. Every day. I close my eyes, inhaling the scent of leather and paper—his scent. It's the only room where he still exists. His chair. His desk. His antique desk lamp. His paperweight holding a picture of Annie and me from the NICU the day we were born. Side by side. Each hooked up to our own ventilator. As fragile and helpless as we look, I've always loved that picture. It was one moment in time when I had a sister.

My eyes wrench open when Dopney's screams start rattling around my head. I blink them away, bury them, send them racing down the dark tunnel to my gut before I start thinking about whether my dad cried out when the Swarm closed in on him.

Hana, Hawaii. I cling to my happy thought and immerse myself in the memory, hearing waves crashing and swishing, seeing white foam swirling across the black rock beach. I smell the fresh drops of rain as they speckle the ocean and watch as the sun peeks above the horizon, bringing light to a deep purple sky.

I stay in the moment, aware of my breath and my limbs until the trembling subsides. When my hand is steady enough, I grab a pen from the desk and push forward.

Extending the timeline, I add today's date and Dopney's name. The two-year gap between my dad and Dopney is longer than any lapse of time.

Charlie barks so suddenly, my hand jerks. The black pen makes a jagged dash along the brown paper backing. I lick my thumb and attempt to rub it off, but it smears, making it worse.

"Charlie," I say through gritted teeth.

The office window overlooks our small side yard. I lift the wooden blinds just enough to peer outside. The last thing I need is to make myself visible for a fraction of a second and risk a camera going off in my face.

Charlie stops barking. Other than a few rustling leaves in my neighbor's yard, the night is still. I tighten the blinds and return to my makeshift crime wall.

I study the snippets. Overly Tan News Anchor was right. Most of the attacks were on tourists. Only four of the victims, not including my dad, were Chicago residents, making nine dead tourists in nine years' time.

After his death, I found a handful of my dad's case files locked in our file cabinet. I assumed someone from his office would retrieve them. Apparently, no one had the backbone to continue the case. The media easily convinced the nation that gangs were behind the Death Mob, and my father had pissed them off enough to make himself a mark. But Emi and everyone else are stupid to think my dad's attack was the only targeted one.

According to my dad's theory, *every* hit was targeted. And the whole operation was run by a sophisticated organized crime cartel—not local gangs. As for Morrell, he was somehow involved, but he wasn't the main guy my dad was after. I've never known whether my dad knew who was in charge before he died. If that's what got him killed.

I scan the articles for connections to Dopney or even Loveland, trying to figure out how he's connected or who he's connected to. I already know before I look that I won't find anything here. I'll have to dig deeper.

I grab four square Post-its. One for Copperhead. One for Black Hat. One for Cropped Hair Girl. And one for the gray-eyed attacker who knew my name. I stick them beneath the heading "The Swarm," next to Lip Spike's name, before stepping back, frustrated I can't picture more of them.

Outside, Charlie's barking reaches a manic level. Our neighbor's boxer is harmless, but his barks sound vicious. He's going to wake my mom, who would have me institutionalized if she saw any of this.

I flip the picture and hang it on the wall. It takes longer than it should to balance the thing. Feeling a bit dizzy, I hurry out of the office and hop onto the living room couch as if I've been there all along.

Charlie doesn't settle easily this time. I chuck a pillow at the door. "Shut up!"

Our motion sensors flip on.

Outside, Charlie's nails scrape against the fence as if he's trying to climb over it. I stare at the thin curtains on our French doors that separate me from whatever is riling Charlie on the other side.

A muffled thud comes from our back porch. Something, or someone, is there. I stop breathing. Flashes of the Swarm closing in on Dopney flood my head, and I pray it's some abhorrent reporter.

"Lia," my mom whispers from the top landing. "What's going on?"

When I don't move, she rushes down the stairs toward the French doors. She grabs a poker from the fireplace on the way. Pausing at the door, she looks at me one last time. She flips the poker in her hand as if finding the right grip and peels back one curtain to peek outside.

My mom looks confident, resolute. For several seconds she doesn't move as I dig my fingernails into the couch, anticipating what she sees. Emi Vega? A camera waiting to snap a shot of me petrified like an idiot? A mob of teenagers waiting to kill me?

She unlocks the door and steps outside.

"Mom!"

She disappears.

For several agonizing seconds, I imagine her screaming, getting attacked, being murdered. My breathing grows rapid. Just as I'm about to go after her, it turns hysterical. I can't slow it down. All the drugs I've inhaled today are suddenly not enough. My lungs burn and pump quickly, in short, constricted bursts. I fall back on the couch. Stretch out. Give them room to take in air until my body is so stiff I can't move. Scenarios reel through my mind—most of them including my mom, the last of my family, dying on the back porch while I'm trapped in my own skin, completely immobilized. The pressure around my chest intensifies. It squeezes my ribs, my throat. I gasp for air, but my lungs are wearing down. I'm losing control of my breath and my body when she walks back inside the house.

"Lia!"

She runs to the kitchen. I lose sight of her as the weight of the world presses down on me. Crushing me. The junk drawer rattles. My throat constricts. Feet brush against the wood floors. There's stabbing pain like my chest is about to collapse. Just as I think it might, my inhaler is thrust into my mouth.

Mist hits the back of my throat, and I breathe in. It trickles down to my lungs, opening them, giving relief. Air pumps in and out. My breathing slows until it finally matches my mom's.

She crouches in front of me. Her voice is hard. "There's nothing out there." She looks me over, assessing the damage. "The trash can lids were knocked off. Probably an animal."

I concentrate on the routine of my breathing and nod.

"Deep breaths," she says. Twice, her breaths mimic mine, and then she watches me, scrutinizing the mechanics behind each inhale. "How do you feel?"

I nod again. "Better."

She heads to the kitchen and comes back with an ice cube. She presses it into my palm and wraps my fingers around it. "Give me a minute to get dressed. We'll go back to the hospital…"

"Mom." I push the words out as the cold begins to sting my hand. "I'm fine."

My mom studies my expression like I might be lying to her. She walks over to the door, locks it, and picks up a bag she must have brought in from outside. She sets it on the armchair and heads to the fireplace to put the poker away.

As if in slow motion, my gaze drifts to the bag—my bag.

Dizziness rushes to my head all over again.

"Where'd you find that?" I force myself to remain calm.

"On the table outside. You need to stop leaving your stuff lying around the porch. Any of those reporters out there would love a chance to rifle through your purse."

I stifle a gasp, but my mom doesn't seem to notice. She heads to the kitchen to straighten and close the junk drawer. She taps one nail on the granite like she's debating whether to drag me back to the ER.

"Turn out the lights when you go to bed," she says at last. She walks up the stairs, her shoulders tight, her bathrobe fluttering behind her.

I look to the armchair and press my back into the corner of the couch as the ice cube slides from my grip, landing somewhere on the floor.

Anyone could have picked up my bag and returned it. Dozens of firemen, police officers, paramedics, and reporters continue to comb the area. And the entire city now knows where I live. But only the Swarm would break into my backyard and leave it on my porch.

Like a deadly addiction, I reach for it. I peer inside to find papers I've never seen before. A packet folded in half that someone wanted me to find.

I should get my mom, call Detective Irving.

Instead I pinch the corner with two fingers and pull it out like a bomb. They're printouts. Newspaper articles.

In one hasty movement, I unfold them, spread them over the coffee table. Three articles. I scan their headlines, wondering what this has to do with me.

"Blogger Killed on Bike by Hit-and-Run"

"Local Beat Reporter Stabbed to Death; Pulled from Chicago River"

"Body Found Near Ravenswood Metra Tracks"

I dig through my purse for anything else, unsure of what it means to find my phone at the bottom.

A tiny spark of hope flickers inside me, and I suppress it. Finding them now, like this, would be too easy. Illogical even. I key in my passcode and scroll through my images. Like I thought, they've been erased. Everything from Navy Pier.

At the bottom of my screen, two thumbnails catch my eye. Pics I didn't take.

I tap the first one. It's me and my mom, fighting in the kitchen. Taken forty minutes ago from outside my kitchen window.

My arms grow clammy. Numb. I swipe right.

The second picture. A close-up of the grill on our back porch. And written in the thin layer of dust covering it are the words, "Back off."

CHAPTER 6

I don't know when I finally fall asleep, but at 3:33 a.m., a loud noise I can't define jolts me awake. I lie in bed, paralyzed, sweating profusely, heart racing.

Something scrapes against the office window downstairs. The sound is slow. Taunting. Then there's rattling. Someone trying to pry open the window just below my room.

I breathe deeply, unable to afford another asthma attack, and ground myself in the plausibility of a murderer breaking in to kill me.

The office window is easily thirteen feet up. Someone would need a ladder, and there are likely still news crews out front. *Whatever I'm hearing, it's not a threat*, I try to rationalize.

I strain my ears, hypersensitive to every creak and rustle around my house. A car starts. Its door opens and shuts—a heavy one from the sound of it. The car doesn't move. It idles. A news van camping out front.

My room is pitch black except for the tiny halo of blue light hovering around my clock.

The scraping comes again, this time accompanied by a low drone—the wind.

A branch from our magnolia tree must be brushing against the side of our house. That's the scraping. No need to be neurotic. But just as I think it, my mind is back on Navy Pier . . . Dopney moans from inside the Swarm. His bones crumble as they beat his face, kick his ribs. Waves crash against the concrete.

I dig my palms into my eyes, trying to block it. I kick off the covers and sit up. I need to get a grip. Grabbing my inhaler from the side of my bed, I tiptoe to the window—to prove that there are no monsters or murderers stalking around my yard, waiting to kill me.

Despite tonight's warning.

Pulling back the curtain, I peek through the wooden blinds and make out at least two news vans below. The windows are dark, with scum reporters likely sleeping inside. Across the street, the tree in my neighbor's front yard rustles, but other than that, the night is still. My yard clear.

I check the parked cars lining the street, making sure they're empty and normal and recognizable—my neighbors' cars, the ones always parked outside.

Two houses down, I notice a black Escalade I've never seen before, its windows suspiciously tinted.

The biker from the article. The dead blogger. He was sideswiped by a dark Escalade.

I lean forward and squint, unable to tell whether I see a hand resting on the steering wheel through the windshield. I try to make out what's inside the car, if anything. As I do, a figure in the driver's seat jerks forward.

I jump back. The blinds clang against the glass as I run to my bed. I yank the covers over my head and try to shake the burning image of two eyes glowing beneath the streetlights, glaring back at me.

massage my temples, trying to stop the throbbing, like it's possible in a lunchroom packed with five hundred juniors.

If my mom had any idea my head hurt this badly, she'd insist I go home. But after spending two days tethered to my neb under her scrutiny, this is a welcome relief. Between her hovering and the reporters surrounding our house, I was itching to escape. Without distractions, I was too easily consumed by everything that happened on the pier, including the fact I had nothing to show for it. No evidence to put Lip Spikes behind bars and stop the Swarm from striking again.

My mom must have recognized my restlessness. When I told her I wanted to go to school today, she didn't exactly approve. But she didn't argue either. Doubtless it's because of what happened two years ago, how bad things got when my catastrophic thinking turned into hallucinations. Instead of anticipating the worst-case scenarios wherever I went, scenes would play out in my head so vividly that they felt real—especially my dad's attack. I couldn't stop imagining it as if it were happening to me. Dr. What's-His-Name convinced my mom that I belonged at Compass Health Center. He said I'd continue to plummet without more support. But before she could register me for their

Intensive Therapeutic Outpatient Program, I started getting better on my own. Proving Dr. What's-His-Name wrong became all the motivation I needed to control my spiraling. I became stronger. Empowered. Smart enough to figure out how to keep it all in check. Even now, with the Swarm threatening to stab me, sideswipe me, or toss me into the Chicago River, I'm not crippled by fear like I might have once been. If they expected to scare me into submission, they failed—an epiphany that came to me late last night after I figured out my next possible lead.

Katie takes her seat at our usual lunch table. Her dark eyes have a haunted expression behind them. She opens her lips and pauses like she doesn't know what to say. But before the words come out, her attention shifts. She quickly nudges her iPad to cover her sketchbook, where I swear I glimpse a drawing of me—an isolated girl, surrounded by people whispering. I avert my eyes, thankful the speech bubbles are too small to read, and pretend not to see it. It's not like she's mocking me. It's just her observation of what the day's been like. And she isn't wrong.

Katie paws her dark, silky hair and collects herself. "When I told you I was going to Navy Pier and you told me not to go, I thought you were…"

"Crazy?" I act like it doesn't hurt. When she texted me her plans Saturday morning and I wrote a million times back, begging her not to go, I could tell, even then, she thought I was irrational—her responses made that clear.

Katie drops her eyes. "You weren't making sense. You didn't say why."

Not that it would have mattered. She wasn't the only one who didn't believe me. It just stung a little more coming from her. "I'm glad you weren't there," I say. Maybe I should sound more reassuring, but I don't have it in me. The entire student body has treated me like some social leper with bad-luck disease, watching me from a distance, whispering behind my back. All of them. Like they passed around a morning memo titled *How to Handle Lia Finch* and they refuse to waver from what everyone else is doing.

I'd still take this over home lockdown.

Katie grabs a black, hexagon-shaped pencil from her backpack decorated with buttons: *Save the Parks, Hate Free Zone, Keep Calm and Be Creative.* She shades the anime avatar on the cover of her assignment notebook—the one of a girl holding a picket sign, who bears a striking resemblance to her. Katie glances at me. "I was supposed to collect signatures for Save the Parks."

I think of Pixie Girl. Where was she when the attack broke out? Did her short, skinny legs run fast enough, sparing her from everything I witnessed?

Adam walks up, completing our trio. "You look so much worse than everyone's been saying."

If there wasn't so much awkward tension between Katie and me already, I'd consider smiling. Adam mocking me for looking too boring or pale or tired feels normal. And right now, more than ever, I need normalcy.

"You should have seen me this weekend," I say.

"Oh, we did. The whole world saw you wretched and waterlogged with seaweed in your hair. Thank God someone had enough sense to give you that coat we all know wasn't yours."

Katie balances her pencil on her stack of books before spreading a napkin to serve as her placemat. She opens her bento box with separate containers for fruit, celery, beans and rice, and rolled sandwiches. As she arranges a bag of chips on the left and a bottled water on the right, I notice tear tracks on her cheeks. I should say something. Ease her guilt. She is, after all, one of the only two friends I have. Instead I pinch the bridge of my nose like it might relieve the tension pressing against my eyes.

Adam cuts his white asparagus pizza with plastic utensils. "How's the head?" he asks, like he's talking about math class.

"Kills."

From our corner in the cafeteria, Adam glowers at the students behind me. "Because of the concussion, or our charming compatriots who have no problem with their lack of discretion?" Adam throws his right hand toward the surrounding tables. "No one is even trying to hide the fact they are gossiping about you." He looks almost vicious wearing a vintage heavy metal T-shirt from a band I've never heard of and black liner around his eyes. "Your pettiness never fails to disappoint," he shouts.

A high-pitched cackle erupts from somewhere behind me. It pisses me off that I recognize Cullen Henking's laugh. The way that self-righteous sociopath mocked my dad's death still grates my nerves.

"And somehow," Adam says, "he's the hero of the story. Lia, how could you let that happen?"

"I was a little busy trying not to die."

Katie smooths the hair falling in front of her shoulder and wrinkles her nose. "I had a Cullen Henking groupie ask *me* what the inside of his house looks like." Her eyes flit toward mine, like she's gauging my reaction, wondering if we've moved past it. "As if I'd ever associate with him or his dad."

"It's gaudy," I say. "You'd hate it."

Katie's smile is weak, but appreciative. As a Save the Parks supporter, she's compelled to hate the mayor. She slides her bag of chips toward me. "Eat something."

"She's right," Adam says. "You look…"

"If you say 'wretched' again, I'll smack you."

"Grayish."

"They'd let you go home," Katie says. Her dark eyes taking on the pitying stare every adult in this school has given me today.

I pull my sweater sleeve over my palm and start wrapping the fabric around my thumb. "I needed to get out."

Shifting in my seat, I grab the chips and pretend to read the nutritional information. Even though I've bumped into them both a couple times today, it's the most we've talked about what happened.

Adam drops his usual roguish expression. "Touchy-feely is not my thing. But today I'd make an exception."

I try opening the bag, but no matter how hard I tug, it won't budge. I envision the huddled masses behind me mocking my ineptitude and throw the chips across the table.

Katie opens them easily and passes them back my way.

I lower my voice. "I took videos at the pier." I address Adam. "I got the Initiators. Shots of the Swarm." Lip Spikes. His dark brow. His pointed chin. The guy with gray eyes. Glaring at me when the attack broke, his face captured by the lens. "I caught enough to give Detective Irving, so he could build an actual case."

Adam freezes. His fork and knife hover over his plate. Both elbows jut out like chicken wings. Katie's jaw hangs slack.

"Don't look at me like that," I snap, sure that everyone behind me is trying to eavesdrop and one-up the gossip mill.

Katie fumbles for a swig of water.

"Took pictures with what?" Adam says.

"My phone."

Adam sets his plastic utensils down on either side of his plate. "Ditch them. Now. They're easy to access, and if the wrong people find those…"

"The images are gone. Pictures, videos, everything."

"Good. For a second, I didn't think you were capable of acting sensibly."

"I left my phone on the pier," I say, shocked he thinks I'd erase them myself. I risked everything for them. "It was returned inside my bag, but the footage was gone."

"Define 'returned,'" Adam says.

"I jumped into the lake without my bag. Last night, it was left on my back porch."

Katie squeezes her water bottle so hard the plastic crackles.

Adam splays his hands against the table. He closes his eyes, his thick, perfectly sculpted eyebrows adding drama to his frustration.

Everyone in the cafeteria must be watching us by now. I thought Adam of all people would understand. He's the only one who knows how much I've investigated the Death Mob. He's even been as obsessed as me at times when I've needed him for tech support. But I guess I don't need him to get it. I just need him to help me with the last piece of tangible evidence I have to go on.

Katie turns to Adam. "Someone erased them?"

"Of course someone did. Lia can't think anything through for the life of her."

"My phone was locked," I say defensively. "They hacked it."

Adam snorts. "They probably guessed your password."

"Just because you knock down firewalls every night doesn't make me incompetent."

"It's *bypass* firewalls—not the point. There are ways to hack a phone, but any idiot can figure out your password."

He acts like I'm technologically impaired. "That's not true."

"Katie, guess her code."

"The date of her dad's death?"

Adam nods, and Katie's face glows with pride.

They're the two people who know me best. That doesn't make it obvious.

"What did your mom say?" Katie asks.

I grab my pendant and twist the chain around my index finger. "I didn't tell her."

"Tell me you at least called the police!"

"Keep your voice down," I say through clenched teeth, certain that by the end of lunch, everyone behind us will have their own interpretation of what we're talking about. It's the side effect of attending a pretentious private school, where people treat Everybody's Business like it's a class they can ace and add to their transcripts.

I'm glad I didn't mention the Escalade. The articles. The warning etched in the dust on my grill. "I figured out another lead. I just need to check into it before I …"

"You realize it was a threat." Adam stares at me with a seriousness I've never seen on him before.

"Sure, but…"

"Lia." His voice is low and severe. Adam, my overly sarcastic, in-your-face friend, adapts an Armageddon-type air of gravity I didn't know he was capable of. "I wasn't planning on giving you this lecture today, but clearly time is of the essence. Whatever you found, whatever you're onto, drop it. At least let things settle down."

It was stupid of me to bring this up here, today, with every gossip mongrel in this cafeteria dying for a scene so they have more to say about the spastic girl and her freaky near-death experience. I throw my bag over my shoulder. "You sound like Maggie Finch," I say, ready to ditch as the entire cafeteria behind us hushes.

Adam and Katie look up.

"What's happening?" I whisper, my face flushing.

"I don't know about you, but today's been exhausting." Cullen Henking sits beside me, facing the cafeteria. He props his elbows behind him on our table and leans back. "All everyone wants to talk about is what happened between us this past weekend."

Cullen grabs a chip from the bag in my hands. He flashes a fake, polished smile and pops the chip into his mouth. "But there's beauty in that." He brushes his hands together, wiping away the salty residue.

I feel blotches crawl up my neck and face as I ineptly search for something to say, assuring he will never ever smile at me that way again.

Cullen swings a leg over to straddle the bench. He moves closer, brushing a chunk of knotted hair behind my shoulder with his finger.

This is my chance to humiliate him in front of everyone at this school. Or at least put him in his place. But my lips won't move and my thoughts are traffic jammed inside my head in a horn-blaring, road-raging mess.

"Here's what I'm proposing. I don't know if you've looked outside yet, but there's a camera crew just past those doors dying for an exclusive. I'm heading out to give them a few words. Wanna join me?"

Again, the smile.

Behind me, no one moves. I imagine five hundred pairs of eyes boring into the back of my head, necks craning for a better look to watch the spectacle in the corner of the cafeteria. His request is so absurd. Surely there are a million different comebacks I can sling at him, and yet I can't think of anything to say.

Not a single word.

"Look, I get that Saturday sucked for you, but you're missing out on a prime marketing opportunity. I, for example, am about to go out there and take advantage of an otherwise unfortunate situation."

"I'd rather stab myself in the eye."

Cullen chuckles like I've said something charming. He turns to Adam. "Better keep that knife away from her." He brushes the underside of my chin with his index finger.

I jerk my head away.

"If you need me, you know where to find me."

Adam chokes on his Diet Coke, nearly spitting it out across the table.

I ball my hands into little white fists. Of course he'd be all about the cameras. No doubt it's why he's wearing another collared shirt to school today.

Adam shouts after Cullen, now swaggering out of the cafeteria. "We'll keep our fingers crossed. Hopefully your performance issue that night was just a one-time thing!"

I'd laugh if I weren't so irritated. And with my head pounding, I can barely think. I would love nothing more than to stomp off and spend the rest of lunch locked in some bathroom stall.

But I need Adam's help.

I'm the closest I've ever been to proving the attacks are organized and the victims targeted. If I can do that, then hopefully someone competent can figure out who's behind them. I just need to make sure my other lead is legit before I hand it over.

Adam cuts a bite of pizza and stabs it with his fork.

I lean in. "Your program found it."

Adam drops his fork and knife. "Seriously?"

"What program?" Katie asks.

"The Search Alligator."

"You make it sound like kids' play," Adam says. He never approved of the nickname I gave it. "It's a search aggregator," he tells Katie, trying to sound annoyed, but his eyes ignite. "You're still running it?"

I pull a piece of paper out of my back pocket.

"The Swarm uses Twitter."

He reaches for the note I've pushed toward him. "It's so old school."

Scrawled in my own handwriting is the tweet I'd discovered: *#13.9.1.1300.41.891466N.87.599709W*

I suppress my smile. Despite his lecture, Adam shows interest like he does with any challenge.

He catches on right away. "Coordinates?"

Katie waves her pencil-smudged fingertips. "I'm still sitting here."

"It's a tweet I found that led me to the attack. The thirteenth one. Hashtag thirteen was one of the searches Adam's program had been running."

"I wrote an algorithm, though not my best one." He smirks. "But still impressive. I basically set it up for social media mining so that it would extract keywords, patterns, phrases—whatever Lia was looking for from a dozen or so different sites. Didn't filter very well." He turns to me. "Which means you've spent more time than I can possibly imagine sifting through that raw data."

I hold my poker face, concealing just how many hours were consumed every night for the last couple years.

"But, unlike Lia's haphazard approach, it was carefully planned and well-hidden."

"Nine one is the date." I address the paper. "Followed by time, latitude, and longitude of Navy Pier."

I think of how vindicated I was when I found it. Then I think of the way the CPD hotline receptionist thanked me for my call and said she'd pass it along to a detective, like I was some delusional little kid.

"I called the police. I tried to warn them." I glance at Katie, wondering if she dismissed my warnings as obsessed and unhinged like they did. What does she think of me now?

"Please," I say to Adam. "Will you figure out where it came from?" I hold my breath, waiting for his response as Adam examines the tweet like there's more to it.

Sophomore year, he hacked our school's emergency system and

sent texts to all the parents saying school was cancelled. Even more impressive, he was never caught. He called it white hat work, justified because we should've had the day off. The roads were ridiculous. As far as I know, I'm the only one he ever told.

"Lia—" he starts in his lecture tone.

I cut him off. "The IP address could lead to the guy who sent the tweet or maybe the guy organizing the whole Swarm." I can't look him in the eye. "I'll turn it over to a detective. I just need to know what it is first. They had leads in my dad's case and never arrested anyone."

Adam's face remains hard.

I think of Jeremiah Dopney in ICU across the city. Fighting to stay alive. My voice breaks. "This can't all be for nothing."

While I wring my hands beneath the table, I focus on Adam's black hair, perfectly molded into several peaks atop his head.

His eyes narrow. "I will do this for you on two conditions."

My lips flicker, and I try not to smile.

"Don't use the program again. Clear it from your device."

"You said it was untraceable."

"It's rerouted pretty well." Adam smirks again. "Really well, actually. But now you've raised attention. Ditch it."

"Those are your conditions?" I can't imagine deleting it completely.

"That's one. My second—every news station and half the city is questioning why you were at Navy Pier during the attack. People are suspicious. Convince them it was a coincidence. Get them off your back. As soon as you do, I'll figure this out for you."

I squirm in my seat. "What do you want me to do? Join Cullen out there talking to the cameras and make some dramatic statement?"

"You need to protect yourself," Adam says. I'm not used to his serious side lasting so long. "One small slip could get you killed."

Like my dad.

"Don't give that half-wit any more attention, but talking to the media might be worth it. The cameras suck—I get that—though at some point, your life needs to be more important than your pride."

I nod reluctantly before turning toward the cafeteria windows. Just outside of them Cullen is giving some kind of statement, his face drawn to imitate concern. I can only imagine what lies he's feeding them so he can play boy hero.

I can only imagine what lies I'm going to have to create myself.

CHAPTER 8

During advisory at the end of the day, while Mr. Mater drones on about a student council food drive and tryouts for the upcoming musical, I count three news teams on the school's front lawn, waiting to ambush me the second I walk out the doors. When my dad died, they were more discreet. Aside from Emi Vega, who nagged me for an exclusive, cameras filmed me from a distance. They wanted nothing more than a shot of the fatherless girl walking around looking sad and pathetic.

They weren't as lenient with my father. Every local station slandered his name. They made him out to be a narcissist and called his case against Morrell erroneous and self-serving.

This time, I can tell they're out for blood. They check their watches beyond the school property lines, ready to swoop in and pick at my wounds like starving vultures.

Like the Swarm.

I grab my phone and key in *Jeremiah Dopney*. It takes two links before I find an update. "Northwestern Hospital spokesperson said Dopney is still in the ICU in critical condition . . ."

He has to pull through. I can't handle spending my life knowing I should have tried harder to save his.

I tap the home button to check the time. Two news banners pop up. The *Tribune*: "Was Lia Finch the Real Target?" and the *Sun-Times*: "Does Lia Finch Know More than She's Letting On?" I toss my cell back into my bag and shove it near the bottom.

Adam was right. News feeds have been speculating all day about whether I knew about the attack. As if that's more important than the Swarm's resurgence. They want to discredit me like they did my dad, dissect me until there's nothing left, without caring what their implications could mean for me.

The bell rings. Chairs and desks screech across the floor as everyone scrambles. Mr. Mater shouts over the chaos—something about Science Olympiad—but no one listens.

I don't move.

The news teams outside inch toward the front door. I'd love to think they're looking for Cullen, someone who relishes his media attention. But they're not.

Kids spill into the courtyard two stories below. Hundreds of teenagers dressed in hoodies, sunglasses, and scarves start filling the space until the courtyard itself becomes a patchwork of unidentifiable milling high school students. The scene is too familiar, the suddenness too reminiscent of yesterday.

Any one of them down there might be a part of the Swarm. They survive on their ability to remain concealed, anonymous. They thrive on people's fear that they could be anyone, anywhere. Because of it, they're never caught. My classmates flood the lawn, and my insides twist like the tight coil of a spring. One—or more—of my classmates buzzing below might have been there Saturday. Or worse. They might have been there the day my dad was murdered.

I grip the edge of my desk. I should look away. Escape out back. But I'm locked in place. Any second, little blue orbs might perforate the brimming mass. Starting the attack. Denoting someone's murder.

And then suddenly, I see him. Broad shoulders. Hooded sweat-shirt. The gray-eyed attacker. His back is to me, but I'm sure it's him. Even from where I sit, immobilized in my desk, I recognize his shape. He leans against the school's stairs, his head bent, shoulders hunched, watching people leave, waiting for me.

I can't move. Can't breathe.

I shut my eyes. Picture Hana. The purple sky.

My throat clenches, restricting the thickening air. I force an inhale, tighten my focus: the black rock beach. Salt water foams and swirls around boulders. Swishing. Fizzing.

Mr. Mater startles me. "Lia?"

It takes several moments to register his presence. He stands behind his desk, waiting for my answer as I remind myself I'm still in his classroom.

I spin back toward the window. By the time I look outside, the boy with the hood is gone. As if he'd never been there.

"Everything okay?" Mr. Mater asks.

I stand—an awkward, jerky motion—and stack my books. "Yeah, I was just…"

Momentarily hallucinating? Flipping out because I watched someone practically murdered three days ago? Wondering where and when someone's going to kill me? There is no way for me to finish the sentence.

Mr. Mater slides his hands into his pockets and steps out from behind his desk. "If you give me a couple minutes, I can walk you out."

I jam my notebooks into my canvas bag. "No, I'm fine."

"Lia," he says quietly. "You've been through quite a bit. It's okay if you're not fine."

I wrap my thin beige cardigan around my torso. I should be used to it—adults always walking on eggshells, asking if I'm all right, like I'm a helpless, injured little bird, too weak to function. Mr. Mater has always been one of the few to treat me like everyone else—not the freak with the tragic backstory.

I consider saying, *"It's okay if you don't force an unnecessary conversation."* But I find that kind of response invites adults to talk and pry more. Instead, with my books tight against my chest, I cast him a sideways glance and mutter an obligatory "bye" on my way out the door.

Mr. Mater gives me that familiar look of pity I've seen all day. I pick up my pace toward the main staircase, eager to get home and scrub away each of those looks with a long shower.

I head to the ground floor, trying to convince myself the guy who tried to kill me or save me or scare me—whatever he did or didn't do—is not outside. More than once I've considered that *he* delivered my bag. So, what's he doing now? Checking up on me? Does he know about the IP address?

I race down the stairs, trying to convince myself it doesn't matter. Because the more I think about it, the more I'm certain I didn't see him. He was a figment of my imagination. Not a hallucination. Just my eyes and my mind playing tricks on me.

I grip the rail, steadying myself, and pause on the last step. Relaxing my shoulders, I take three deep, meditative breaths until my heart rate steadies. I fumble for my inhaler, shoot the medicated mist into my lungs, relieving the tension in my chest. Then, I turn the corner.

When I hit the school's main corridor, the hallway is near empty. I rehearse my statement and my saddened, comatose expression. But as I approach the front doors and peer out the window, I second-guess my game plan. Maybe I should call Katie to meet me around back with her car. I could sneak out, lose the cameras, escape.

Except Adam won't find that IP address for me until I shut the media up. And if I wait too long, he might become preachy and decide that helping is somehow bad for me. Besides, if anyone is out to kill me—like the guy I didn't see waiting for me in the courtyard—no one will do it on camera.

I'm about to burst through the doors when someone grabs my elbow. I spin around, ready to punch, and find Cullen Henking.

He flashes a one-dimpled smile, clearly amused by my reaction. "Easy, there. You don't want them to catch you looking jumpy and spastic on camera." He clucks his tongue. "Somewhat suspicious—like you've done something wrong. Bad for the image."

I straighten my sweater, my bag. "I almost died Saturday," I say, angry with myself for sounding too defensive.

Cullen's smile deepens. "Good thing my dad pulled you from the lake when he did," he says in a sarcastic way, like we both know it's a lie.

I turn toward the window. At least Emi isn't out there.

Cullen steps beside me. "You know, my car is on the other side of the fence." He gestures to his black Lexus parked in front of a fire hydrant, two steps past the courtyard's exit. "We could walk right past the cameras," Cullen says. "I'll take you home."

I snort. "You can't be serious."

He leans against the doorframe. "I'm willing to bet you'd do just about anything to avoid those reporters, which includes accepting a ride with me as much as you'd despise it."

I scrutinize his expression, trying to figure out his angle. Either I've grossly underestimated Cullen's narcissism or there's something more to his charade.

"In seventh grade, you posted a picture of me yawning on Instagram and called me the ugliest girl in school."

Cullen breaks out laughing. "Oh God, I forgot about that." He bends over like he can't control himself. "I'm sorry, but have you ever seen the face you make when you yawn?" He puts his hand on my shoulder. Composes himself. "Would it help if I told you you're pretty, Lia?"

I jerk away. "I hate you more than I do those cameras." I lift my chin. "I'm actually about to give my statement."

Instead of looking surprised, Cullen opens the door and stands aside. "Fair enough. Your funeral." He winks, still snickering. "Too insensitive for the girl who 'almost died'?"

I grab the straps of my bag slung across my torso and brush past Cullen through the second set of doors. Before I hit the third step, the news teams rush toward me. Three cameras crowd my personal space. Their black lenses and tiny red lights. I'm caught halfway down the school's front steps, worried if I keep walking, I'll miss a step and fall down the concrete stairs.

Three reporters talk over each other.

"Amelia, how do you feel today?"

"Why were you at Navy Pier on Saturday?"

"Did you know there would be an attack?"

The questions jar me. I'd expected them, but not so abruptly.

I mask my face. Sullen. Lifeless.

"My father," my voice squeaks. "My father," I say again, sounding somber, "loved Navy Pier. He started his career in the Navy." Not what I'd rehearsed. "He was an attorney for the Navy." I can sense red blotches creeping up my neck. "He loved to go there on weekends."

All three camera lenses swell. "I wanted to spend a holiday meant to celebrate working men and women honoring his memory. My father worked hard for this city."

A burning sensation ignites behind the bridge of my nose. I clench my gut. "That's all I have to say."

I try to sidestep them, but they inch closer.

"Can you tell us what you saw, Lia?"

"What was it like watching what happened to your father?"

"What's your reaction to alleged gang affiliate Rafael Nuñez being brought in for questioning?"

I step back, nearly tripping over the stair as I climb it. I don't know who they're talking about. "What?"

"What did the Death Mob members look like?"

"What did you share with police that implicated the Latin Royals?"

I search for my next sentence, my next move. "I didn't." I sound too weak, uncertain.

The cameras move closer, as if to swallow my head with their little black mouths.

Cullen steps in front of me, forcing them back. "As I told you earlier today, Lia has been through a traumatizing ordeal. She's answered everyone's burning question, but now, understandably, needs time to mourn the loss of her father and pray for Dopney and his fight for life."

His response sounds calm, rehearsed, like something his dad might say. How didn't I come up with something so simple?

"Now, if you'll excuse us," Cullen says.

Maybe I should shove him away. Proclaim I want nothing to do with him in front of the cameras. It's not like he actually cares about me or my father or Dopney. But the courtyard is thick and claustrophobic, and my inadequacy handling the media is glaring. Cullen guides us away from the reporters shredding me with their questions, and I let him.

He loops his arm around my shoulder in a way-too-intimate gesture. I imagine viewers watching at home, fawning over his chivalry, speculating about a relationship between us, and I jerk my shoulder.

He chuckles under his breath. His hand slips away as I focus on placing one foot in front of the other, desperate to escape this moment I'm sure will be broadcast a million times over tonight.

Cullen pulls his keys from his pocket. His Lexus beeps twice. The engine starts.

"No way," I say, refusing to get in a car with him.

I backpedal, eager to walk home and put this all behind me, when a WGN news van passes. It parks a few cars down, and Emi Vega jumps out in four-inch heels.

This can't be happening.

Cullen opens the passenger door. "The lesser of two evils?"

Emi snaps at her cameraman and darts into the street toward us.

I've loathed Cullen Henking since middle school, which is all I can think about as I bite the inside of my cheek and duck inside his car. Sinking into the leather seat, I hide behind the tinted windows. The reporters yap at their cameras in the courtyard while Emi Vega picks up speed, trying to block us.

Cullen climbs in. The car revs and peels off in the other direction, making a dramatic escape.

Adam's not going to let me hear the end of it.

"Where to?" Cullen asks, as though he doesn't have a care in the world.

I brace my feet against the vacuumed floor mat and fumble for the seat belt. There's no way he cleans his own car.

"You love this, don't you?"

His grin widens. "Love what?"

"Acting like you're rescuing me." I'm so angry for letting it happen, I stutter.

"Is that how you see me?" He squeezes my knee. "Lia, I'm touched."

I slap his hand away.

Cullen chuckles and turns left, away from the school.

"It's a game, Lia. They're so hungry to tell a story that sucks people in. Why not create that story for them? The one you want to tell. In my story, I get to rescue you." He flashes his irritating one-dimpled smile. "In your story, you get to hang out on Navy Pier for no other reason than to celebrate your late, hard-working father."

In the thirteen years we've gone to school together, it's the most honest thing I've ever heard him say, and I wonder if I did enough to silence the media's speculations. My dad was so good at spinning stories, controlling what the media reported. Why didn't I inherit that?

We pass beneath the "L" track. "Head toward Division and State."

"Gold Coast? Interesting. Didn't expect that."

"What's that supposed to mean?"

Cullen looks me over and shrugs. "Didn't peg you for a rich girl."

I cross my arms. Of course, the entire Henking family would snub anything without a designer label. "You're a jerk." I try not to squirm in my tight jeans, T-shirt, and cardigan sweater.

"And you're quite the actress. Quit changing the subject. I don't believe for two seconds that you knew nothing about the attack before it happened. And I certainly don't believe you couldn't identify anyone there."

I cast him a dirty sideways glance. "I don't care what you think."

My phone chimes in my bag. Twice. I dig through it to find texts from Adam.

you let CH help you?!?
your story was pathetic BTW. Somehow I think it
worked.

Nice to know they didn't waste time broadcasting.

"Go ahead, Lia. Tell me your little secret. How did you know there'd be an attack?"

My phone chimes again, but I'm too caught up wondering if this has been Cullen's motive all along. Today's teasing, his fake comradery, helping me with the cameras, taking me home—I can't help but think he orchestrated it so he could ask me my secrets in a moment like this. And for what? So he can spill them to reporters, monopolize the attention?

We pass Second City and hang a left on North Avenue. My phone chimes, nagging me to check the incoming text. **Theyre making you sound like a couple. I hope ur not still w him.** Followed by, **Dont ignore me. I got something for you.**

Cullen's phone buzzes too. "We've already made the news. According to Celia Green, I looked very attractive."

??? I text. He must already have the IP address. My heartbeat thumps in my temples as I wait for Adam to fill in details.

Search Alligator?
I'll ditch tonight!! Spill!

Even if the IP address doesn't link to the guy in charge of organizing the attacks, it will at least tie to one of his lackeys. Maybe a house. Or apartment complex? Even an office building is a lead.

Cullen leans over like we're exchanging secrets. "Did I look attractive, Lia?"

He runs a light as it turns red. Two cars honk at him.

I grip the door, bracing myself. "Watch the road."

Adam texts, **Took 42 minutes. New record.**

Cullen accelerates. "Where to in Gold Coast?"

With one hand still clutching the door, I silently curse Adam for taking so long.

"Am I supposed to guess?"

Then at last: Snapchat from Adam Cohen.

Of course. He has to make this difficult.

Grabbing a pen from my purse, I tap the notification, half convinced they wiped my account for inactivity. It's a picture of numbers. I scribble *24.192.0.28* to my wrist before the image switches to a scrap of paper with Adam's handwriting: *creepy demonic building ;)* The second snap vanishes faster than the first.

In true Adam fashion, he's ambiguous on purpose in case my phone isn't safe, but I know exactly where he means. The Harold Washington Library. The giant Gothic owls perching along its roof freak Adam out. He calls them spawns of Satan, mostly because he knows they fascinate me.

"Change of plan," I say. "Drop me off at the Brown Line." It's not the lead I'd hoped for. So many people use the Harold Washington Library computers each day that it might be another dead end. But it's the only thing I have to go on.

Cullen scoffs. "I'm not a cab."

He yanks the wheel to the right, shooting across three lanes of traffic. I brace myself as cars screech and swerve to avoid us. Cullen stops at a curb, in front of an Italian café.

"And you say I'm crazy." I go for my buckle, but he clamps it down and holds it, trapping me in place.

A woman in a tight suit looks up from her patio table. She watches me as she sips her red wine.

"As I said, I am not a cab. I am, however, all about negotiating."

"Let me go." I claw at the straps of my belt.

"How did you know there would be an attack?"

He tries to pull off a playful smile, but there's something sinister behind his narrowed eyes.

I grit my teeth and glare at him. "I didn't know about the attack. It was a horrible, cruel, ironic fluke I was there. Now let me go before I give you a different reason to be on the news tonight."

Cullen lets out a low chuckle and releases his hold on the belt. I unbuckle, fling open the door, and nearly jump out of the car, trying my best to look more pissed off than panicked.

Cullen shakes his head and puts on a pair of expensive-looking sunglasses.

"So many secrets, Lia. Don't think I won't get them out of you." He leans across the passenger's seat and drops his voice to a near whisper. "I'm pretty good at getting what I want."

I slam the door as hard as I can, as if I can somehow hurt him. Instead, it draws the attention of the café's half dozen patrons enjoying a late-afternoon meal.

Cullen cranks up the music before cutting off a car as he pulls away from the curb.

I swear I hear him laughing as he speeds away, leaving me behind.

Alone.

And even worse, exposed.

burst through the doors of the library. Rushing past the main lobby to the nearest staircase, I take the stairs two at a time to the third-floor computers and find an empty table in the corner. I throw my stuff down, slump in the chair, and release the breath I've been holding since getting off the "L." Nervous energy prickles beneath my skin. I slide my hat off and unravel my scarf, keeping my hands busy so no one notices how badly they're shaking.

After Cullen abandoned me in the middle of downtown Chicago, I concealed my face with the hat and scarf stowed in my bag. I kept my head low, watching for anyone trying to sneak up behind me. Stab me in the back. Throw me in the river. Toss me near the Metra tracks.

It took an hour navigating the two miles. I hugged storefronts and imagined all types of common accidental deaths: a mugging, getting caught in gang crossfire, a nudging into oncoming traffic. When I got to the "L," I sat against the chain-link fence with my keys laced through my knuckles, ready to maul anyone entering the station to murder me.

I squeeze the sides of my head as if that will stop the paranoia. I need to focus. The computer that matches that IP address. It's here. I need to find it. And once I do, I'll figure out the very small detail of how that's going to lead me to whoever sent the tweet.

Something *has* to come of this.

Standing, I flip my chair away from the table so it's facing the center of the room, making it harder to sneak up behind me. As I do, someone slams books on a table. I grab my bag, ready to make a run for it before noticing some weedy-looking kid throwing his own little tantrum at an empty table near the edge of the room. It takes several seconds before I'm able to loosen my white-knuckle grip on the chair while Weedy Boy makes a big show of ripping open his book bag and yanking out materials in some passive aggressive way to get back at life's unfairness. Any other day, the scene would be comical.

I exhale, trying to release the tension pulsing throughout my body. But as I scan the room, I notice the entire floor is packed. Eighty, maybe a hundred desktops—most of them occupied—line tables stretching across the center. Bordering the computers are smaller tables, also full, and on the far side of those, clusters of bookshelves.

Pressure squeezes my chest like a blood pressure cuff, cutting off circulation one second at a time. I didn't expect so many people. The low drone of their keyboard clicking becomes deafening, maddening.

And then somewhere from the middle of the pit, a phone rings. It's piercing. Heads snap toward the intrusion. I watch for more chimes, more blue lights, more calls. I pore over the patrons to see who else is checking a phone and who is about to stand, spin, and swarm me.

I close my eyes, and lock my knees to prevent collapsing.

This is not Navy Pier.

Just a crowded room. A phone.

These people are not about to kill me. They are students completing homework, lone adults seeking quiet refuge, study groups carrying on like it doesn't matter that the Death Mob reemerged and nearly killed someone a few days ago.

I push the fear back down the black, twisty tunnel. *Get it together, Finch.* I can't flip out like this every time I see a crowd or hear a phone ring. I live in Chicago.

"You look so familiar."

I swing my bag on instinct and find a man in a plaid shirt with a hooked, pockmarked nose sitting at a nearby table.

"Sorry." He smiles derisively. "Didn't mean to startle you." His fingers curl like talons around his book. His eyes bug out like some predatory bird's.

"It's fine," I whisper.

I can't stop looking at his hands.

Bird Man tilts his head. "Are you an actress or something?" he says in a way that makes me suddenly thankful for the packed room. "I've seen you before."

It isn't a question. It's awkward, intrusive. I tuck my stringy, whiteish-blonde hair behind my ear and am about to excuse myself when I notice the books on his table: *Lethal Violence in Chicago, True Stories of Chicago's Most Brutal Murders.*

I take a step back as I read the title of the one he's holding: *The Psychology Behind Mob Mentality.*

Bird Man's eyes gleam. "Human psychology," he says, tapping the book in his hand. "A crazed mob destroys our inhibitions so quickly, making us all do things we wouldn't otherwise do." He leans forward. "Fascinating, isn't it?"

My shoulders knot. Who is this guy? He doesn't fit the Swarm profile, but I have a burning desire to put as much distance as I can between us.

He grabs his glasses from the table and draws out the act of putting them on. "I'll figure out who you are." He stares at me longer than he should before wagging his finger. "I always do."

I sling my bag over my shoulder and flee Bird Man and his creepy fixations before tonight's news features my abduction by a child predator.

Heading toward the sea of computers where patrons stare at their screens like lifeless fish, I realize that checking the IP addresses of all these computers is near impossible. And even if I found the exact computer that was used, what good would that do?

That's when I look up and see the security cameras hanging from the ceiling. If I find the computer, Detective Irving can access the footage and cross check it with the tweet's time stamp. Irving will have the image of the guy who announced the attack, and I can somehow salvage the disaster I've created.

Excitement flutters in the base of my stomach, and I squeeze my gut. No need to get ahead of myself. I scan the room for where to begin. One kid, maybe fifteen, sits a few computers down wearing sunglasses. He's bigger—muscular—and wearing a hooded sweatshirt. I walk faster, making a beeline for him, half expecting to see the Twitter account open on his desktop with a tweet about the next attack. But when I pass his computer, he's reading a site on Henry Wadsworth Longfellow.

He's filled an open notebook with notes and lines of poetry in handwriting neater than mine.

Focus, Finch. It's not like I've uncovered the Swarm's hideout. I need to be vigilant, not neurotic.

Scoping my surroundings, I continue past him toward the far side of the room where fewer patrons sit. A murderous tweet wouldn't be sent from a screen as visible as these to anyone walking by.

I stop at the first open desktop. Signing in with my library card, I navigate the system preferences to find the internal IP address. I pull my sleeve up and compare it to the numbers on my wrist. No match.

I inch along the row, trying four more computers, and fail. Just as I'm about to hit the fifth, giggling snaps my attention away. Two people are making out at the far end of the aisle I'm standing near. They have their tongues shoved so far down each other's throats, it looks like they might choke each other.

That's when I spot a set of ten computers tucked between rows of books, far removed from the rest of the room. If someone wanted to conduct nefarious activity on the third floor at the Harold Washington Library, these would be the computers to use.

I cut down the aisle and make my way to the island of desktops. The cubbies are empty, except for a faded Loyola sweatshirt folded over a chair and a green notebook resting on the keyboard.

Starting with the computer in the corner, I tap the space bar, enter my library card, and check the IP address. I move down the line—no match after no match—until I'm down to the final two. I shake the mouse, waking the ninth screen in front of the spiral notebook and hoodie. Someone's signed in, with only six minutes left of their hour block.

I search for the user. No one's lurking. This area, for the most part, is undisturbed.

Sitting down at the tenth desktop, I check its IP—another no match. I glance back at computer number nine. Six minutes is easy to waste. Booting up the Internet on the screen in front of me, I check my email—twenty-three spam messages and one from Emi Vega. I'm irritated before I even open it.

Hi, Lia! she begins, sounding like a high school student instead of a thirty-something professional.

I would love to sit down and chat with you.

I delete it, unable to read any more. She's not getting an exclusive.

I scan the room for anyone paying too close attention to me. No one's watching. No one's sneaking up behind me. I'm ignored. And other than the sweatshirt and the notebook, I'm alone.

I search yesterday's attack. The reporters at school mentioned CPD bringing someone in for questioning, like I should know about it. But I had no idea who it was.

The top story reads "Are Latin Royals Behind the Death Mob? Gang Leader Rafael Nuñez Brought in for Questioning." It includes his picture, a mug shot, likely from a previous arrest.

Clicking on the link, I skim the article. The more I read, the more cynical I become. According to the article, Nuñez was brought in for his alleged involvement in Dopney's assault after claims that dozens of Spanish-speaking, dark-skinned teenagers dominated the tip of Navy Pier just before the attack. Which is a lie. I don't remember anyone Latino when the attack broke out. Certainly not dozens. Even with their faces covered, enough skin was exposed for me to know the

Swarm was diverse—white, black, brown. The city's always been quick to implicate gang activity, but they've never been specific about any one gang. They've never taken it this far.

I fall against the back of my chair. It's a diversion. They're pushing their only theory, that gangs are behind the attacks. And for whatever reason, they're going after the Latin Royals. It feels like an attempt to thwart the investigation. But why? Why take it to this new level?

"I figured it out," someone whispers in my ear. A bony hand slides over my shoulder.

I jerk around to find Bird Man peering at my computer screen.

"I should have known. You're quite famous."

I can't breathe, or swallow. I can't put enough space between me and his talonlike claws.

"Don't worry." Bird Man leans down and picks up the sweatshirt and the notebook. He tucks them underneath his arm. "Your secrets are safe with me." He stares at my face, which I'm sure is pale and clammy and desperate. I scoot closer to the wall. My shoulder prickles where he touched me. Like spiders crawling on my skin.

Bird Man makes an attempt at winking and walks off—back to his books on murder. I swear the air grows colder as he leaves with—was it *his* notebook and sweatshirt? Or was he simply collecting them as an excuse to taunt me?

I stare at the empty chair next to me, like it holds answers, before sliding into it and entering my library card number. A jittery rush races through me as I look up the IP address of the desktop Bird Man was using. I know before I read the numbers it's going to be a match.

And it is.

I throw my hair into a ponytail with the rubber band around my wrist and access Twitter. In the early 2000s, when flash mobs shifted from innocent dances to teens looting stores and mugging tourists, Twitter was used to communicate. Whoever organized this last attack must have known that. I guarantee he thought his little nostalgic shout-out was clever.

But I'm clever too. As I try to type *ZX_81412JT*, my fingers shake. They slip on the keys, taking me three times before I get it right. When I do, the tweet is gone.

It doesn't exist. I type in *#13*, wondering if I somehow screwed up the username. But the tweet's been removed as if it never existed. There has to be a way to retrieve it. A stored cache on my computer or Adam's computer. All I need is an image of it with that stupid time stamp. Why didn't I print it?

But when I look around for the camera Detective Irving would access to cross-check the time stamp from the tweet, I can't find one aimed at these computers. I spin in my chair, craning my neck, possibility sinking with every passing second. That's why these computers were used. Whoever sent that tweet knew exactly what they were doing. I want to cling to the hope that they used their library card to sign in. But my instinct that it would be another futile pursuit is too strong.

I smack my palms against the keyboard. This can't be it. There has to be something I'm missing.

My cell phone chimes in my bag.

Behind me, there's cackling. I snap toward it and catch the couple who was making out earlier running through the shelves in a flirtatious game of chase. The girl's hair, streaked with purple and dotted with metal barrettes, swings back and forth as she dodges her boyfriend. I roll my eyes as my cell chimes two more times.

I'm not ready to admit my failure on both leads to Adam or whoever is calling. To acknowledge that Jeremiah Dopney is fighting for his life and I have nothing to show for it.

"Give me a freakin' second." I grab my phone out of my bag and am surprised to see three texts from a blocked number:

GET OUT
NOW!!!!!
STAIRS TO YOUR RIGHT—RUN!!

I spin, searching for the threat or person texting me. But no one looks out of place. No one's paying attention to me.

I snatch my bag and fling it around my torso.

I scramble for my scarf as I half run, half walk toward the exit sign. My chest tightening, restricting my lungs, I twist the scarf around my neck and chin.

Just as I get to the door, I freeze.

It's a trap.

Someone wants me in the stairwell so I'm alone. So he can kill me. Throw my body down the stairs. Watch it ricochet off the railings three stories down.

I turn away from the exit only to slam into someone's chest. It's hard and muscular. He reaches around me, yanks open the door, and shoves me into the stairwell.

stumble, fighting to keep upright as I'm thrown into the stairwell. I grab the rail, catapult myself down the stairs, and take off sprinting.

He follows me. His steps hammer the cement. They ricochet around the concrete walls—drowning my thoughts, my ability to think.

I'm not fast enough. My feet are too tiny and weak. Four stairs from the landing, I jump, hoping to gain ground as I spiral down the empty staircase.

He does the same, landing behind me with a massive thud.

My heart sinks. He's faster than me. I'll never make it down three flights.

I round the stairs to the second-level exit. Willing my legs to move faster, be quicker, make it to the door. My life depends on it. I jump the last three stairs, hurling myself forward. Just as I grab the handle, he catches my wrist and yanks me back.

I start to scream. But his other hand reaches around and clamps my mouth shut.

He's tall and strong. He locks me in an iron-clad grip impossible to escape. I kick at him, hoping to shatter his kneecap or split his shin, but instead I'm a cloth puppet dangling in his arms.

"Calm down," he says.

His voice is deep and rough. He's trying to soothe me. He needs me to stop fighting so he can break my neck or throw me down the remaining two flights of stairs.

He takes a step forward, trying to control me. Refusing to give in, I lift both legs and kick off the wall. He loses balance and falls back against the railing of the stairwell, grunting. I rock my shoulders, flailing hard, but he tightens his grip.

His breathing accelerates. But he steadies himself with ease. He pins my arms and presses my back tight against his chest. My toes brush the ground.

I rack my brain for what my self-defense instructor would tell me to do to incapacitate him before conceding I'm completely defenseless.

"Stop fighting." He leans in as he talks, just like the boy from the pier. His cheek presses against my head. His lips brush the top of my ear, sending chills down my back, and I know without a doubt it's him. He's come to finish what he started Saturday.

"Swarm are all over this library. If they see you, they'll find out why you're here."

I thrash back and forth. Without a doubt, this is the guy who threw me off Navy Pier.

"Did you use your own account?"

He sounds angry. A short temper must be a prerequisite for the Death Mob.

"To sign in," he adds impatiently.

The fight in me deflates. My library card number. He's right. If anyone checked my account history, they'd see how many computers I signed into, that I checked IP addresses, that I'd searched for the tweet that announced the attack. Those dots aren't hard to connect.

I think of the articles that were shoved in my bag. They were meant to threaten me, prevent me from doing what I did here tonight. This is all they'd need to justify killing me. Once again, I've screwed myself over with my inability to think things through.

I nod.

My head spins, flashing through all the faces I scrutinized on the third floor. I combed that room. I didn't see anyone after me. None of them fit the Swarm's profile. Breathing becomes increasingly labored as I search for a reason he would lie to me about this.

He lowers me to the ground and loosens his grip on my arms and mouth. "I'm going to let you go."

The second he does, I jump away and spin around to face him.

The boy with the steel-gray eyes stands against the chipped blue railing of the stairwell. I press my back against the concrete, trying to keep as much distance between us as possible.

"Who are you?"

"Someone who's helping you."

I search his face for a sign of deceit, but his expression, half-hidden from the florescent lighting by a faded White Sox hat, remains emotionless and unreadable.

"I don't believe you."

His bulky hoodie—the one he wore the last time I saw him—masks the strength of his arms, which moments ago rendered me helpless. "If I wanted to hurt you, I would have."

"I don't need your help."

"Had you hacked into someone else's account to check all those computers—maybe you wouldn't," he says, like I've somehow jeopardized him.

I'm tempted to lunge at him, punch him, kick him for throwing me off the pier. "You nearly killed me."

"And you're acting like you want to die," he says, his voice intensifying as he echoes the same ludicrous thing my mom said to me yesterday. His square jaw sets. The muscles ripple beneath his skin.

I glance at the second-floor exit, assessing what it would take to escape, but he steps to the side and blocks my view.

"That couple you kept looking at?" His eyes narrow into crescent-shaped slits. "They're part of the Swarm. You're lucky they're too into each other to notice you or what you were reading."

It doesn't make sense. They were out in the open, making a scene.

"We don't walk around concealing our identities all day."

I grit my teeth, refusing to let this guy make me feel stupid. How did he know I'd seen that couple? Or what I was doing here? "How do you know so much about me?"

"Anyone with a TV knows who you are."

"Are you following me?"

He steps toward me as if to intimidate. "I don't think you get the danger you're in."

I straighten my shoulders and lift my chin, extending my 5'5" frame. "You didn't answer my question."

Above us, a door rattles in the stairway. I jump at the intrusion. Before I have a chance to look up, he grabs me and spins me around to face the second-floor exit door. With one hand clenching my bicep, he stands over me almost like he's blocking me from whoever could be coming. My back presses against his chest, only this time it feels oddly protective. My nerves thrum with adrenaline. We stare at the third-floor door hovering ajar.

"You're seeing things," a whiny female voice says on the other side of the door. "She's not here."

I think of the couple running through the bookshelves. Their silly little cat and mouse game.

"I don't want to take the stairs," she says. "C'mon."

The door rattles.

And then just like that, it closes. No one is coming.

"Was that them?" My words come out as an exhale.

"I don't know," he says, his voice low and rough. "Let's not find out."

He nudges me forward, but I plant my feet. "Why are you doing this?"

His eyes flit back and forth between mine. "I knew your dad," he says quietly.

For a moment, his words tug at my heart and I believe him. "He's dead," I say in a near whisper. "There's no way to prove that."

Facing each other, this guy towers over me, making me feel little and inadequate. He looks about my age, but he's already proven to be stronger and faster than me. If he is lying and this is all some kind of trick to kill me, I don't know how I'll escape.

He glances at the floor before staring at me with an intensity that almost makes me squirm. "He helped me once." His face remains hard-set, but there's emotion behind his expression. For whatever reason, I can't pinpoint what it is.

My dad was a prosecuting attorney for the city. Most likely—if this guy is even telling the truth—my dad cut a deal to get him out of whatever offense he'd committed: drugs, theft, murder.

Several seconds of awkward silence pass before he says, "We need to move."

He's right. That couple could change their minds and burst through these doors any second.

I dig through my bag, trying to settle the shake in my hands as I put on my hat, my scarf.

In one swift motion, he pulls his hooded sweatshirt over his head and holds it out to me. "It's big, but you'll be less…" He looks me up and down, making me self-conscious. "Noticeable."

Something about putting on his sweatshirt terrifies me.

"This"—I gesture to my disguise—"has always worked for me."

His lips twist into a scowl. "Consistency will get you killed."

I grab his sweatshirt with reluctance and throw it on over my head. "Says the boy wearing the same shirt he had on last time."

"You're the most recognizable girl in the city. No one's looking for me." He scrutinizes my new look in his sweatshirt, which is so long it hits my knees. He's once again expressionless. "You're breathing loudly."

His perception throws me. I'm paralyzed for several seconds before I dig through my bag, grab my inhaler, and breathe in the puff of cold mist.

He reaches out and pulls the hood over my head as I toss my inhaler back into my bag.

"Keep your head down." He grabs my hand, which feels fragile in his calloused grip, and I follow him down the last flight of stairs.

"Where are we going?" I still don't trust him. Whatever his plan is, I need a backup that includes running far away from him the second things look sketchy.

"The 'L.'"

"Then where?"

"You're going home." He pauses at the stairwell exit. "You ready?"

I nod. He puts his head down, tightens his grip on my hand, and shoves the door open.

He walks with deliberate ease, but his strides are long. I need to skip every few steps to keep up. We snake our way through a large common area toward the atrium that marks the library's epicenter. As we pass a cluster of tables, he swipes a backpack resting on the back of a chair. His movements are so fast I do a double take to make sure he grabbed it. Without slowing our pace, he slides it over my arm and onto my back.

I glance over my shoulder, but the chair looks undisturbed. No one seems to have noticed we just stole their belongings.

He tugs on my arm so I look ahead. "Keep walking."

Again, I shuffle to match his pace. I want to search the tables, the groups lingering near the outer edge of the room, see if I can spot the Swarm's attackers with a new lens. But I'm too panicked about looking suspicious. Instead, I keep my head down and think casual. Nonchalant.

We circle another long table. He swipes a baseball cap lying upside down on the table. His movements are so subtle, so expert, I can't imagine people noticing. At the same time, stealing everyone's stuff is hardly inconspicuous.

We leave the common area and enter the hallway. He grabs my

hand, pulls me into a mosaic alcove, and flips me around so my back is pressed against the tiled wall. I clutch my bag, trying not to brush his shirt as he shields me. He swaps my hat for the baseball cap.

"It's too big."

His fingers catch in my tangled hair as he tucks it beneath the hat. I'm not sure whether to be embarrassed it's knotted or annoyed he's so rough. His focus is tight, intense. I can't look at him. I squeeze my gut and try not to shudder every time his thumb sweeps along my neck, my ear. He breathes through his nose. Short, rhythmic bursts. His breaths are accelerated, but not labored.

"I'm not sure if I should be more scared of someone recognizing me or of wearing their things you just stole." I mean to break the tension, but my voice sounds strangled.

His expression shifts from intense to cold, metallic. He stares at me for several seconds, letting me feel his glare. "It's crucial no one recognizes you."

My breath gets trapped in my throat.

He grabs my hand, scans the hallway, and pulls me behind him.

When we enter the Grand Lobby, his eyes shift around. An older, well-dressed couple circles the opening in the center of the room. They lean over the brass railing, peering down at the floor below. A few others sit on benches lining the wall. One woman takes pictures of the ceiling with her phone. Everyone here is too old for the Swarm.

As we pass the marble help desk, neither librarian looks up. No one here gives us a second glance. We walk down another long hallway, toward the "L" platform. I reach for my CTA card in my back pocket when suddenly he yanks my arm, swinging me through a glass door.

We land in some empty conference room with long tables and chairs and no one to stop him or help me. He spins me around, and again I'm thrown against the wall, my back thudding. This time, he leans in. His forearms press the wall around my head. He drops his face near mine. For a second, I think he's going to kiss me. My stomach flips. His lips start to move, and I'm hyperaware of the space shrinking between us.

"Don't move," he whispers.

His head stays bent near my face, while his eyes watch the glass door. His breath, warm against my cheek, quickens. Just past the glass door, a group of people laugh and jeer. Four of them, at least—maybe more. Their voices come from the entrance near the "L." His body tenses, his expression severe. The jeering gets louder as the group gets nearer and then seems to fade again as they pass.

His eyes flicker to mine, but I can tell he doesn't see me. With his deadpan expression, he seems to listen for what's happening outside.

He grabs his phone from his back pocket and flips through it. "There's a Brown Line train coming in two minutes. Ready?"

I nod, my mouth too dry to speak.

We bolt through the glass door, down the hallway. He clutches my hand. I trail a step behind as we begin jogging.

When we hit the library's exit and spill out onto the city sidewalks, the train is already rumbling above us toward the station. We break into a run—a half block to the train, up two flights of stairs. With each breath searing my lungs, I push legs that are threatening to collapse like my life depends on making this train.

It pulls in as we hit the turnstile. He runs toward the car, holds the door, and peeks inside, checking, I assume, for his friends. Then he straddles the platform and the train and waves me in.

As soon as I'm on, I grab a seat and put my head down by my knees. I don't even watch the "L" train doors close behind us.

CHAPTER 11

We sit across from each other, but don't speak. A cold chill creeps down my spine as I consider everything this guy seems to know about me. I don't even know his name.

We ride around the Loop, rocking back and forth each time the train jerks and turns. The city blurs by. Parking garages. Offices. A patchwork of sleek black windows taped together with stone and steel. Commuters pour in at each station. They huddle around me, clutching the bar overhead as my knees knock into their legs.

I concentrate on breathing and try to ignore the claustrophobic sensation clawing at my throat.

Scanning the passengers flipping through their devices, I remind myself they are harmless—everyone except him. He's a part of the Swarm—the epitome of everything I hate and want to destroy. And for whatever reason, he's helped me. Twice. It doesn't make sense.

I don't trust it.

Being in the right place at the right time, knowing my name, my phone number, where I live, telling me he knew my dead father, which I have no way to confirm—it's all too convenient.

Our train rounds the corner, past Trump Tower, toward State and

Lake. People make way as he maneuvers across the aisle. He grabs the backpack at my feet and the baseball cap from my head in one swift movement. His moves are so subtle, I might not have noticed he'd swiped the hat if it weren't on my head.

"Let's go," he mumbles without looking at me. "Take the stairs to the Red Line. You lead."

Grabbing the nearest pole, I pull myself to stand. The train slows as it nears the station. I squeeze my way toward the doors, steadying myself as I walk, while noticing he looks perfectly balanced without needing to hold on. When I get to the exit, I grab my hat from my bag and adjust it in the reflection of the train doors. I smooth the hair along the sides and twist the rest so it falls like a ponytail down my neck and into the sweatshirt. My hair is too white, too recognizable. I don't need that kind of attention.

The train shudders, jerking me sideways. I grab the pole again to steady myself.

He stands behind me, his reflection in the darkened glass towering over mine. His T-shirt isn't exactly tight, though it hugs the muscles in his arms and chest. I keep my eyes hidden beneath the lid of my hat. I can't stand the thought of him seeing me look at him. Even in the reflection, his eyes are unmistakably bright.

I shift my gaze to an advertisement above the train doors. It's a panoramic view of Chicago at sunset showcasing six of the eighteen million-dollar mansions lining the lakefront. I can just make out the mayor's house. It's farther from Navy Pier than I thought.

The train doors open, and I step onto the platform. He tosses the backpack and baseball cap into a trash can as he walks by it and waits for me to go ahead.

I fall in line with the crowd heading down the stairs to the street and the Red Line—one of the actual subways in the city. It's late, but plenty of commuters are still heading home from the business district, making the station thick with passengers. The place rattles with trains coming and going. A chorus of chimes and automated voices on the overhead intercoms blur together into loud, indistinguishable background noise.

He stays a few feet behind. I don't see him, but I sense him lurking like a shadow. He's so inconspicuous, I can't help but wonder if he's followed me before. Then I remember earlier today, at school. I saw him. He'd been following me then. My stomach knots.

I saw him at my school and dismissed it as my imagination. It's mistakes like those that could get me killed, and yet I can't stop making them.

I lift my chin as my foot hits the sidewalk. Across the street, lights from the Chicago Theatre's marquee bursts through the dimming twilight. Descending the Red Line stairs, I push my way through the turnstile and take the escalator down to the platform. Hundreds of people pass me going up, headphones snaking into their ears, messenger bags slung across their torsos. None of them seem more frightened or alerted than on any other day. I'm half expecting someone to recognize me as the girl from the pier, the girl found on the mayor's dock, the girl whose father was savagely murdered exactly two years and eighteen days ago. But no one takes a second glance.

I look for Swarm, unable to find anyone who fits the stereotyped profile I've created for them. And it worries me. I have no idea who they are. Stepping off the escalator, I squeeze my way to the front of the platform, taking my place beside a tiled pillar.

I glance over my shoulder. He stands behind me, several rows of people back, not looking in my direction.

Train lights flicker in the tunnel to the right. The air is stale and warm. Sheets of discarded newspaper flutter on the tracks below. A rat scurries to take cover. Across the platform, the same Chicago ad from the train takes up most of the wall. It promotes Phase Two of the Lakefront Project, listing ways the project has benefitted the city like it's justifying the next group of mansions they're about to build. Someone has spray-painted *Save the Parks* across the entire poster in green.

I'm trying to figure out how someone crossed the tracks to spray-paint their message when the train's rumbling grows into a booming, rattling noise that overwhelms the station.

The first several cars pass as it slows to a stop. Every car is crowded. Standing room only. The car that stops in front of me is especially packed. Teenagers with hard, scowling faces stand behind the door beneath the train's putrid florescent lighting. Dozens of them. One guy glares at me with ferocity. I've never felt so hated. His lips are pressed together. His nostrils flare.

They're here for me.

They stand two feet away on the other side of the train doors, ready to mob me, to beat me to death. I try counting them, to determine my odds, but I can't stop staring at the lead boy. He's the one who will throw the first punch. I try to step back, but too many people push me forward from behind. I can't move. No one lets me move. And then the train chimes, the doors open. People flood out of the car.

Someone collides with the right half of my body, spinning me around. It knocks me off balance. This is it—the start of my attack. Not a punch or a hit, but a shove, knocking me backward. I'm falling to the ground and my death. I can't breathe. Can't run.

And then *his* arm reaches out and catches me. I don't hit the platform. His chest and his bicep hold me upright. I clutch his shirt, bracing myself for the next hit. Dozens of people file out of the train, pushing me, knocking into me.

But they go right past us.

Every. Single. One.

No one hits me or kicks me or shoves me down. Instead, each passenger rushes out of the train and up the stairs to catch their transfers.

They aren't trying to kill me. It's just a crowded train full of people shoving and racing and not paying attention like any other rush hour train on any other day. And it's that realization that makes me lose it.

I've been holding my breath for too long, and I gasp for air so abruptly I start to cough.

He guides me into the train while I wring his shirt, gulping oxygen, looking like some frenetic lunatic. I stumble as he leads me to a seat in the back of the train. A burning sensation explodes behind my nose. I start crying and shaking. It's all too much—my dad, Dopney, people who want me dead. The pain of it pours out in a horrific, ugly deluge of snot and tears and coughs.

Everything seems to fade into the background—the scene I'm making, the commuters staring at the freak show I've become, and the fact that he tilts my hat to cover my face as I cry into the chest of this guy whose name I still don't know.

Somewhere along the way, the train emerges from the city's tunnels. Dusk hits the windows, pouring into the dark and dingy car as the Red Line becomes elevated like the others in the city.

With my crying under control, I keep my face against his chest while our train travels to the north side of the city. My breakdown is humiliating enough. Last thing I need is seeing it all over tonight's news broadcasts because some jackass with a camera phone recorded my meltdown. If the city's reporters are desperate enough to jump into some fictional romance between me and Cullen Henking, I can only imagine what they'd do with this.

We're approaching Fullerton when he nudges my elbow. "We're getting off."

I lift my head. The sun's soft orange glow reminds me of how red and puffy my eyes must be. I can't get off this train fast enough.

When the doors open, he grabs my hand. Head down, eyes down, I follow him to the elevator at the end of the platform.

"Give me the sweatshirt."

The elevator doors close behind us.

"I thought . . ." My words catch in my throat. I clench my teeth. Hand over his sweatshirt. "I just thought back there . . ."

He faces the elevator door, waiting for it to open as it hits street level. "I know what you thought." His voice is dry, quiet.

Of course he does. I rub the tear stains on my face. He knows exactly what I thought because he's in the Swarm. He's seen it happen a dozen times.

I follow him for several blocks to a parked Audi that beeps as he unlocks it. I'm not sure what I expected—not exactly a black Escalade with tinted windows, but not a silver car either, much less a nice one with leather seats. It feels normal, too normal, for the nameless gray-eyed attacker who seems to be stalking me.

He opens the passenger side door.

I tense. My first instinct is to run. There are a million different ways to get home from here—bus, taxi, on foot. The second I get in his car, I'm trapped. He could take me anywhere. Do anything to me.

But hasn't he had those chances already? On the pier? In the stairwell? So far everything he's done has gone against the Swarm's MO. This guy holds answers I've spent the last two years searching for. He knows how the Death Mob operates, who's heading the organization. With both of my leads dead, I can't walk away from that. I'm not sure he'll say more than a few words at a time to me, but it's a risk I have to take.

He moves around the back of the car and climbs in the driver's side without glancing my way.

Pushing my shoulders back, I step inside, hoping this isn't the last time I'm ever seen again.

He starts the engine. Satellite radio blares acoustic rock.

It can't be his music of choice. This car has to be stolen. I stare at the blue lights on the dashboard, waiting for him to turn the station to some kind of angst-ridden punk. But he doesn't. He doesn't adjust the seat or the mirrors either. Instead, he tosses his sweatshirt in the back and shifts the car into drive.

"Why exactly are you helping me?" It's the lamest of my questions, but by now, he must know what I've been trying to do.

He pulls away from the curb and starts driving like a normal person in a very anti-Cullen Henking way. Dropping his shoulders, he leans toward the window and releases a little of the edge he's carried with him since the library. "I told you."

"You were vague."

The sun is low. The dusk has turned gray. Shadows pass over his face, making his unreadable expression more difficult to interpret than usual as we drive down a street lined with brownstone homes.

"Is it some type of guilt thing? You feel guilty for the horrible things you've done and helping me somehow makes up for that?"

We stop at a red light. For several seconds, he says nothing.

I refuse to speak, my silence demanding an answer.

At last he turns to me with his stoic expression. "Yes."

Not a shrug or a maybe or a yeah. It's a full-out yes—with eye contact.

I'm not expecting it, and my mind blanks. The glow illuminating his face turns from red to green, softening his features. He looks away, and the car lurches forward.

I grab the pendant around my neck and start twisting it around my index finger. I wrap the chain around and around, letting blood pool in my fingertip.

This guy is a murderer, not a hero. He hurts people—kills people. He's the reason my dad is dead. And I let him console me. I cried into his chest. So he could feel redemption from his crimes? "I'm not going to let you use me to absolve your guilt over murdering people."

"And I'm not going to let you get yourself killed," he snaps, shattering his mask of indifference. "The only reason your dad didn't die sooner was because his investigation was high profile. Yours isn't," he says with contempt. I can't tell if he's threatening me or not. Either way, he knows what I've been up to. "He risked his life protecting people in this city. That included his daughter," he says, like I'm the one who's done something wrong.

It's so hypocritical. Ironic. And the most he's ever said to me at once. "My dad died putting people like you away."

He snorts. "You're more clueless than I thought."

"What makes you think I won't turn you over?"

His eyes flash at me, slicing into me. He leans closer to the door, indicating the conversation is over. "I don't," he says, his even, dispassionate tone returned.

I can't tell what he means. He knows I'll turn him over? He doesn't care? He doesn't think I will? I have no allegiance to this guy. I didn't ask him to throw me off the pier. Or yank me into the stairwell. And I still have no idea why he did either.

Realizing he isn't going to reveal anything I want, I stare out the passenger window. Maybe I don't need to know more. I already know the details of his face—enough to give a sketch artist. It's better than nothing. And if that's the only tangible evidence I have, I'm not afraid to turn it over. Regardless of whether he knew my dad.

Every home we pass is dark, with the exception of a hall light or a front room lamp, casting the impression that people are inside. Usually the sidewalks are busy with runners or dog walkers, but tonight the streets are empty. Several blocks away, a halo of light rises above the buildings. I'm sure it's my house, the brightness thanks to reporters still camped out front, eager to grill me about my lust for Cullen Henking.

He jerks the steering wheel, and we come to an abrupt halt on the side of the road. "You need to be smarter."

He turns toward me, his eyes glistening against the ill-lit street. They don't feel distant and cold—emotion lies behind them, one I still can't pinpoint. And it drives me crazy. I'm usually better at reading people.

"They're watching you closely. Make yourself irrelevant."

We sit a few feet apart, his coffee house rock playing softly in the background. For a second, it almost seems like we're fighting on the same side in a war against the city.

"Were you following me today?"

"Yes."

I didn't expect an honest response. "Were you following me yesterday at the pier?"

"No."

"Were you there to kill Jeremiah Dopney?"

"I was part of the Swarm."

I clench my jaw, trying not to wince at the thought of him beating Dopney to his death. I can't forget who he is and what he does. We'll never be on the same side of anything.

"Were you there when my father was killed?"

"No." He looks in the direction of my house three blocks away. "If I were . . ." He turns back toward me and my heart leaps in my chest. "I would have done everything I could to save him." He sounds sincere, like it's the most important thing he's said to me all evening.

He nods at the passenger door. "Time to go."

"What's your name?"

He remains silent, like he's used up his allotted word quota for the day.

I unbuckle, reach for the door handle, and wait. I won't leave without an answer. At the very least, I need to know what to call him.

His steel eyes flash at me like a wolf's. "Ryan." He points to my house. "Looks like you've got company."

CHAPTER 12

Ryan grabs my wrist as I climb out of his car. "Lia." He holds on as if to emphasize his point and looks at me like we've known each other forever. "Don't trust anyone."

"But I should trust you, right?"

Something flashes behind his eyes. Amusement? Deception? Irritation?

He lets go of my wrist and turns away. "You don't trust me, so it doesn't matter."

"You don't look like a Ryan."

Ryan is a safe name, a wholesome name, a name for a guy who plays soccer and wears crew neck sweaters. Ryan is not the name of a murderer or stalker or a guy with eyes the color of metal who expresses no emotion when he talks.

Before he can respond, I slam the door and tuck my hat and my scarf into my bag. I creep along a series of wrought iron gates guarding each home. At least eight vans with satellites that reach toward the sky idle in the street, waiting to broadcast my latest secrets to the greater Chicago area. My lawn, which is big for a city lawn, is littered with reporters and camera crews. They light up my house like a sacred architectural dig site. Some of them are busy reporting. Others are waiting. For what? Has my train meltdown already become a viral sensation?

All of them ignore the sleek black town car parked outside my house. I imagine whoever was inside the car is now inside my house.

When my dad was alive, we had visitors all the time. Any of them might have been the type to take a town car to our house. But since his death, no one visits, which means whoever came in that car is here because of what happened Saturday.

At two blocks away, I zigzag—right down a side street and left past the corner house and into the alley behind our home. Even though I try to keep my steps light, gravel crunches beneath my feet.

I slink against my neighbors' detached garages. Motion sensor lights flip on two of them, their giant spotlights exposing me. As I reach for the latch on our wooden gate, Charlie starts barking like a maniac—the angry, foaming-at-the-mouth kind. Any other night I'd yell at him to shut up. Tonight, I'm more worried his bark will out me. Reporters will catch on, start herding toward me with their trivial questions. I unhitch the door, slip past my garage, and hurry onto the back deck, where I take the stairs two at a time up to our first floor. Charlie barks the entire time, but no one comes—a sign of the media's idiocy.

The curtains on our French doors block my preview to what's waiting inside. I lean over the wooden porch rail, propping myself on my stomach to peek in through our kitchen window.

Inside, a man with short sandy-brown hair that sticks up in the back sits at our kitchen counter, bent over what I assume is his phone. Richard. Behind him, my mom amicably smiles at our breakfast table and nods while clutching a paper coffee cup. It's out of character. She hates overpriced coffee or basically anything not made in her own coffee pot.

The mayor must be in there.

Playing nice with Cullen's dad is the absolute last thing I'm in the mood for right now.

I hop down from the railing and smooth out my shirt. If Cullen's inside, I'm running the other way. Never seeing him again would be too soon.

When I open the door, my eyes are drawn to Richard first. He's fixated on the TV in our living room. I assume it's about Dopney—his condition, his tie to Chicago, but instead the news anchor is talking about some city event. ". . . expecting an announcement later today regarding the fate of the annual Save the Parks Gala, originally scheduled for next week . . ." An older woman's face flashes on the screen with her name, Sydney Cornell, highlighted in white beneath it.

Richard sets his cell on the kitchen counter and stands when he sees me, his shoulders hunched like he's hiding his height. He smiles, a real one, his face bending in accompaniment.

The mayor and my mother stand in unison.

"I was just getting ready to text you," my mother says. "The mayor stopped by to check on you."

She shoots me a warning look behind the mayor's back, indicating best behavior, manners, don't pull your I'm-too-tired routine this evening. It's a look I know well.

The mayor steps forward. "Amelia." He puts out his hand. "Allow me to formally introduce myself. Jim Henking."

The mayor's undeniable presence makes my kitchen and living

room feel small and inadequate. His dark hair is combed back to the left, highlighted with the right amount of gray, as if a hairstylist colored it that way. Crow's-feet around his eyes deepen when he smiles, somehow making him look charming, not older. His white teeth gleam. He's like a walking billboard for whitening toothpaste.

When we shake, my hand feels babyish in his grip.

He pulls out a chair from our table. "Please, join us."

I throw my bag on the floor and sit, unsure how I feel that he's offering me a seat at my kitchen table.

"Would you like something to drink?" He holds out a hand to Richard, who brings him a cardboard cup holder filled with drinks. "Let's see. What do we have?"

He lifts each one to read the label.

"A vanilla latte." He returns it to its place before picking up the next. "A caramel macchiato . . ." Drink two is put back. "Or a green tea lemonade? The coffee drinks are decaf with skim milk." He waits for my choice and smiles. It's too warm, too congenial, like he's spent an exorbitant amount of time perfecting his smile in front of the mirror.

"Your mom took the chai tea latte. She didn't think you'd want that one."

My mom smiles at a drink I know she can't stand.

When I still don't respond, the mayor holds out his hand again. Richard brings over a plastic grocery bag. "We also brought a Diet Coke and a Sprite, in case you're not a big coffee drinker."

"I thought you might take the green tea lemonade," my mother says with the practiced pretense of manners and class. She's always been able to turn it on when needed.

The mayor puts the drink in front of me. "All right then . . ." He takes the latte for himself and gives the other to Richard, who returns to the kitchen counter. Richard shrugs and grins and doesn't touch his drink.

The whole thing is bizarre. The mayor of Chicago treats me like a guest in my own home and offers me one of six different drinks he picked up before coming here. My mom can't think this is normal either, not that I can tell by her expression.

The mayor takes a sip. "I came over tonight to see how you were doing, Amelia. Saturday was a tough day for our city. For you especially, I'd imagine."

The ice in my cup is near melted. Only a few flat discs left. While I like green tea lemonade, I can't bring myself to drink it. "Don't you have people for that?"

My mom shoots me a warning look.

The mayor smiles. "This is something I wanted to do myself."

So camera crews could film him being chivalrous, no doubt. It's something Cullen would do. I've never met the mayor. The only thing I know about him is that I don't like his son. Maybe not a great reason to dislike him, but something in my gut feels off.

I fold my hands in my lap. "I'm managing."

"That's an admirable answer. You're clearly a strong young lady," he says in a smooth, steady voice. "Like your mother."

He nods to my mom playing the part of the resilient widow.

"Appearances can be deceiving." I'm not sure who I'm trying to insult—the mayor? My mom? Myself? This conversation that feels phony for a million different reasons?

The mayor's smile widens, reminding me of Cullen. "You don't give yourself enough credit. When I picked you up from our dock, you were in bad shape. We were all worried it was too late. But here you are today, alive and well, walking, talking, ignoring the drink I brought for you." He gestures toward my cup. "I'd say that takes quite a bit of strength."

Watching him say it to my face, like he's trying to convince me that he carried my limp, unconscious body in his arms—I'm more certain than ever. Definitely wasn't him. Maybe Richard. His height is more accurate from what I remember. But Richard's arms are rail thin. I'm not sure he's strong enough.

I imitate the mayor's artificial smile. "I'm not sure if I got the chance to say this Saturday—I hardly remember you being there at all—but thank you so much for carrying me into your home."

Richard's eyes flicker toward me. The mayor, however, doesn't flinch.

He adjusts his suit. Tailored. Expensive. "You seem like the kind of girl who would do the same." The crow's-feet at his eyes make him look congenial as ever. "I was just talking with your mom about your dad's service."

For a moment, I don't follow what he's saying.

"You told reporters earlier today you were at the pier to honor your dad for his service to the Navy and our city," he says, clarifying like he knows I'm not sure what he's talking about. "I knew Steven well. We didn't always see eye to eye, but he was still a good man, your father." He pauses as if to honor him with silence.

I lace my hands together and squeeze. I'm sure my knuckles are turning white, but I refuse to look away from the mayor.

He leans toward me, and for a second I think he's going to grab my hand and hold it as we speak. Instead, he folds his hands together in a way that mimics mine. "You know, Lia, if there's anything you can tell us about Saturday's attack that would help our own investigation, our city would be indebted to you as well." He speaks quietly as if it's just us two BFFs sipping glorified coffee drinks, trading the intimate secrets of our lives.

Very convenient of him to finally get my name right. Very convenient of him to bring up my lie to the press after I call him out on his. But the mayor's face remains pleasant and trusting. His lips are curved in a half smile. He's handsome, like Cullen—without the transparent arrogance. His is subtle. If my gut weren't telling me otherwise, I might consider confiding in him. Or Richard at the very least. Only, right now I have nothing to tell. No images. No tweet. Turning over what I know about Ryan—if that's even his real name—is flimsy at best. Before I say anything to anyone, I need proof that someone big is orchestrating these attacks.

"I told the police everything I know already." My words come out smaller than I intend.

The mayor glances at the TV behind me. I'm tempted to look at it myself to see what he's watching, but his focus returns to me. "You know, Amelia, I grew up in this city," he says, very politician-esque. "I met my first wife at the very school you and Cullen attend. She was something else—smart, passionate, opinionated. She wanted to change the world. I asked her to marry me two months after we graduated college." He looks down as if reminiscing.

"It was her idea I get involved in politics. I started by running for alderman of Ward 51 and won. Pretty easily. Shortly after I took office, she was caught in gang crossfire while bringing home takeout from our favorite Indian restaurant. It happened in Lincoln Square—a proclaimed safe place to live and raise a family, which we never got to do." Again, he pauses.

"After that, I vowed to do whatever it took to put an end to gang violence in our city. I'm still just as committed to that cause. But I need the support of the people of this city—of you, Lia—to help me do that."

My palms press so tightly against one another that I feel the burn running up my arms. I boil inside as I fight to keep my expression even. It feels like a jab. Gangs had nothing to do with the attack. He knows my dad was out to prove that, and he must know I won't endorse that phony theory. Is that the real reason he's here? To get me on his side of the debate?

Of course, he, of all people, *needs* gangs to be responsible. He *needs* the city to be in control, taking action.

I'm tempted to say it, to clarify exactly what I *didn't* see—that there wasn't a huge Latino population on the pier during the attack like the papers are claiming. But a warning in my head screams to keep my mouth shut about this. He isn't interested in the truth. Not until I can prove it. If he's even the person I can trust with the evidence once I have it.

"That was a campaign ad, right? For your last election?" I cock my head. "I'm sure I've heard that story before—word for word."

"There was an ad that referenced my first wife's story, yes. A family history like that, well, it empowered *me* at least to do the right thing."

My mom sips her drink, breaking the quiet tension.

The mayor holds his hand out to Richard again. "Richard, give them our number."

Richard slides two cards toward my mom and me. The cards have Richard's name and number on them, not the mayor's, which I'm thankful for.

The mayor stands. "If you think of anything at all, please call. We're all on the same team here."

Once again Richard focuses on the TV, and I wonder how someone like him got involved with the mayor. They seem like complete opposites.

I turn to find Cullen and me on the screen. Emi Vega, who wasn't even there at that point, has footage of the pathetic interview I gave after school. Cullen completes his spiel about my family and me needing privacy. His schmooze is more overt than his father's. I can't believe anyone falls for either of them.

The mayor bows his head. "I'm glad Cullen was there to help you. These reporters can be real bastards." His voice is different, and when he smiles for a brief second, it's sadder. Distant. Genuine? I start to wonder if I'm wrong about him.

"I really am glad you're okay, Amelia."

The mayor buttons his jacket and walks toward the door. Richard follows.

"Mrs. Finch, thank you for having us in your home tonight. It's always nice to see you."

The mayor reaches out and shakes her hand.

She dips her chin. "Very kind of you to check in on us."

My mom begins walking toward the foyer as well, but Richard holds up his hand for her to stop. "You might want to stay back. The

second I open this door, those 'bastards' out there are going to attack."
For the first time, I notice the dark shadows beneath his eyes.

Richard brushes the lapels on the mayor's jacket. The mayor smiles, showing his teeth, as Richard bends his knees to check them—for food or coffee stains, I'm not sure. I can't believe I'm witnessing one grown man groom another.

The mayor slicks down the hair on either side of his head, as if a strand might have fallen out of place during his relatively brief stay, before Richard gives him a head nod indicating he's ready.

The mayor winks. "Good night."

Richard waves, an almost awkward gesture, before opening the door. Once they're outside, lights flash and glare like an out of control nightclub I don't want to be anywhere near.

I wait for my mom to scold me for being rude, but she's already walking toward the living room. She grabs the remote and turns the TV volume louder. We watch the mayor as he stands on our front porch fielding questions—mostly about me.

He holds up his hands to quiet them. Richard stands off to the side as if in deference.

"Miss Finch is doing as well as can be expected right now. This past Saturday was a difficult day for her and for this city. As I told Miss Finch, we will continue our zero-tolerance policy toward gang violence and work to bring Mr. Dopney's attackers to justice."

The mayor pauses, allowing several reporters to shout further questions. One woman, louder than the rest, gets his attention. "Mayor, do you believe she was there to honor her father and that her encounter with the Death Mob was coincidental?"

The mayor smiles. "I have no reason to believe Miss Finch is gang affiliated, so yes, of course I believe her."

"What about her relationship with your son?"

Richard steps forward, signaling to the mayor that his time is up.

"If you'll all excuse me, I must be getting home to my own family."

Richard clears a path through the reporters, who continue to shout questions that the mayor ignores. Their voices seep through the brick and echo on TV. Now I'm sure the mayor only came here for his photo op.

"Your dad and I—" my mom starts, and then seems to get stuck on how to finish. She turns off the TV and heads to the kitchen, where she grabs her full chai tea latte and tosses it into the trash. "We voted for the other guy."

CHAPTER 13

My cell buzzes like it's having a seizure, pulling me from a deep sleep. I should mute it or chuck it across the room, but my arms are heavy. The noise needs to go away so I can drift back to sleep in a world where my head doesn't hurt and I don't have to think.

Like a puppy who wants to be fed, my phone won't shut up. This is exactly why I don't have a dog. With my head planted in my pillow, I slap the nightstand three times before reaching it.

Adam. Of course.

Grunting, I roll onto my back and brush the hair from my face. I can almost hear the panic in his voice as I scroll through the texts he's fired off in rapid succession.

Broke into attendance. Why rn't u @ school?
What happened last nite?
LIA!!! Where r u??
Googled u. READ ur ditching school today.
Our friendship has hit a new low.

It's 10:15. Adam's in the middle of English class, breaking into the school's attendance records, texting me, and likely pissing off Mrs. Greenberg. Knowing Adam, he's not discreet about it either.

taking a personal day.

Seconds after I hit *send*, Adam texts back: **Something I should no b4 press. BFF rights!!**

I chuck my phone at the lump of covers. I love Adam, but I'm not getting into it with him right now. He doesn't understand failure. How heavy that weight can feel. How it threatens my sanity.

I had pictures of the Swarm—of Lip Spikes. Despite his hood and glasses, I caught his face when he lifted his head. Lip Spikes should be locked in a county jail.

If I would've chucked my phone into Lake Michigan, the pics would still be online. I should've planned a better escape. Or used a stolen card to sign in to the computers at the library.

I shove a pillow over my face and scream. It's muffled and strangled—not like Dopney's. When he cried out for help, it was terror-stricken, like he knew he was going to die.

And I did nothing.

Sounds of the attack trickle into my head: Tourists shrieking. The Swarm cheering. Dopney wailing, howling in the center of the pit.

I bite the cotton fabric and sob into it. I picture Dopney's face—the one shown in all the news reports. Dark hair and scruff. Bright blue eyes. And his smile. That smile haunts me most. Dopney looked like the friendly type. I bet he went out of his way for people—offered them rides, gave money to the homeless, walked his neighbor's dogs when they were out of town. He wouldn't have stood forty feet away while someone was getting pummeled to death and allowed it to happen.

The pain of it all writhes inside me as I cry like a five-year-old who's fallen off her bike. Like Dopney's family is probably crying over his unconscious body. Like I cried two years ago when some nameless doctor in teal scrubs pronounced my dad dead.

After my dad's death, I cried every night for months. I became skittish. Couldn't handle being alone. I'd go days without showering to avoid the reeling thoughts.

I promised myself I'd never be that girl again. And despite everything that's happened in the last several days shoving me toward that breaking point, that's one promise I still will not break.

Wiping my eyes, I slide out of my sheets and make my way to the front of the house. My mom's room is empty and gray despite the sunlight seeping in through the cracks of the closed blinds. Her bed is made, the comforter tight and creaseless across the mattress. My father's picture, free of dust, sits at the perfect angle toward her bed. While my floor is littered with dust bunnies and week-old clothes, hers is spotless. Immaculate.

I tiptoe across the hardwood to the window as if the reporters outside have secret X-ray cameras that might detect me. Careful not to move the blinds, I peek through the crevices for any sign of news crews. I spot three, a significant cutback. Still, their presence aggravates me.

Last night before I fell asleep, three different networks posted pictures of me with Cullen Henking and called our speculated relationship "breaking news."

Because that's what our city should be focusing on.

I peek one more time, just to be sure. No Escalade.

Grabbing a bra, I loop my hair in a constricted ponytail on top of my head and brush my teeth. I ignore the new bottles of magnesium spray and lavender soap, my mom's idea of calming agents that she's strategically placed next to the sink, and head downstairs.

Today isn't about resting. Or relaxing. Despite my mom's not-so-subtle hints.

According to my dad's files, he'd traced most of the Death Mob's victims back to a city resident. The connections were obscure—a daughter's ex-boyfriend, an old college roommate, a former colleague. One time the Swarm attacked an old woman who barely spoke English. That one really fired people up. My dad discovered she was a childhood nanny to a city alderman.

If my dad's theory was right and all the attacks were targeted, the Swarm wanted to warn or get revenge on whoever Dopney was connected to. As far as I can tell, my dad couldn't figure out their motive beyond that. But maybe he just needed one more connection.

I grab a bowl of Raisin Bran and head to the living room—a room, according to my mom, reserved for sitting, not eating, as if I might spill white milk on her white linen couches and ruin them. Sitting cross-legged on the floor at the edge of our square coffee table, I pull my laptop over.

With the Swarm likely monitoring my online activity, I can't exactly search "Why was Dopney in Chicago." But reading articles about the attack and its victim is hardly unreasonable. It'd be more suspicious if I was avoiding updates.

I type "Jeremiah Dopney," producing over six hundred thousand hits. I click the first link from the *Tribune* posted an hour ago and shovel a spoonful of cereal into my mouth.

The article says a whole lot of nothing. Dopney… still in the ICU… family with him … It's long. Redundant. No mention of his trip or why he was visiting Chicago. I skim for his chance of survival, which is shared at the very bottom. *"The next forty-eight hours will be crucial for Dopney as doctors work to restructure his jaw and assess the long-term effects of his injuries. He remains in a drug-induced coma until his future becomes clearer."*

I squeeze my eyes shut, realizing how unprepared I am to spend the day reading articles about Dopney and the attack I didn't prevent.

But it's necessary.

Drumming my fingers on the base of the computer, my nails click the aluminum in a speckled cadence as I skim through the next few sites. Most of the articles mention me and my dad and sound more like tabloids than serious reporting. One even speculates my involvement with gangs.

I snort. Of course they'd go there.

At some point, I notice the small wooden box resting on the table. Lifting the lid, I find stainless steel Chinese medicine balls. Another passive-aggressive gift implying I'm too stressed. That I might have another asthma attack. The lid thuds shut. I shove the box, which skids across the table.

As the day drifts by, I read through news articles, blogs. I even scan reporters' social media sites, despite their nauseating and self-indulgent content, but my research is futile. Not one person even tries to speculate Dopney's reason for his visit, whether he knows people in the city, whether he came here often.

Two hours into my search, I find a related link at the bottom of an article: "Amelia Finch is lying," right next to Emi Vega's immaculate face staring at me in a way that makes my skin crawl.

She *would* call me out on CNN and get my name added to the top of the Swarm's hit list. Emi Vega's so desperate to skyrocket her career out of this city and into the national market, she'd sell her soul. Or mine.

I grate my teeth. While my dad never openly talked with me about his case, I once overheard him tell my mom that whoever ran the Death Mob also made sure the attacks received very little national attention. At one point, my dad convinced CNN to run a story about it—something his critics hailed as self-indulgent, which wasn't true. More exposure would have pressured this city into action. He was interviewed, but the segment never aired. As much as I would love for this story to be exposed to a national audience, I don't trust Emi or anything she has to say.

I click the link and press my temples.

A split screen shows newscaster Gregory Irwin and Emi side by side with the little banner in the bottom right corner promoting the CNN logo. Emi's about to say something ludicrous and exaggerated for higher ratings. Of course, CNN is willing to air *her* side of the story.

I ball my hands at the sides of my head.

Irwin introduces the interview. "While others believe that gangs are not involved in the return of Chicago's Death Mob, Chicago-based investigative reporter Emi Vega believes the Latino gang that has been implicated in these attacks is being falsely accused."

Thinking I misheard it, I start the clip over and turn up the volume. Emi is *against* the gang theory?

Irwin continues. "What's your stance on this, Emi? Do you believe city officials are wasting time pursuing gang involvement?"

The screen narrows in on Vega, sporting a more toned-down look than she typically flaunts for Chicago news.

"Yes, I do. Every gang in Chicago, including the Latin Royals, has denied any affiliation with the Death Mob murders. In fact, gangs have not claimed responsibility since the flash muggings in the early 2000s. Those assaults involved anywhere from ten to twenty participants, smaller numbers than the attacks that have plagued the city for the last decade. My sources insist gangs have had no part in these murders, and there is plenty of evidence to substantiate that."

A nervous energy rushes through me. I can't believe she just disputed the whole thing.

"What kind of evidence?"

Emi cocks her head. "In the last five years, Chicago has spent over half a million dollars placing high-tech surveillance cameras around the city. Yet none of these cameras have captured an attack. Every attack has occurred just outside the cameras' view. Anywhere from fifty to one hundred teenagers participate in these mobs, but there's been no footage to identify any of them."

Greg Irwin leans in. "Are you suggesting the attackers have intimate knowledge of the city's surveillance?"

Emi lifts an eyebrow and tilts her head. Her caramel-colored hair doesn't move. "I've heard claims that cameras were repositioned just before an attack. Gangs are well connected, Greg. But this suggests a sophisticated level of organization and involvement beyond the capabilities of local gangs."

I've waited months—years—for someone to agree with my dad's theory. And of all people, it's Emi Vega. I gnaw on my bottom lip and wait for the part about me.

Irwin overgesticulates with his hands. "Has this ever been brought up before?"

Emi nods her head. "Yes. It was part of Steven Finch's investigation before he died." For once she doesn't rhapsodize a tangent, which makes me uneasy. She knows more about my dad's case that she isn't sharing. Things I don't know.

"Let's talk about Finch's daughter, who's now the sole witness to the first attack proceeding her father's. Finch claims this is a coincidence, that she was at Navy Pier to honor her father's service to the city. Do you believe her?"

I inhale a sharp burst of air.

"It seems too great a coincidence for her to be on that pier at the exact time and place of the first attack since her father's murder."

They flash to pictures of me leaving the mayor's house. My Tory Burch coat. Cullen Henking and me outside my school.

Heat crawls across my skin.

"You're saying that Miss Finch knew about the attack ahead of time?"

"I am, which also implies she successfully predicted what local city officials and the FBI could not. If I'm right, what she knows could be enough to reopen her father's case."

"Then why do you think Miss Finch doesn't come out and share what she knows?"

"According to Steven Finch, these attacks are run by people with power, wealth, and resources. They pull off premeditated attacks without consequence and frame gang activity for them. If his theory is right, and Amelia Finch has information that threatens the Death Mob's infrastructure, she could be at risk."

Irwin smirks like this is amusing, an entertaining event. "Some might accuse you of being a conspiracy theorist."

Emi nods. "Let me put it this way, Greg. If something were to happen to her, it would show the world that the Death Mob is bigger than any of us have speculated. Steven Finch's case would be reopened, and I'd imagine the city of Chicago would be under a tighter federal investigation than our city has ever seen before."

The video flashes back and forth between Greg Irwin and Emi Vega, who continue to talk like they're experts on my life, but I don't hear them. I can't get past the fact that Emi just sold me out to millions of people as a liar and a marked girl.

I jump to my feet and pace. She's going to get me killed. For whatever reason, I think of my mom and what another family death will do to her. Then I envision Emi beaming over her own success at breaking into the national market without giving a second thought to what this has done to us.

I grab one of the Chinese medicine balls and chuck it across the room. It crashes into the doors on our TV stand. Glass explodes like colorless fireworks, spewing shards around my living room floor.

I stand there in silence, immobile and terrified, barely aware of the neighbor's dog barking like he's about to lose his mind, when I hear the loud and sudden rapping on our back door.

CHAPTER 14

They've come to kill me. Right now. In the middle of my living room. A hit man with a gun waits for me to open the door and end it all, while my body refuses to budge, trapped by the certainty that I'm about to die.

Then logic kicks in. What kind of hit man knocks first?

I shake life into my limbs and inhale the courage back into my spine. Halfway to the door, a searing pain shoots into the ball of my foot. It burns like hell, but I keep hobbling toward the door, unable to feel anything until I know who it is.

A muffled silhouette waits on the other side of the sheer curtains.

"Lia?" The voice is familiar. "Are you okay?"

Ryan. I halt. Knowing who it is should relieve the tension, but it doesn't. And I don't know why. Because I can't figure him out? Because I don't trust him?

The neighbor's dog won't shut up. It grates against my already frayed nerves. Someone needs to give that animal a sedative before a reporter from the front finds a guy from the Swarm on my back porch.

Ryan bangs on the door again, making me jump. "Lia!"

I unlock the door and open it a few inches. Ryan wears a brown

130

crew neck sweater and fitted jeans. His hair is styled. His massive frame, capable of rendering me helpless yesterday, looks slender, athletic.

I partially close the door, narrowing his view of me—my rickety T-shirt, my pajama pants.

He peers inside like I'm hiding something—or someone.

I cross my arms over my chest, hoping to conceal the gaping hole in the armpit of my shirt. At least I put on a bra this morning.

"I heard a crash." The concern on his face and in his voice throws me. Yesterday, through everything that happened, he remained serious and calculating.

I don't know how to respond. Ryan looks like a guy I'd go to school with or have a crush on, not a killer or a stalker or whatever he is.

Then, like flipping a switch, his expression turns hard. He puts one hand on the door. "You're bleeding."

I look down at my foot. Blood smears the floor beneath it.

"I'm fine." I lift it to find a shard of glass jammed into the ball of my foot, surrounded by a line of dark red. "I threw something at the TV." Seeing the wound makes me realize how badly it stings. "It hit a glass cabinet."

Ryan pushes the door open and glances at the TV as if to assess the damage. He makes a noise—either a grunt or an attempt at laughing, I'm not sure. Then he stalks into my house—uninvited.

"What are you doing?" I hobble after him. Even if he's dressed like a normal person or someone I'd know, he can't just walk in.

Ryan surveys the glass, stepping over the broken pieces, and retrieves the stainless steel medicine ball from the floor. He sets it on the coffee table. Somehow, it doesn't roll off.

Ryan scrutinizes the living room and kitchen.

I limp over to the table and set the medicine ball back into its little wooden box. My foot throbs harder with each pathetic attempt to walk.

He rounds the corner into our main hallway.

"Where are you going?" I call, wanting to chase him down and shove him back outside.

His footsteps head toward the front of the house, followed by the opening of doors—the office, the hall closet, the bathroom.

I prop myself against the arm of the couch. "You can't just barge in and walk around like you own the place."

The pain in my foot intensifies. I brush fallen strands of hair back into my ponytail before inspecting it. Of course. I managed to step on the longest piece of glass, which has burrowed itself under my skin like a parasite.

Ryan returns to the living room. He leans over me to study my foot. His shoulder grazes my hair, making me hypersensitive to the narrow space between us.

Thank God I brushed my teeth.

"You need tweezers."

I make the mistake of breathing. He smells clean, outdoorsy. My stomach flips—a disturbing reaction for all kinds of reasons. This guy is in the Swarm. "Why are you here?"

Ryan walks over to the kitchen cabinets next to our fridge and opens them. He pulls down our first aid kit and rifles through it. "You weren't at school," he says, like I'm not aware of that.

"Why aren't *you* at school?"

I doubt he goes to school at all. For all I know he lives on the streets—except he's well-dressed and drives a silver Audi with leather seats.

He grabs a handful of God knows what before closing the lid. "Wanted to check on you. Tweezers?"

It takes me a second before I realize he's gathering all of this for me. I'm not the damsel in distress he's making me out to be. "I'm very capable of taking care of myself."

"You can barely walk." His tone is dry and condescending.

I'm about to point out that sitting on a couch all day doesn't require a lot of walking, but somehow that makes me sound pathetic. "How did you know where our first aid kit is?"

Ryan shrugs his left shoulder. "Everyone keeps it in the kitchen." He goes toward the front of the house and heads up the stairs.

"Now where are you going?" I shout after him.

I think of my room littered with clothes, my underwear lying in the middle of my floor. "Tweezers are in the bathroom at the top of the stairs. Left drawer." A hint of panic taints my voice, which I hope he doesn't recognize.

If he stops at the guest bathroom, he won't pass my room—if he's even looking for tweezers at all. For all I know, he could be upstairs planting bugs or cameras around my room for the Swarm, who wants a tighter hold on my activity.

I listen to him rummage through the drawer in the bathroom. Then everything is still.

I hop off the arm of the couch and limp toward the front of our house. Just as I turn the corner to the hallway, I run into him. I stumble backward on my stupid injured foot. My leg buckles, and my hand flies out to brace myself against the wall. But Ryan catches me by the wrist. His grip is solid. It immediately steadies me.

He pulls me upright, one hand pressing against my right hip to balance me as if I might fall again. His hands are cool, drawing my attention to how thin my pajama pants are.

Goose pimples fan across my hip, my stomach.

I shake his hands away, grit my teeth, and hobble back to the couch. "I couldn't hear you." I fall into the couch and prop my leg on the coffee table.

Ryan sits on the edge of the table and lifts my foot. His hand is rough—from years of fighting, I imagine—but he's gentle as he studies it. Maybe I should shake him away and kick him out, especially with my body overreacting every time he gets close. But with Emi's claim that I'm lying, the Swarm could be on their way over to find out what I know. It suddenly makes being alone less appealing. As long as Ryan's not the one here to kill me.

Ryan picks up the tweezers. "Were they showing clips of you and Cullen Henking?"

I try to avoid his eyes narrowed in concentration, the straight line of his lips.

"What are you talking about?"

"You threw a metal ball at your TV. I'm guessing you saw something you didn't like."

I tug at the bottom of my shirt to cover my midriff. Heat creeps up my neck at the thought of him seeing that charade with Cullen. I feel like I should defend myself, make it clear I would never actually date that pompous politician-in-training. Ryan and everyone else in

Chicago must think I'm some flighty, superficial schoolgirl like all Cullen Henking groupies.

The tweezers grip the glass, which tugs at my skin. When he slides it out, my foot feels like it's being sliced open. I clench my jaw, hoping he can't tell how much it hurts.

"Emi Vega called me a liar," I say, trying to keep my voice from sounding strained.

Ryan's expression remains controlled. He concentrates on my foot and the giant shard of glass he just pulled out.

"She told the whole world I know something about the Death Mob."

He glances up at me before depositing the glass on a paper towel next to him. It's thin but longer than I expected—an inch at least—and smeared with blood.

Ryan picks up a wet washcloth—from our linen closet—and presses it against the cut. After a few seconds, he pulls it back and examines my foot. I'm acutely aware of his fingers wrapped around my heel and ankle. His hand is still cold, but every nerve ending in my foot ignites where he touches me. I adjust myself, trying to sit taller as he begins dabbing the wound.

"I'm not saying my lie was good, but…"

Ryan stares at me with an intensity that clamps my mouth shut. His dark brow furrows, and his grip on my heel tightens. I can't help but wonder whether I've made a mistake by sharing.

It feels like forever before he looks away. He tosses the washcloth aside and picks up a bandage. "It's deep," he says, applying the adhesive sides. "Probably could use stitches."

"I'm not about to spend another minute in the ER."

His eyes flicker back to my face. That intensity again. I press my back into the couch and pull my foot away.

"There has to be a reason," he says, so quietly I almost miss it.

"For what?" It takes me longer than it should to realize what he's talking about.

"Vega liked your dad."

The way he says it, like he knew my dad, like he knew things about him that I didn't know, angers me.

"Emi Vega wants a national spotlight," I say, like it's not the most obvious thing in the world. "She's unethical. She'd do anything to boost her fame." Including sell me out to a band of savage teens that probably wants me dead.

Ryan grabs the glass, the bandage wrapper, and the washcloth and heads toward the kitchen.

I get stuck on the washcloth. If he went through our linen closet, he definitely passed my room. I turn my entire body toward him, staring him down. "How did you know my dad again?"

Ryan throws the trash away beneath our kitchen sink. "I told you."

"You're the one who told me not to trust anyone."

"I got in trouble. He helped me out," Ryan says, heading toward the pantry. When he comes back with a broom and dustpan, it hits me. He's too comfortable in my house.

I jump up, forgetting about my foot until I've already put weight on it and it's burning. "How do you know where everything is?"

Ryan's steps hitch for a fraction of a second.

"The first aid kit? The trash can? The broom?"

I know before he says anything that it's from watching me. He's been stalking me for who knows how long. I glance at our kitchen windows and imagine him outside in the dark, staring at me as I eat dinner, do homework, watch TV. Is he the one who took the picture? Wrote the warning on my grill? I become self-conscious, as though millions of insects are crawling all over my skin.

"Get out." I choke over the words.

"Lia . . ." He starts toward me and speaks in a calm, collected voice like he's speaking to a child.

I grab the phone and dial 911.

"It takes the cops exactly seven minutes to get to my house. I suggest you get a head start."

CHAPTER 15

Ryan's eyes are callous, metallic, the color of stainless steel. "Put the phone down."

My thumb hovers over the send button.

"I've been here before," he says, "with your dad."

It's a trick. I'm sure of it.

"*You* took pictures of me with my phone outside that window and left the articles to threaten me."

"You didn't exactly listen." He steps closer, looming over me. A shiver runs along the base of my neck. "You're running around the city daring them to kill you."

"Like you're daring me to turn you in?"

"There is a car parked down the street watching your house. They are following you, monitoring online activity, noting where you go, who you talk to. In case they want to hurt someone you care about."

"Who's *they*?"

"I don't know."

Of course he knows. He has to. I lift my phone, threatening the 911 call again.

"You won't get answers if you do that." Ryan's expression is serious. Sterile.

"Then tell me *who* I should be afraid of. Who's in charge?"

"I don't know. No one does."

I narrow my eyes. He's lying. "How can you not—"

He lowers his voice and cuts me off. "I was trying to help your dad figure that out."

I blink several times. It's not what I anticipated. Every scenario I concocted in my head explaining the relationship between Ryan and my dad involved Ryan cutting a deal with my dad to avoid punishment for whatever crime he committed. My dad made them all the time.

I lower the phone, keeping it clutched in my hand, ready to hit *send* any second.

Ryan scratches the back of his neck just beneath his hairline. He props the broom and dustpan against the French doors and walks toward me, dwarfing me with his size. He perches on the coffee table and gestures for me to sit in the armchair. Across from him. Face to face, captured beneath his gaze. I push back against the cushions, creating distance between us.

"I wanted out," he says, his voice low and rough.

I square my shoulders, scrutinize his face, looking for the smallest tic to indicate he's lying. People always give away their lies in their faces.

Ryan looks down at his hands. The thumb of his right hand massages the palm of his left hand, like he's trying to clear away a smudge. "Your dad thought he could help me."

"Why did you need help?"

He glares at me with the accusation I'm stupid for asking such an obvious question. "The people running the Swarm are dangerous. Those articles weren't hypotheticals. The guy they stabbed and threw in the river was a beat reporter looking into the attacks. And the man by the Metra tracks? He worked for your dad."

The body was found only a year ago. Had someone in my dad's office continued the case? After his death? I thought everyone dismissed his work, abandoned it.

"You can't just decide you want out and expect them to be okay with that." He clasps his hands together. His knuckles turn white. "These people do whatever it takes to get their way."

He defends himself with anger and raw emotion, like he's scared, which I didn't expect. He's been alert and decisive in situations that have paralyzed me.

"I used to come here in the middle of the night and tell your dad what I knew. Every Monday."

I try to picture Ryan hanging out in my living room with my dad. He was protective when it came to my mom's and my involvement. Wasn't he? Would he really have arranged clandestine meetings in our house with a guy from the Swarm while my mom and I slept upstairs? "He wouldn't have allowed that," I say, wanting to believe the claim.

Ryan shrugs his left shoulder and looks at his lap. "He thought it was the safest way to meet."

"For who?"

Ryan's expression deadpans. His ability to wipe his face clear of all expression unnerves me. "We were careful," he says after another long pause. His lips remain in a perfect straight line. "I snuck in through your basement. We met in his office."

"What sort of things did you tell him?"

For several seconds, I think he won't respond.

Ryan rubs his palms back and forth on his knees. "I described the attacks, how we were notified, how we got involved."

A flurry of thoughts and facts rush my head. References in my dad's case files, particularly to a man named Paul who served as my dad's lead witness, begin to have meaning. I try to connect invisible dots and can't help but wonder if Ryan and Paul are the same person.

"How did you get involved?"

"It's complicated."

His vague response infuriates me. "So is my life, if you haven't noticed."

Like everyone else, he assumes I'm not smart enough or tough enough to handle the truth. The whole thing pisses me off—that he knew my dad, that they met in secret, that it all happened right under my nose.

"Did you know the Swarm was planning to attack him?"

"No." The word is hard. His nostrils flare. "I knew there would be an attack. I had no idea it would be on him." His eyes search the floor. He shakes his head and exhales. The skin is so tight against his knuckles, I can make out each bone and muscle beneath its almost translucent surface. Ryan closes his eyes like it's some deliberate, meditative reaction before leaning forward with his elbows on his knees. "And if I did," he says, "I would have warned him." His eyes look into mine like they share the pain of my father's death. "Your dad meant a lot to me."

I clench my teeth. Swallow. I'm so used to people slandering him when they talk about him.

For the first few weeks after his death, the city honored my dad as one of the county's best chief prosecutors, who put away terrorists, drug traffickers, contract murderers. But then the media's focus turned bitter. It started with a cheap shot: someone called his courtroom flair sanctimonious. Then like an infectious disease, the smear campaign spread. Critics said the evidence against Morrell was circumstantial. My dad was called a media hog who only pursued the case for the notoriety, citing his Porsche, his tailored suits, and his designer shoes as evidence. He was blamed for Morrell's death and defamed until his friends and coworkers distanced themselves from his memory, leaving no one left to defend him but me and my mom.

"He meant a lot to me too." The words come out garbled and sad.

Ryan nods like he understands, without saying anything artificial to cheer me up or make me feel better like everyone else tries to do any time my dad is mentioned.

It rips at my chest like the picking of an open wound—how much I miss my dad, how lonely I've been since his death, how more than anything I want the people responsible for his murder to rot in prison for the rest of their evil, horrible lives.

An image of myself slumped in this same chair after my father's death flashes through my mind. My arms at my sides in a state of surrender, like some dark force had drained me of energy and life. I push it away, take a deep breath, and bury the pain like always.

Ryan's foot brushes against my injured one and lingers. He doesn't seem to notice.

"How did I end up on the mayor's dock?"

Ryan clears his throat. "I didn't throw you far enough off the pier. When you went into the water, you didn't come back up."

"You jumped in."

"When I brought you to the surface, you started coughing right away, but your breathing was rapid." He rakes his hands through his short dark hair. "I swam as fast as I could away from the pier before anyone saw you, but you needed help."

"So you dumped me on the mayor's dock?"

"I didn't have many options. I had no idea how long you had without your inhaler."

"How did you know about my asthma?"

"I check in on you," he says. "Sometimes. After your dad died, I didn't know if they'd go after you or your mom."

He doesn't flinch or look away or give any hint that he's making it all up.

The rhythmic whirl from the oscillating fan fills the room. I wish he would've worn his ratty sweatshirt instead of something so normal looking. My foot throbs where it touches his. When I can't take it anymore, I pull it away, setting it on the coffee table. I expect him to scoot over so my calf isn't pressed against his hip, but he doesn't. My entire leg begins prickling.

"I took pictures and videos of the attack. Did you erase them?"

He nods.

"They were good ones." I tried to recover them, but he'd been thorough wiping them from my phone and the cloud.

His eyes look so intently into mine I'm tempted to look away. "If they found out you had those images, you'd be dead." He pauses, allowing the weight of his words to sink in. "All those people on Navy Pier, taking pictures, and the cops don't have anything? The Swarm is good at covering its tracks." Ryan scoots closer, brushing against my leg, a detail I'm trying hard to ignore. "I need to know if you answered the tweet about the attack." There's an edge to his voice, like everything rides on how I respond.

Answered the tweet? I shake my head and pretend to know what he's talking about.

"If you signed in, if they knew you'd be there . . ."

"I didn't." My words are tiny and weak as my head reels with the implications of what he's saying. "Did you?" I have no idea what I'm asking, but I try to look assured, hoping his answer reveals something. At this point, I'm desperate for anything that could turn into a lead.

"I didn't have a choice." His voice is low and remorseful. His eyes stay hard.

Captured beneath his stare, I fight the urge to squirm beneath it.

"They're trying to figure out how much you know."

"I know the Latino gang isn't behind it."

"Don't repeat that. Not to anyone. You need to prove you're not a threat or that you're scared out of your mind and won't say anything."

"That killing me would be more complicated for them than keeping me alive," I say. I've spent the last two years finding out everything I can about the Death Mob. Now everyone expects me to stop cold turkey like a chain-smoker who just found out she has cancer. It's not that simple.

Ryan points to my necklace—the one my dad gave me a few weeks before he died. "I saw your dad the night he gave that to you."

I reach for the silver pendant, tracing the imprinted four-leaf clover with my index finger.

"He said he didn't believe in luck, but he'd do anything to protect you from the bad guys."

A sting forms behind my eyes. I clench my stomach to keep from crying. My dad was well-connected. Made promises. Might have been able to protect Ryan if he really wanted out like he claims. But the sentimental way Ryan talks about my dad indicates he might have known a more personal side to him. The man I knew, who ate Lucky Charms and sat cross-legged with me on our living room floor when we ate our cereal, who taught me how to water ski and picnicked with me at the outdoor concerts in Grant Park.

Most people never got the chance to see that side of him.

"Your dad didn't scare easily, but he was scared for you."

I remember the night he came home and put a tiny brown box in front of me at the dinette table while I was studying. He stood across from me with his hands tucked into his pockets, waiting for me to acknowledge it. Deeply etched lines surrounded his eyes and the corners of his mouth. His hair seemed grayer, and I remember realizing how much of a toll this case was taking on him. He smiled and nodded at the box. "Just a little something."

I opened it to find the necklace, its simple silver disk resting on a cotton square.

"For luck," he said as I lifted it out of the box and let it twist around my fingers.

Instead of thanking him or telling him how perfect it was, I said, "You don't believe in luck."

He walked around the table, lifted the chain from my hands, and fastened it around my neck. "I'm pretty lucky to have you," he said, kissing the crown of my head. Without another word, he went upstairs to change out of his suit.

I wore the necklace every day after that.

Ryan looks down at my leg touching his thigh as if noticing it for the first time. He and my dad might have been close, and Ryan might have saved my life because of it. But that doesn't make Ryan innocent.

"Have you ever hit anyone during the attacks?"

Ryan's jaw clenches, making his face look hard and angular. "Yes." His knuckles turn white again. I imagine his hands covered with the blood of someone helpless—an unsuspecting tourist visiting Chicago for fun, only to be attacked by a mob of savage teenagers. I fight back the urge to flee. Those hands also pulled me from Lake Michigan and kept me afloat for a mile away from the attack.

Ryan catches me staring at them. He wipes his hands on his pants and stands without looking at me. "Your mom might come home for lunch." He retrieves the broom and dustpan resting against the French doors. The glass tinkles as he begins sweeping it into a pile.

She'll be at a luncheon today for the art gallery, but I don't correct him. "I can clean up my own mess." I stand less gracefully.

He doesn't look my way. "Sit down."

Just as I'm about to protest, he adds, "If you need to run for your life, it'd be good if you're able to do it."

Between my slashed foot, my concussed head, and my crap lungs, I'm not sure I could outrun a sloth if it decided to take me down.

I sink back into the white armchair and watch Ryan sweep my mom's floor. "Does the name Paul mean anything to you?"

Ryan's shoulders drop. He turns and looks at me as if he's trying to read into the question. "Why?"

I try to sound nonchalant. "Just trying to make sense of everything."

Ryan shuffles a piece of glass into the dustpan with his foot. "He was my older brother."

My chest tightens. "Was?"

Ryan keeps sweeping as if the conversation is trivial. "He died when I was two." The strain in his voice chips away at my defenses.

"How did he die?"

Ryan's movement hitches, then stops altogether. "Asthma attack."

He keeps his head down, sweeping, while I avert my gaze and remind myself to breathe.

When he's done, he returns the broom and dustpan to its place in our pantry. Just as he's about to walk out our French doors, he pauses and stares at me. His lips part slightly.

The air between us bristles as I anticipate whatever is about to come next, like it might change everything between us.

But Ryan's eyes drop, and he leaves without saying anything at all.

CHAPTER 16

After Ryan leaves, I prop my foot on the couch and try to distract myself, but bad daytime TV only lasts so long. Every time I try to make sense of his nightly meetings with my dad or his insinuation that the Swarm has some sort of sign-in process for the attacks, I'm filled with a nervous energy that muddles my thoughts.

Too restless to sit, I hobble down the back stairs to take out the trash. Glass clinks around the bag, keeping time with my uneven cadence. Each step is awkward, but manageable if I shift my weight to the outer edge of my foot—at least that's what I tell myself.

I open the door of our heavy wooden gate. I'm about to toss the bag like I do every night when I notice a thick, padded manila envelope lying on top of one of our trash bins.

I look both ways down the narrow drive, stand on my tiptoes to check the neighbors' yards past the fences. No one is around. The alley is empty.

The package isn't addressed.

A voice in my head begs me to leave it alone, to dump the trash in someone else's bin and hide in my house for the rest of the day. It's late afternoon. Neighbors will be coming home soon. My mom.

Instead, I reach for the envelope, a slight tremor in my hands. I try to convince myself it's empty—a discarded piece of trash. But as soon as I pick it up, I notice how heavy it is. And it's sealed.

I throw the trash inside the bin, craning my neck left and right. Still no movement in the alley. The air is stale, warm, still. I wipe my palms on my pajama pants before pulling the seal open and peeking at what's inside. I can't tell. I tear the rest open and pull out a black iPad.

My heart thumps. It's a trap—the Swarm giving me a device so they can record my activity.

But I'm not that naïve. No one is. They'd have to know that.

My back tenses as I press the wake button to light up the screen. A video appears with the words *press play* projecting across the title page.

My breathing quickens. This has to be a video of me, caught doing something they don't want me doing. Going to the library? Meeting with Ryan? They've seen Emi Vega's interview and are sending me a message.

Again, the tiny voice in my head begs me to run, to call the cops, to do anything other than follow its instructions.

But it's a futile argument. There's no way I'll walk away now.

I press play.

A figure emerges, heading down the city sidewalk past a stone office building. Four American flags jut from its ledge over a row of giant revolving doors. My stomach makes a slow roll. I recognize him by the way he walks—it's my dad.

A pang of longing shoots through my chest. On the video, my dad scrolls through his cell with one hand and clutches his messenger bag with the other. His sandy brown hair ripples in the wind.

I realize what's about to happen a split second before it does as three Initiators stomp toward him.

He doesn't see them. My dad's face relaxes. He smiles at something on his phone.

The lead guy, bigger than my dad, winds up his hand to punch. He swings. My dad flinches away, dodging the hit. The second guy, Lip Spikes, anticipates it and punches him from the other direction. My dad's glasses fly from his face. He falls, his body crashing against the sidewalk.

A strangled cry catches in my throat.

Lip Spikes punches him in the face. Again. And again. I wince and gasp as the Swarm materializes out of nowhere. Dozens of them. They surround my dad in a matter of seconds.

Screaming erupts. I can't see them. But I hear them. Evening commuters run in the opposite direction, fending for themselves.

The Swarm closes in. My dad protects his head as Lip Spikes kicks him in the gut so hard that I'm sure something inside him burst.

And then my dad's gone. Blocked from the camera's view.

I drop the iPad.

Double over. Heaving.

Anguish rips through my body as if I'm the one being attacked. The world spins as horror and shock and images eat me alive. The smile on his face before he's taken down. The blow to his cheek he never saw coming. The punches and kicks that tortured him in his final moments.

I try to picture Hana, like it has any chance of calming me or steadying me or preventing me from spiraling, but every detail of its sky or beach has escaped me.

Then realization hits.

Someone *left* this for me. Wanted me to suffer. Wanted me to watch my dad pummeled to death as some threat or warning to scare me into submission. These people murdered my father for trying to stop them. And they wanted to remind me of that in the most gruesome way possible. For what? To cripple me? To send me to the psychiatric center where I can't pursue them?

Something coppery and rancid wafts into the alley.

Blood. My dad's blood.

I hold my breath. Shake my head. No, it isn't real.

Dopney's screams echo from inside the pit.

Not. Real.

I shut my eyes. Count backward. Bury the delusions. Push them out of my head.

Five . . .

My dad moans.

Four . . .

His desperation.

Three . . .

Torture.

Two . . .

The Swarm cheers.

One.

My eyes wrench open to where the iPad lies on the ground. *File Corrupt* flashes on the screen. Incessant beeping punctures the empty alley. The file is being erased. I grab the iPad and slam it against the brick lining of our garage. Glass pops, shatters, and clinks across the gravel.

I chuck the device in our neighbor's trash bin, making sure that thing stays away from my house and my mom and me. I hate them. I hate them all. The ones who attacked my dad, those who sent me this video, and whoever is calling these sick and twisted shots. Hot tears flood my eyes. I scour the alley one more time, wondering who's watching, who is reveling in my torment right now. Bursts of air pump in and out of my nose. I clench every trembling nerve and muscle, determined to keep it all in. Balling my hands at my side, my nails digging into my palms, I march, one foot in front of the other, back into my house, where I collapse behind my locked door and crumble into a million pieces.

CHAPTER 17

I wake the next morning, heavy and drained, like I'm experiencing the morning after my father's murder all over again. Only this time, instead of imagining what his final moments were like, I relive them. Every vivid detail. In a way that happy thoughts can't replace. He was smiling right before the first hit. At what? A text? From me? My mom? Lip Spike's blow batters him. My dad's body slams against the concrete. His face, once handsome, pummeled, bleeding.

I bury my head in my pillow. Part of me wants to sink into the down feathers and sleep away the next few years of my life. Free of thinking and memories and agonizing pain that shoots through every part of my body.

The Swarm would love for that to happen—it's what they're hoping for.

With every part of me broken and resistant, I push my head and shoulders off the pillow. I slide out of bed, determined to start my day, go to school, do whatever they'd least expect.

The Death Mob will not control me.

For the first time in my life, I dab concealer beneath my eyes to hide the red puffiness and I do a treatment without my mom's prodding. I grab an outfit off my floor—something I wore last week or this week, I forget—and limp down the stairs.

Spinning around the staircase, I catch a shadow as it ducks into my dad's office. A silver glint flashes in the light from the spikes in his chin.

I squeeze my eyes shut, tighten my grip on the banister, and ground myself. I concentrate on the cool, smooth wood beneath my hand. The gurgling of our Keurig machine as it drains water into a cup. The pungent smell of my mom's Mahogany coffee mixed with the faint perfumed scent of her face cream. These things are real. *The shadow,* I rationalize, *is not.*

When I step into the kitchen, my mind already feels stronger. My mom, on the other hand, pinches the skin between her eyes and leans over her coffee on the granite peninsula. "You should stay home and rest," she says to her cup.

I pour myself a glass of juice. "I'm fine," I say, already believing it. "I'll stay off my foot."

She looks me over. The cut on my foot. The stitches on my head. My torso expanding and contracting, taking in air like it should. "Your head and lungs could use an extra day too."

Like she needs to remind me that my body is defective.

My mom, always put together, wears an ivory cashmere sweater and pencil skirt. Her golden hair is slicked back in a ponytail, but her eyes are squinted like she's battling a migraine. She presses her palms against the countertop for support as she stands. "I called Dr. Ericson's office. They said he could squeeze you in on Monday."

Dr. What's-His-Name. "No."

She reaches out and puts her hand on mine. "You might need someone to talk to."

I glance at her, caught off guard. It's a plea, not a command, not a way to control all the things she can't.

How do I tell her I'm better off on my own? Ericson might have given me a few good strategies to fight my demons, but even before the whole therapeutic-setting debacle, his weekly sessions were draining and ineffective. His idea of talking was to repeatedly prod about my nonexistent relationship with the dead twin sister I never met. With my dad savagely murdered, he wanted to talk about things that didn't matter, and I don't have time for that right now. I roll my shoulders back. "I'm fine."

She wraps her fingers around my hand and squeezes. "No one's expecting you to do this alone." She waits, giving me a chance to respond, but I don't know how to. We've dealt with everything so differently and for such a long time, I have no idea how to begin bridging that gap.

Her hand slides from mine and just like that, the moment has passed. She walks to her purse and rummages through it. Pulling two twenties out of her wallet, she lets them drop on the counter like leaves falling from a tree. "At least take a cab today."

I have a sudden urge to warn her. Of what, exactly, I'm not sure. Don't open any random packages delivered to the house? Don't walk alone down our back alley? Don't be surprised if someone tries to kill me today?

"Sorry again. About the cabinet."

"Don't think you're off the hook," she says, heading back upstairs for unnecessary last-minute touch ups.

I grab the money off the counter. Closing my eyes, I allow myself one more moment of gut-wrenching self-pity. Then, without anyone's help, I swallow it down, sneak out the back door, and hobble down the stairs.

Mist floats in thick swells like waves around our backyard and alley. Like Pavlov's dog, the second I see it, my lungs start burning. Each inhale scrapes against the back of my throat despite my morning cocktail on the nebulizer.

I follow the brick pavers that cut a path across our yard and imagine heavy clouds concealing the city's height, lingering around the tops of buildings on Michigan Avenue just a mile or so in the distance.

Our back gate creaks when I open it. Before passing through, I strain every sense, scrutinizing the alley for anything that feels off. A chill creeps along the back of my neck, but I ignore it. It's just the weather.

Shifting my backpack on my shoulders, I head toward the nearest street. I make it two steps before the gate slams behind me, clanging against its latch. The pop cracks like a gunshot. I jolt back, stumbling on my injured foot. Stinging sears through me the moment I press down.

Determined to get out of the alley, I walk as fast as I can. Gravel crunches beneath my feet in an uneven cadence as I curse my beat-up body and the air for being so chilly and damp.

At the side street, the mist thins and hovers low over the road. Aside from that, it's empty. No movement on the one-way street or its sidewalks. I hang a left and head toward the nearest intersection for a cab, hobbling along like a complete idiot at a ridiculous, slow pace. My foot still burns, but like everything else, eventually I'll become numb to the pain.

I hone in on my destination, the heavy morning traffic two blocks away. As I do, someone turns the corner heading toward me on the sidewalk.

I freeze.

The deliberate way he walks at me. His height. His face dipped beneath a baseball cap.

He's part of the Swarm.

A block and a half away, I can't outrun him. Even without an injured foot, I won't make it home before he chases me down. My eyes flit up and down the street. The nearest house—I need to run to it, bang on the door, hope someone answers in time.

Before my legs have time to react, he lifts his head.

Ryan.

I cough, unaware I'd been holding my breath.

Yesterday, when I heard his voice on my back porch, I was skeptical, uneasy about opening the door. But as my heart rate steadies, relief settles over me at seeing him today.

I don't know why. Because he hates the Swarm—or so he claimed? Because he wanted out? Because he didn't try to make excuses or defend himself for the horrible things he'd done? Because he saw a side of my dad that I thought I'd lost? My dad must have trusted him if he was willing to harbor him in our home at night. As the distance between us closes, I can't decide whether I'm ready to trust him too.

Ryan's eyes are relaxed, inviting even. His mouth lifts into a tentative smile, transforming him from someone menacing into someone I'm almost glad to see. I consider telling him about the video. It's not like I'm going to confide in Dr. What's-His-Name.

Behind me, tires squeal.

Ryan's eyes dart past me, his face tightening at a car speeding down the one-way street. He breaks into a sprint, and I know without needing to look the car is for me. I need to move, run, escape, but my legs don't work. My feet are anchors, stuck to the cement.

Ryan chucks his backpack and closes the space between us faster than seems humanly possible.

Music blares as the car speeds up, getting closer.

How stupid to make its approach so obvious.

And then at thirty yards away, Ryan halts. He ducks into a side alley that's crammed between brick apartment buildings as the car skids to a stop beside me.

The music thumps in my chest. I turn as the door of a black Lexus springs open and Cullen looks up at me from behind the wheel. "Get in."

I'm so taken aback, I can't respond. A second ago I was sure someone was coming to abduct me.

I glance at the alley Ryan turned down. No sight of him—only his discarded backpack lying upside down in someone's side yard.

"Lia," Cullen shouts like I'm unable to process what's happening. "I'm giving you a ride to school. Get in." He smiles and his whole face lights up, reeking of confidence and making me wonder if he's rehearsed this look hundreds of times before.

"I'm fine." I walk away, careful to hide my limp. Putting weight on my foot kills, but I don't want to look weak in front of Cullen.

He turns down the music. His car rolls alongside me at my snail's pace.

"C'mon, get in." He sounds annoyed to ask more than once.

"I said I'm fine." I'd love to be the first girl to turn him down. "Katie's picking me up," I lie. She has a.m. Art Club, but he doesn't know that.

Cullen snorts. "You'd be safer driving with me."

I narrow my eyes. "Who are you insulting exactly? Asians? Girls? Or both? I can't tell."

Cullen looks amused.

"You missed the cameras. They hang out in front of my house."

"Lucky for me, there's a camera crew at school," he says. "If you're fine with me talking to them without you, I'll take off. Speak on your behalf. A lot of people are interested in us right now."

I halt. He sounds congenial, but he's threatening me. I'm sure of it. If Cullen talks to the press, he'll say whatever he wants. At best, it's humiliating. And at worst…after that package, I don't want to consider the worst outcome.

Cullen glances at himself in the rearview mirror. He props his elbow on the middle console and smiles at me, waiting for me to give in.

I close my eyes and think of Adam's lecture. Right now, my life should be more important than my pride. Despite how much the sight of Cullen disgusts me, my priority should be ensuring Cullen doesn't make everything worse with the media.

Scanning one more time for any sign of Ryan—nothing—I head toward Cullen's car. "Can you guarantee I'll get there in one piece?"

Cullen leans over the passenger's seat, pressing his hand against his chest. "You have my word."

I want to walk off, showing him what his word is worth. Instead, I climb in, buckle up, and let the self-loathing begin.

"I will get you there in one piece, and I will do it in record time."

Cullen winks. The car lurches forward as he slams on the gas and turns down the same alley Ryan's hiding in.

"Where are you going?" I brace myself, worried that we're going to expose Ryan or hit him. But by the time we take the corner, Ryan is walking, head down, hands tucked into his pockets. Nothing connects him to me or makes him look suspicious. Nothing outs him as the Swarm. He looks normal, like he belongs walking down this alley at this hour of the morning.

Cullen pays him no attention. "Main roads are too crowded at this time of day."

As we pass Ryan, his eyes flash up at me, making me wish I were trapped in a car with him instead of Cullen, who's driving like a complete lunatic.

I inhale sharply as Cullen turns down another one-way street, almost hitting two trash bins. "This was a mistake."

"You'll get used to it."

"This is the last time I ever get in a car with you."

"Lia," he says in a condescending tone. "If we're going to be a couple, we're going to have to start acting like it."

He narrowly avoids sideswiping a parked car.

"I came with you to end this stupid relationship story." I should keep going, emphasize my point, but I'm too busy worrying he's going to hit something. Or someone.

"You need to start reshaping your image."

Cullen slams on the brakes for a red light. My body lurches forward and catches on the seat belt.

"Excuse me?"

"Vega made you look like a Death Mob stalker. Created a level of suspicion you don't want," Cullen says, all serious.

His perception throws me. "You don't know me or what I want," I say, my back flattened against the passenger's seat.

"Sure I do." He turns toward me while I stay clenched, anticipating the light turning green. "You want the press to go away, which they're not going to do. Like it or not, you have thousands of people desperate to read anything with your name in it."

"You realize you're contradicting yourself."

"Don't interrupt. You can bet the press will exploit a citywide audience like that. So either you give them something to talk about, or they'll start digging."

My nails claw into the leather. I fixate on the red signal and try to appear nonchalant. "I have nothing to hide."

"You and I both know you have plenty to hide. But you still have control here."

I glare at him from the corner of my eye. "What are you talking about?"

"Were you online last night at all? We're a hit. I woke up with two hundred more followers than I had yesterday. Everyone loves us, and they want more. The press eats that stuff up."

That's exactly why I avoided the Internet. Blogs. Social media. Tabloid frenzy. I can only imagine how I've been portrayed, dissected, profiled. It's enough to make me reconsider leaving my house. Ever. Again. And Cullen's relishing it.

I watch the light, bracing myself for the moment he takes off. "You act like you're doing this for me."

"I am."

"You like the attention."

"Sure." He shrugs. "Maybe I'd do it for any girl at our school with sixteen camera crews camped in her front yard." Cullen turns back to the road and the light, now green. He slams on the gas. The car peels off, and I jam my fists into the seat cushion, fighting to stay upright.

Cullen flashes a smile. "Or maybe I like you."

I want to vomit. His intentions are one hundred percent self-serving. "You're a terrible liar."

"Have you watched your sad attempts at lying? That bit about your reason for being on Navy Pier? You're lucky I rescued you."

I refuse to defend myself and give credit to his claim as Cullen swerves in and out of rush hour traffic on the two-lane road.

"Doesn't matter why I'm doing it. It's good PR." He winks. "Which you could use after Vega's interview."

We jolt to a stop behind a line of cars and inch our way toward a busy four-way stop.

"Your dad knew how to handle the cameras. I'm sure you inherited some of it."

He says it with reverence, but his words hit the wrong nerve. "Leave my dad out of this."

"It's a compliment. Your dad was smart, an expert at manipulating the media. When he spoke to cameras, he did so in twenty- to thirty-second bites, tailor-made for the evening news. Your dad made bold choices, but he was smart. Everyone in this city knows that."

He says it like my insides aren't twisted, like all of that wasn't eventually used against him. I can only imagine what the media would say if

I started flaunting my five minutes of fame. With Cullen Henking of all people.

Cullen's phone pings. He grabs it from the cup holder and scrolls through texts. "All I'm saying is that a lot of successful people control the spotlight instead of letting it control them. Why wouldn't you?"

When I was little, my dad and I were watching him on TV one night when I asked him if he was famous. Instead of answering, he loosened his tie and told me it was important for the public to see that those who do wrong get punished.

If I sold out to social media and reporters, things I despise, my reasons wouldn't be as just. But would it be worth it? Would it distract news feeds or anyone else who thinks I stalk the Death Mob? Are people so desperate for gossip that a ridiculous, pseudo-relationship could accomplish that?

The music bangs around Cullen's car, muddling everything. I press my knees together at the thought of Lip Spikes, his eyes flickering up at me, his tongue running along his bottom lip like he's about to devour me whole.

Cullen flashes me a picture. The two of us from yesterday. "We're almost up to eighty-two hundred likes." He laughs. "That's nearing celeb status."

"A bunch of high school kids fawning over you hardly makes you a celebrity."

The car rolls closer to the stop sign. "Doesn't matter who it is. That's eighty-two hundred people interested in you, despite your little Swarm fetish. And all they care about is whether I'm driving you to school today. Don't underestimate the power of that."

I turn away, desperate to escape the conversation. I'm nauseous for even considering it. Ryan told me the Swarm didn't kill my dad sooner because of his high-profile case. Would making myself relevant at least buy some time to figure out my next move? The media and their audience are among the groups I despise most, but the real enemy is the Swarm. Aren't I willing to do anything to take them down?

We approach the intersection, where a handful of protestors stand on the corner. High schoolers, I'm guessing. A couple twenty-somethings. They hold poster boards declaring atrocities committed by the Lakefront Project. A girl with tiny french braids swirling in intricate designs around her head shouts, "Save our parks," most of it drowned out by the chaos coming from the stereo.

"Don't encourage them," Cullen says flatly.

"Got something against freedom of speech?"

"I got a thing against people bashing my dad. Maybe you can relate."

One protestor nears our window and shoves the sign at the car. "On with the gala!"

"What gala?"

"A party set up by self-righteous housewives who need an excuse to get dressed up and have their picture taken in the name of 'park preservation.'" He rattles it off while scrolling through his phone. The car creeps forward, closing in on the bumper of the car in front of us. "You realize they're bashing the mayor's efforts to save the city on sidewalks that were repaved with Lakefront Project funding. This city was billions in debt before my dad took over." Clearly, he's had this discussion with his father before.

He tosses his phone in the cup holder and flashes me a fake smile. "Good stuff for my girlfriend to know."

As we inch along, I spot Katie in the back of the protestors, wearing a thick headband and ruffled skirt. She looks empowered as she folds her Save the Parks sign painted in perfect beveled letters and tucks it into her backpack with its trio of buttons. Her cheeks are flushed, her eyes ignited. For as quiet as she can be at school, she's in her element out here, defending a cause she believes in.

I duck, not knowing how she'd react if she saw me in Cullen's car. I can't imagine she approves of any interaction I've had with the mayor's son. What would she think if I went along with this horrific idea and pretended to be his girlfriend?

Cullen rolls through the stop sign and slams on the gas, cutting off the car to our left who has the actual right-of-way.

"I haven't agreed to anything."

"You have about sixty seconds to make up your mind." Cullen jerks the wheel, and we vault into the school parking lot, packed with students heading toward the building. We drive past them, toward the front line of parking spaces, which by now should be full. Cullen turns right down an open lane, taking the corner much too fast. The car jolts as he slams on the brakes inches away from a girl with cropped black hair and a cropped green jacket.

My chest bangs against the seat belt again.

The girl slams her fist on Cullen's trunk. Her mouth falls open as if to scream at him, but as she looks inside the car, she stops. Her eyes dart back and forth between Cullen and me, making the hairs on my arms and neck bristle. She drops her head, wraps her jacket around her chest, and hurries toward the building. Something about her seems off. And somehow familiar. But just as I'm about to wonder why she's so afraid of

Cullen, I see the camera crews. At the far end of the parking lot camped outside an empty spot.

"You called them," I snap, pissed that I got in his car, pissed that I made this so convenient.

Cullen faces me. Once again, his tone is serious. "I'll come around and open your door. I'll stay on your right side. Hold on to my arm, and no one will notice that limp or the puffy eyes you're trying to hide."

Cullen stares at me in a way that, for the first time, doesn't feel completely smarmy before hitting the gas and speeding toward the cameras like he's late for school. The crew shuffles aside as Cullen eases up and rolls in. He smiles at the reporter and leans toward me. "Ready?" He kisses me on the cheek.

I flinch, fighting the impulse to wipe it away, and try to reassure myself that ditching the target on my back is necessary if I want to destroy the Swarm.

Cullen steps out of the car and flirts with the lead reporter. When he opens my door, light from the camera shines in my face. I grab for Cullen's arm so at least my wounded foot isn't plastered all over the station as the next bit of something "newsworthy."

I keep my head down—partly in resignation that I'm lowering myself to something so humiliating.

Cullen does the talking. I tune it all out, forcing myself to smile once or twice and willing myself to hold on to his arm instead of running the other way, far from the absurdity of what I'm doing. I hear Cullen say, "I guess we both lucked out that she ended up on my dock," and decide to hyperfocus on walking like I don't have a jolt of pain shooting up my leg. The camera with its glaring light and the reporter with her trivial questions follow us like we're famous. Before I know it, it's over, and I feel the need to shower.

"See? It wasn't so bad."

I can't look at him. "Sure." I keep my head down, anxious to put distance between us.

Cullen chuckles as we go our separate ways.

The walk to my locker feels extra long, either from the pain in my foot or the general unease that makes my skin itch. I feel disconnected to everyone around me, to what just happened in the parking lot, to the series of terrifying events over the last couple days that have somehow become my life. It isn't until I get to my locker that I pinpoint exactly why I feel so uneasy.

The girl with the black cropped hair and the army jacket is the same girl I saw in the Swarm five days ago—right before I jumped off Navy Pier.

CHAPTER 18

The blood drains from my face. The hallway chaos of students brushing past each other, shouting to friends, opening and closing locker doors fades into background noise. Someone from the Swarm is at my school.

And she knows I'm here.

I stand at my locker, spinning the dial as the white numbers blur together. I can't remember my combination. What if that girl is here to kill me? Last night's package wasn't a warning. It was a way to torture my final days.

I don't know where to go, where to hide—whether to stay at school or run for it. I picture her at the pier. She was wearing sunglasses, a stocking cap. Black hair stuck out beneath it. And the way she'd stood, clutching her bag—she had the same posture today. It was undeniably her.

"I just saw a news reel of you and Cullen Henking walking with his arm around you. I almost threw up my smoothie."

I recognize Adam's voice as he approaches, but I can't bring myself to look at him.

He notices my near-catatonic state and drops the sarcasm. "What are you doing?"

I can't respond.

"Lia?"

Adam grabs the lock from my hands, spins the combination, and opens the locker. He eases my backpack off my shoulders and starts stacking the books I need for first period.

"There are worse things than being Cullen Henking's girlfriend, I'm sure. Nothing comes to mind, but don't worry, we'll fix it."

"I saw someone," I whisper, "from the Swarm." My head and body feel light, like a buoy swaying in water, anchored by my feet.

"Here?" His voice is urgent. He grabs my arm. "Let's get you out." He swipes my bag and tugs me toward the hall, but my feet stay planted. I can't shake the image of Cropped Hair Girl during the attack. She'd stood along the outskirts of the fight, her distress palpable.

Katie walks up, clutching her sketchbook. "What's going on?"

Her words barely register. I can't shake Cropped Hair Girl's reaction to seeing Cullen and me in the car. The second she saw me, she rushed off like she was uncomfortable in her own skin.

"Lia?" Katie says, but it feels like she's in another world.

"She didn't want me to see her." Ideas begin to shape themselves. This has nothing to do with the package last night. "She doesn't want me to identify her."

Adam tugs me again. "Who cares. Let's go."

"Who didn't want you to see her?" Unease escalates in Katie's voice. "What's going on?"

Ryan claimed he doesn't want to be in the Swarm. If Ryan's forced to participate like he says ... I think of the way Cropped Hair Girl looked during the attack—like she didn't want to be there, like she didn't belong.

Adam tugs harder. "She saw someone from the Swarm, and we're getting out of here."

Katie gasps. "Here?"

I pull away from Adam's grip.

"Katie," I begin.

Somewhere down the hall a locker door slams shut. Someone screams—a high-pitched cackle. I jump and spin toward the noise. Two students are doubled over, laughing.

I turn back to Katie. "Do you know anyone with black hair, choppy, just above her chin? She was wearing an army jacket."

Katie fumbles. She looks back and forth between Adam and me, unsure of what to do. "There's"—I can almost hear her mind spinning— "Stella Mangrove? Or..." She hugs her sketchbook as if it might shield her. "Sadie Lasky? But they're not in the Swarm," she adds with uncertainty. "Are you sure you saw her right? Don't the Swarm disguise themselves?"

Adam rubs the back of his neck. "I can't believe we're having this discussion. Even I can think of at least three girls that fit that description of the hundred or so people I know by name. But that leaves eleven hundred other students I can't vouch for who may or may not be here to kill you."

I grab my backpack from Adam. "I need you to find her for me." A game plan begins to take shape. "Take a picture of anyone who might look like that. I need to know who she is."

"Maybe Adam's right..."

I halt. Katie's light-tan skin blanches. She looks petrified. Even if Cropped Hair Girl is no threat, I can't involve Katie and risk her becoming a target. My eyes flicker to Adam, hoping he'll volunteer, but his face is set in pissed-off mode.

I slip my backpack on one shoulder at a time. "Forget about it." I shut my locker and start limping away, surprised my foot hurts so much. "See you guys later."

"I never said I wouldn't do it."

I turn back to see Katie retrieving her cell phone from her backpack. Her thumb shakes as she types like she's scheduling "find girl from Swarm" in her calendar. "I can do this." Katie smiles nervously. Her silky dark hair drapes over both shoulders, making her look too innocent to hunt down Swarm members.

"No, I'll think of something else—"

Katie cuts me off. "You'd do it for me. Besides, I owe you one." Her eyes flicker down before settling on mine. She still feels guilty for thinking I was crazy when I told her not to go to the pier. Or maybe it's because she had friends there—people she didn't warn.

I try to convince myself I'm not endangering her life by allowing her to help. The truth is, I need her.

I give her a weak smile. "Don't be . . ." I struggle with how to finish. "Obvious."

"Covert. Got it." Katie's eyes sparkle for a moment. "I always wanted to be a spy."

Katie is the last person I'd ever peg for espionage. Still, I feel a small sense of relief. I avoid eye contact with Adam and head toward the library, my game plan focalizing.

If the Swarm was hoping that video of my father's murder would cripple me, they were wrong.

Adam starts after me. "Where are you going?"

My steps are awkward. "The library."

"Then I'm coming too."

"I'm fine. I'm just—"

Adam cuts me off. "I think you're an idiot. You should flee the premises, but I'll be damned if some girl wearing a nasty, second-hand-store army jacket is going to off my best friend today."

I bite my lip, grateful for their comradery. Adam and Katie are the only two people in this entire school I'd want on my side. Katie in her thick headband and her ruffled skirt. And Adam in his tight black jeans, faded Black Sabbath shirt that's ripped at the collar, and leather bands tied around his skinny wrists. As if deliberately contradicting his outfit, his black hair is sculpted into a side pompadour and he's wearing thick-rimmed Tom Ford glasses. He picks up on what I'm thinking.

"I might not look like much of a threat, but my intellect is unmatchable."

Adam walks beside me without asking why I'm going to the library or what I plan to do there, which is good. I wouldn't have an answer for him if he did.

"I hope you know what you're doing with Cullen Henking."

"I don't even know how we're going to get into the library without a pass."

"You have the greatest sob story of anyone at our school."

He's right. It's about time I start using that to my advantage.

Adam references a picture of Jeremiah Dopney standing on the Skydeck's Ledge. "He was in Chicago three years ago."

After spending the first four periods scouring Dopney's social media sites, Adam finds a picture of Dopney's feet hovering over a bird's-eye view from the Skydeck's glass balcony 103 floors above Wacker Drive. Makes me nauseous just looking at it. No caption, no mention of anyone else he was traveling with or visiting. Just the picture that, luckily, Adam recognized.

"Two trips in three years? He must have been visiting someone," I say with more conviction than I feel. The truth is, I need Dopney to have a connection so badly I'm almost willing to invent one for him.

I prop my foot on a stepstool Adam stole from the biography section and shift in the boxy wooden chair. It has to be the most uncomfortable chair ever created, like the school needed another way to torture its students. On a desktop tucked into the back corner, I scroll through old yearbooks uploaded in our library's database, looking for Cropped Hair Girl while Adam sits beside me manning his iPad. At his insistence, both of us are signed in to his school account, not mine.

I point to a strip of electrical tape over the camera on his iPad. "What's with that?"

"Precautionary measures. These things are incredibly easy to hack. This"—he flicks the tape with his finger and raises his eyebrows like I should be impressed—"prevents anyone from picking up the feed."

Adam's cell phone buzzes. He checks it before flipping it around to show me the latest picture Katie sent of a girl with short black hair. This one has a nose piercing, heavy purple eye shadow. I shake my head. To Katie's credit, she's had five passing periods and already sent half a dozen pictures of girls who fit the description. Unfortunately, none of them have been close. Same with my yearbook search, though I'm not sure I'd recognize Cropped Hair Girl with a different haircut. More than once, I've wondered whether I hallucinated this morning, made associations that don't exist.

I think about what Cullen said about me—that I used to pretend my twin sister was still alive. He was right. I remember creating elaborate scenes involving the two of us having tea parties in the basement and dance competitions around our swing set. I remember talking to her about the routines we performed. I pictured her facial expressions when I dictated instructions, basically making her my backup dancer. She would nod like it was a good idea. I guess that's the thing with an imaginary dead sister: she'll do whatever you want her to do.

Adam scrolls through Dopney's online picture galleries, many of which showcase pictures of rare birds he'd come across. "The guy's a homebody. Other than his two trips to Chicago, he's completely boring—except for his bird fascination." He flips his iPad so I can see the screen. "Look at this one," he says, referencing a bird with a crazy wingspan about to take flight.

Adam's phone buzzes again. I glance over, already prepared to dismiss it when I see a picture of Cropped Hair Girl—the actual one I'm looking for—pulling a book out of her locker. I jump in my chair and grab for the phone, but Adam beats me to it.

YES, he writes. Get her name.

How??

My body shakes with anticipation.

Adam stares at the picture. **Never mind.**

"What are you doing?"

Adam swipes at his device. The school's homepage. The staff intranet. He keys in a password and continues clicking. "For the record, she's wearing an army-green jacket, not an army jacket."

He hits the link: *Locker assignments.*

"How are you doing this?"

Adam looks at me through his designer glasses. "Mrs. Greenberg's an idiot. Her password is one, two, three, four, five. What's the locker number?"

I grab Adam's phone and zoom in on the number above the locker Cropped Hair Girl is rummaging through. "Two, five, one, zero."

Adam smirks like he just did something sinister. "Amy London. Junior."

I turn to the desktop. The real research begins. My hands shake as I type Amy London's name into the Internet toolbar and hit enter.

Katie sends another picture. A caricature of herself in a Sherlock Holmes cap and a tweed cloak fluttering behind her like a cape. Beneath her sketch, she's included *#elementary.*

I should text her back, validating her impressive detective skills, telling her she's the best friend in the world for what she's done. Instead, Adam and I fix our concentration on our devices. I search media databases. Adam attacks social media networks. Neither of us says anything.

The first page of results proves worthless. None of the sites have anything to do with the Amy London I'm looking for.

Adam flips his iPad around. "Her social media activity looks like a short-lived phase in middle school." She posted a few photos of her with a younger boy I'm guessing is her brother. "She has one group picture from seventh grade with fifteen nitwits we know. But the posts stop right after they started."

"Surprising for anyone at this school." Everyone here seems obsessed with social media.

Like Cullen and his 8,200 likes.

"Sure—except for you."

I shrug my left shoulder, and think of Ryan. The way he shrugs his shoulder like it's a signature move. I straighten my back, click *images*, and search again for Amy London. Halfway down the page, I find a poorly pixelated photo of a nine-year-old Amy London standing with a giant 54 hanging around her neck. Amy London's hair is long and pulled back in two side braids. She looks so different I'm not sure if it's even her.

"Give me your phone." Adam hands it over, and I hold up Katie's text next to the screen to see if the pictures are of the same person.

Adam peers at the comparison. "Braids are hideous, but it's her. Not exactly Swarm material."

I click on the image, and it takes me to someone's personal blog. Adam and I both lean in to examine the picture. Next to her, Amy's well-dressed father stands with his hand resting on her shoulder. The headline of the post reads "My Niece: Cook County Spelling Bee Finalist."

"You've got to be kidding me," Adam says under his breath.

I skim the rest of the post by Amy's aunt, who spends most of the time talking about her brother, Daniel London, being a proud parent and remarking that Amy's spelling bee trophy, for being among the top ten, is among the family's high accomplishments.

The tone of the post feels pathetic. She didn't even win. "This is weird, right?"

Adam squints like it might clarify everything. "Google the dad."

The search produces over three hundred thousand hits including images. I click on one of the links and begin reading.

"An architect?" I'm surprised. By the way he is dressed and posing for each of his pictures, I'd anticipated something more lucrative and smarmy.

Adam points to a list of awards on Daniel London's company page. "The kind that wants everyone to know how important he is."

"Did you turn in your passes to the front desk?"

A library assistant with heavily dyed dark hair and red lipstick peers down at us. I scan the library for the other library assistant, the one I first talked to when we came in. I want her to wave her friend off, but she's nowhere to be seen. I can't remember her name to even reference her. Just like this library assistant, they tend to blend in with every other nameless adult wandering the hallways of our schools. It would be so helpful if they wore nametags like waitresses at a diner.

"Mr. Mater gave us permission to be here." I try to hold her eye contact so she doesn't look at my screen and find our search has nothing to do with science.

"How long did he anticipate you'd be here?" Her voice is thick with skepticism.

I can't help but stare at her scalp, which looks as if she poured dark brown hair dye all over her head and forgot to wash it afterward.

"She's Amelia Finch. Maybe you've heard of her?" Adam answers with so much condescension, I'm sure she's going to kick us out just for being rude. "She's kind of had a rough week."

"I have an injured foot," I say before Adam can continue. "Mr. Mater said we could stay as long as I needed. You can call him if you'd like." Mr. Mater said no such thing, but as my science teacher and advisor, he's my safest bet if she calls my bluff and talks to him.

Nameless Library Assistant's expression softens. She must recognize my name. I begin to wonder what kinds of emails the entire staff has been sent regarding how to handle me.

She offers a weak smile. "As long as someone knows you're here," she says before shuffling away.

Adam glares after her. "You realize she's about to call the school social worker about the crazy girl hiding in the corner of the library."

"Not the first time it's happened." I shrug and return to the screen, knowing our time is now limited. "There has to be something that gives us a clue to why his daughter is involved in the Swarm." I scroll through the results on Daniel London, looking for any sign of a strained relationship. Maybe he kicked Amy out or left her mom to marry someone young and horrible, who locked Amy in her room every night. The spelling bee picture portrays them as a loving father-daughter team, but something must have happened for her to go rogue and join the Swarm. Unless, like Ryan, someone's forcing her to participate.

"I give us five minutes, tops." Adam directs my attention to the library assistant returning to the circulation desk. She whispers to her anonymous colleague, something about us that causes Library Assistant Number Two to glance my way with a look of horror and pity. One of them picks up the phone.

"Five minutes is generous," I say.

I hit *images* as my final attempt to find something out about this family.

I scan through the hundreds of pictures—all of which portray Daniel London as a guy in love with himself.

Adam grabs my forearm and points to a tiny thumbnail image of Daniel London standing among a team of seven men. "Isn't that . . ." Adam stops midsentence.

I click the link to enlarge it. "Bill Morrell." The words come out as an exhale. Bill Morrell, the man my father was in the process of prosecuting when he was murdered. Bill Morrell, the man responsible for my father's death. Bill Morrell, the man who committed suicide like a giant coward just after my father died, basically confirming his affiliation with the Death Mob and my father's murder.

I click on the link. It takes us to an article from the *Tribune* dating back five years, about the ground breaking for Phase One of the Lakefront Project. The article celebrates the project as the savior of our city that would bring tourism and industry back into Chicago.

My hands shake as Adam leans over and hits command-print on the keyboard.

"Recognize anyone else?" Adams whispers, like we're on the verge of uncovering the city's most dangerous secret. Like who heads the Death Mob.

I'm filled with such an adrenaline rush I can barely read the names listed below the picture: Frank Davies, Maximilian Horowitz, Daniel London, Edward Cunnings, Bill Morrell, Clyde Jennings, and Harry Hewitt. All the men stand in suits in a kind of semicircle. They have the same smile spread across their faces and seem to share in some kind of comradery.

I don't know any of them. I shake my head before looking up at the circulation desk. Both library assistants are absorbed with their computers. Before a social worker or principal comes to whisk me away to a private room where I can discuss my feelings on the tragedies of my life, I need to at least figure out who the rest of these men are.

"You take the first three." My words are breathy, barely audible, but Adam picks up on it.

"What are we looking for?"

"I don't know." And I don't. I wish I had at least four more hours to research each of these men.

"Frank Davies," Adam says as he skims through his findings on the iPad, "is the general superintendent and CEO of the Chicago Park District."

I blink, unable to add it all up.

"He had"—he pauses to read—"a scandalous divorce from a very wealthy woman before remarrying someone half his age—a few years older than his daughter, who looks our age."

"Edward Cunnings," I say, scrolling through the links that come up when I google him. "Owns a lumber company in the burbs." I click the first link and keep skimming. "He worked on the first eighteen homes to line Lake Michigan in Phase One of the project." I return to the search results and click on the fourth link down. "One of his sons committed suicide two years ago."

I read more closely. Jamie Cunnings was sixteen and went to a nearby private school. From his picture, he looks handsome—the kind of kid who could get away with anything based only on his looks. He doesn't look the type to commit suicide. Of course, they never do.

Just as I'm about to search my next guy, I see Mr. Mater walk into the library.

I nudge Adam, who sits up straighter in his chair.

I'm not ready to stop—not yet. My eyes jump to the last two faces in the picture like I'm about to lose them forever. Something about the last guy looks familiar, though I can't place it. I type in *Harry Hewitt* and hit *search*, certain I'm teetering on the cusp of something big.

According to the top result, Harry Hewitt started his construction company just six years back. I click on the link to his company and see three of the Lakefront mansions plastered on the front page.

Mr. Mater starts talking to both library assistants, who once again flash me a look of pity.

I click on the *Meet the Team* link at the top of the site. The second the page pops up, a tight, little gasp escapes me. Harry Hewitt has a professionally photographed picture of his entire family, and they are beautiful, stunning even—especially their son, Ryan.

My head spins, making me so dizzy I can't think. Ryan's dad. He's involved. Is that why Ryan's forced to participate? Is that why my dad approached him? I hit *print* and log off the computer just as Mr. Mater begins walking toward me.

Adam slides around his chair. "I'll get our stuff from the printer," he says, abandoning me.

I grab my bag and try to stand, as if I'd been planning to leave the entire time.

Mr. Mater sticks his hands into his pockets. He tilts his head to one side. "I got a call that you and Adam Cohen have been here for a few periods."

I refuse to look at him. Instead, I watch Adam taking his time over at the printing station. It's clear he's ditched me during this conversation with Mr. Mater, likely so I can play up the woe-is-me angle. But for whatever reason, it's a bit harder to do with Mr. Mater.

"I hurt my foot last night. Walking on it really hurts." I look him in the eye for as long as I can before my gaze breaks away. "It's not like I can concentrate in any of my classes."

I slide my backpack over my shoulders and straighten it on my back.

Mr. Mater's eyebrows purse. "Lia, I don't mind writing you a pass if you need it, but I'd feel better if we all knew where you were while you're here at school."

I look at the tables of scattered students and the rows of multi-colored books—anywhere but at Mr. Mater.

When I don't respond, he fills the awkward silence. "I can write you a pass to see the social worker if you want."

"No." My answer is curt.

"I got you in at twelve thirty, but you need to leave now," Adam calls out across the library like he's in a giant rush. "Here are your intake forms. The secretaries get all fussy if you don't bring them." He throws papers from his dad's practice down on the table, ignoring Mr. Mater and the serious conversation he's trying to have with me. I try not to look confused.

"Hey, Mr. Mater," Adam says as he grabs my arm like he's helping me walk.

I grab the stack, noticing the picture of Ryan poking out from the bottom.

"My dad generously squeezed Lia in to take a look at her foot."

"What happened to your foot?" Mr. Mater asks with doubt in his voice.

Adam answers for me. "Giant gash. She needs stitches. Crazy week for her, right?" I wonder if Mr. Mater recognizes Adam's condescending tone or that he's making it up as he goes. The wound has closed. I don't need a doctor.

Mr. Mater rocks back and forth on his heels. "Sounds rough."

"Luckily, she's well connected to a nationally recognized plastic surgeon." Adam flashes a giant fake grin as I wonder if people actually hire plastic surgeons to stitch up a cut on the bottom of a foot.

"Good thing."

Mr. Mater is just going along with it at this point.

As Adam leads me out of the library, I accentuate my limp as if it might sell the story.

"See you later, Mr. Mater!" Adam says, laughing at his own rhyme.

I follow Adam through the turnstile and out of the library, clutching the printouts of the Lakefront team and of Ryan's family like my life depends on it.

CHAPTER 19

When Adam and I walk into the lunchroom, we're assaulted by the smell of grease and cooked vegetables. We snake our way toward our corner table with our packed lunches, where I have every intention of spending the period on Adam's iPad. But as we get closer, Cullen Henking approaches Katie from the other side of cafeteria. Her bottom lip curls into her mouth as she sketches in her notebook. He leans over the table and says something to her. Her body turns rigid. She glares at him.

Adam grabs my forearm. "Go home. I'll rescue Katie."

I open my mouth to protest as Cullen flashes his one-dimpled smile and winks at me.

"You don't need this," Adam says, lifting a brow. "And I happen to relish every chance I get to remind him of his deficiencies."

I want to hide in our corner like I usually do and bury myself in research. One of the men in that picture heads the Death Mob. I know it, and I need to figure out who. I owe it to Dopney and my dad and every other dead victim.

Adam adjusts his black-rimmed glasses. "Go," he says, leaving me behind.

If I ditch, I can find a computer. I can avoid Cullen and reporters and anyone else who wants something from me. Hoping Katie will forgive me for abandoning her, I turn and leave.

As I navigate the halls, no one stops me on my way or asks where I'm going. The corridor to the front doors is nearly empty. My shoulders prickle with expectation, waiting for a hand to grab me. Reroute me back to lunch. I glance behind, looking for a teacher or vice principal. When I turn back around, a girl in an army-green jacket walks out of the bathroom and into the main lobby thirty yards ahead.

Amy London glances up. She freezes at the same moment I halt.

We stare at each other. Neither of us dares move.

The air around us stops stirring like we've entered some giant vacuum. Amy's jaw hangs slack. I've caught her in the middle of something. But what? How is it possible she's suddenly the only thing blocking my getaway? This can't be coincidence. But the way her hands dangle limp at her sides, she looks as shocked and terrified as I feel.

I don't know what to do. Turn and run? Walk past her, pretending she's another student at this school, not someone I saw in the Swarm at the pier? It's too late for that.

Amy tugs the bottom corners of her jacket and steps toward me. Like she's approaching me. Like she's going to say something. Like she isn't my enemy, about to knife me as I pass.

Steeling myself, I take three steps toward her before a blurry streak of fiery red bursts into the lobby from the hallway on the right, barrels into Amy London, and shoves her into the girls' bathroom, out of my sight.

Amy grunts from inside as she thuds against the tile barrier. I flinch.

185

Copperhead. The flash of red is Copperhead. From the pier. I'm sure of it.

Where did she come from? And what is she doing to Amy? Aren't they on the same side?

I need to run. Leave. Amy London might not be here to kill me, but is Copperhead?

My heart thrashes against my ribs. It echoes in my temples.

Light streams in from the front doors just past the girls' bathroom like a beacon pulling me toward it.

I shuffle, then pick up speed as I near the girls' bathroom. I can't help but look inside. The tile barrier blocks everything, but I hear whimpering. Crying. "I wasn't going to say anything," a girl pleads.

A stall door bangs as something or someone crashes into it.

"Please don't," the voice begs—for mercy, or life, I don't wait to find out. I take off running.

Bursting through the front doors, I hobble on my burning foot down the concrete stairs, where another student waits, presumably for his ride. The rest of our school's courtyard is empty. If Copperhead chases after me, at least there's one witness.

I take deep breaths, trying to slow my pulse. Not look so conspicuous. I'm halfway down the school's wide semicircle of steps leading to the sidewalk when the guy at the bottom, who I suddenly notice wears a hooded sweatshirt beneath a jean jacket and some kind of baseball hat, tucks his cell away like I've caught him doing something. He starts to glance at me. Then stops. Instead, he seems to regard me out of the corner of his eye, but for whatever reason, he avoids turning around.

Tiny strands of hair bristle at the nape of my neck.

I stare at the back of this kid's head as if I can see into his thoughts. Other than a creepy spider tattoo behind his right ear, nothing about him seems out of the ordinary. He's just a kid who goes to my school, waiting for his ride.

A gust of wind blows sideways along the school's brick façade. It whips my stringy blonde hair across my face and creates a dull hum in the air.

I'm being paranoid. Not every sketchy person I come across is in the Swarm. And I can't exactly go back inside to Copperhead and whatever she's doing to Amy London.

Rolling my shoulders back, I continue down the stairs, determined to walk two blocks to Division, where I can catch a cab. Get home. Lock my doors. Hide in bed beneath my comforter for the rest of my life.

Spider Tattoo pays no attention to me. When I pass, he looks away—a forced gesture.

I pick up the pace and continue walking with quick, uneven steps, vowing to slather Neosporin all over my cut and prop it for the rest of the afternoon if I make it home alive.

For whatever reason, I wish Ryan would do his thing where he appears out of nowhere. Walk with me till I catch a ride. Watch my back in case Copperhead sprints down the stairs after me or Spider Tattoo tries to gut me.

I turn around expecting to see Spider Tattoo listening to his music at the bottom of the steps, but instead I find him walking twenty or so paces behind me. He keeps his head down—definitely on purpose—and tucks his hands inside the pockets of his coat.

I hobble faster across the courtyard. Pressure builds in my chest. I think of what Ryan said about running. There's no way I could run for my life if this kid starts chasing me.

A cab turns down the street. Just as I feel a twinge of hope, a black Escalade pulls in behind it.

Spider Tattoo quickens his pace to match mine.

I throw my hand up, hailing the cab, but it doesn't slow. Bracing myself for this kid to hurl himself at me from behind, I break into an awkward run as the cab passes the front entrance of our school. The Escalade picks up speed.

"Hey!" I scream, my throat burning as I round the brick pillars that lead to the sidewalk.

I glance behind me. Spider Tattoo is closing the gap between us, glaring at me like a bull about to charge. And then, from the corner of my eye, I see red brake lights. The cab stops. I chase after it. Foot throbbing, lungs constricting, I wrench open the back door and plunge inside.

"Where to?" the driver asks, casting a deadpan glance at the frenetic high school escapee in his back seat.

I dig through my purse for my inhaler and give him my address. I peek out the window. Spider Tattoo walks down the sidewalk with his head down, his hands in his pockets like that's been his plan all along. I'm about to sit back when the Escalade pulls up beside him. Spider Tattoo glances up and glares at me for several prolonged seconds before getting in.

The cab takes off. I collapse against the seat. My breathing is quick and short. Keeping my head low, I risk a peek out the back window. The Escalade turns down a side street and speeds off.

I sink into the faded upholstery and inhale my medication before I have a panic attack and stop breathing altogether.

The cab loops my block a few times as I watch for the Escalade, but the only noticeable cars are two news vans parked outside my house. Hoping it's left me alone for the time being, I have the driver drop me off near the back alley. Despite the pulsing ache in my foot, I hurry past the first two houses, furtively glancing in all directions with each step. When I reach the fence to my backyard, I lean on its wooden gate and roll my ankle around.

Charlie starts barking. Just as I'm about to scream at him to shut up, a woman's voice from the other side of the fence says, "Charlie, sit." She snaps her fingers twice, and the dog is silenced.

Our neighbors never try to quiet Charlie. Or do they have the authority over their own dog to make him stop on command like that.

I lift the latch to our wooden gate and ease it open a tiny slit, ready to turn and run if I see another teenager waiting for me. Instead, sitting on the top of the stairs just outside the French doors to our living room is Emi Vega.

She tosses something to Charlie, who chases it down and eats it. The Bluetooth in her ear and phone in her other hand suggest she's listening to something, which explains why she hasn't noticed my approach. She wears black dress pants, a red boatneck shirt, and dark lipstick—camera ready at all times. I take a quick glance around my backyard in search of her crew, but she appears to be alone.

I could retreat. Circle around front and let the other news teams film me walking into my house alone. Maybe give them a statement to piss Emi off. But since she sold me out to the entire nation as a liar and a marked girl, the video of my dad's murder was left on my trash can and three Swarm members showed themselves at my school today.

Lifting my chin, I walk through the gate eager to unleash on this woman.

Emi looks up with a wry smile.

"Jerky." She nods toward the neighbor's lawn, where Charlie is silent like he's waiting for the next command. "No dog can resist beef jerky."

Emi stands to greet me much like Mayor Henking did a couple nights ago. She brushes her palms against each other and takes the Bluetooth out of her ear. What is it with people feeling overly comfortable at my home?

I cross my lawn undeterred, careful to hide my limp. I'm sure Emi would just love to share with the world that I'm incapacitated.

"You really should take the front door every now and again to vary it up. It's only a matter of time before the press realizes your whole back-door strategy."

The closer I get to her, the tinier she looks in person. I'm small for a sixteen-year-old, but Emi's waist is smaller than mine. I guess I shouldn't be surprised. Last year she competed in the Ironman World Championship in Kona. WGN did a whole feature on it, airing interviews with Emi and her equally perfect and supportive wife, along with clips of Emi's training. All I could focus on was her ponytail that held so much hairspray, it didn't move when she ran.

"I always come around back." I reach the bottom of the stairs and realize she intends to stand her ground. "I have nothing to hide."

"How about that cute little Hewitt boy you've been sneaking in and out of here? That would put a damper on your whole Cullen Henking lover-boy story."

I lower my head, infuriated she not only knows about Ryan, she figured out who he is quicker than me. I ball my right fist and walk up the steps, tempted to hit her as I pass.

"Using the press is a smart move on your part, but you could use some help."

"Help, right—like outing me as a liar to the entire world and inviting the Swarm to assassinate me?" My mom's hanging baskets full of freshly planted mums swing above her head. I imagine one of them falling and knocking her out.

Emi smirks. "You saw my interview." The pride in her voice sickens me.

The closer I get, the more I think I'm going to hit her. I picture her powdered face with a swollen black eye. That would slow down her chances at a national spotlight. Adrenaline pumps through my veins. I narrow in on her pinched cheekbones—a perfect target for my right cross.

Then I get a vision of the Initiators delivering the first hit to Jeremiah Dopney, to my dad—the ones that knocked them down, set them up for their brutal beatings. No matter how much I hate this woman, I could never do what they do.

"Who do you think you are?" I reach the porch, unleashing my pent-up anger and shame. "You set me up to get killed. All to boost your own reputation, because you're that desperate for fame. And now you show up pretending like you want to help me?" A stinging sensation forms behind my nose. I lift my chin, swallowing it back.

We stand face to face on opposite ends of the porch. If she weren't wearing such high heels, we'd be the same height.

Her eyes narrow, mimicking the perfect mean-girl glare. "That's the thing with you. You've always acted like everything is all about you."

"This is about me!" I snort at how ridiculous she sounds. "It's my life you're screwing with. *My* father died in the Swarm."

She closes the three feet between us in one stride. "Didn't you ever wonder why your father's case closed after he died?"

It catches me off guard, and I stand there like a giant idiot unable to think. "Bill Morrell killed himself." I give the standard answer—the one the media proclaimed was the end of the Death Mob era.

"That suicide story was a cover-up. Bill Morrell was a fall guy, which you already knew, or else you wouldn't be stalking the Death Mob."

I've waited two years to hear someone agree with me, that Bill Morrell wasn't the actual head. Now that it's happening, I don't know what to say. Emi Vega is certainly the last person I expected it to come from.

Emi lowers her head and her voice without losing any force behind her words. "Your dad's death confirmed the attacks are organized, but the whole thing got swept under the rug. There were plenty of people working with your dad who could've taken over the case, but they were either scared away or bought off. The one intern who did pursue it ended up dead. Another supposed suicide. And the whole world went back to believing that gangs were behind the Swarm all along. You and I both know that means there are some people pretty high up in this city who wanted this thing to go away two years ago. Those people haven't disappeared."

"You just put a giant target on my back!"

Emi's face tightens. Her eyes flash. "Get over yourself and this naïve woe-is-me routine. I brought your story to the national market and expanded your audience. Because of me, millions of people are interested in what happens to you."

"They're interested in a juicy story—not me."

"They are *interested* in whether you live or die, which is all that matters."

She sounds like Cullen, glorifying public opinion.

Emi leans in and narrows her heavily lined eyes. "If something happens to you, the nation will not ignore that. They'll have questions and want answers. Whoever's in charge of the Death Mob knows that. That's the best protection you're going to get. Never mind the target I put on my back by putting you in this position."

I feel my face flush. "So now this is about you?"

"What? They can silence a prosecuting attorney, but a news reporter is off limits? You poor little Gold Coast white girl. You still don't get it." She throws her hand out as she makes her point. I think of the beat reporter who was stabbed. Dumped in the river.

"This is bigger than you. An entire community has been vilified, scapegoated. The fire at the Latino community center. The church vandalism—smashed windows, spray paint all over the alter. Racial profiling is running rampant in this city. All because someone blamed these murders on a Latino gang."

I struggle to process everything she's saying. Everything I missed. "I didn't know."

"Try reading an article that doesn't have your name in it."

She's right. I didn't know it was happening. I've not spoken out about what I saw. I've been quiet. To protect myself. But in doing so, innocent people—beyond the city's gangs—are suffering the repercussions of my silence. I open my mouth to speak, but nothing comes out. I don't know what to say.

Emi takes a deep breath and claps her hands together as if praying. Only there's nothing divine about her. "I knew your father. I admired him and what he stood for…"

"You slandered him!" My voice shakes as I scream at her. "He was a good person and an excellent lawyer, and you shredded his reputation."

Emi doesn't flinch. "It wasn't me."

"You said he had an enemy list a mile long," I say as proof.

"He did. Watch the clips. I never spoke against him."

I try to remember who said what, which reporters said the worst things, but it all blurs together as the worst time in my life.

"Look, if we started working together, maybe we could get a lot farther than either of us has been able to do on our own."

"Work with you? You're a reporter."

"And you're sixteen. Not my idea of a perfect scenario, but neither is living in a city where organized crime controls mobs of teenagers who attack and kill people."

I stare at her, trying to recall her speaking against my dad, the specific words she used that made me hate her so much. She hounded me for an interview, wouldn't leave me alone, but I can't think of what she said about my dad. My sense of reality tilts. First Ryan claims to have respected my dad, now her? How is there so much I didn't know about my dad and who he impacted? I'm not sure whether to feel awed by his ability to motivate people or betrayed that criminals and reporters have insight about him that I don't.

"Look." Emi relaxes her face, like she's trying to calm herself. "I know you don't like me and probably don't think you can trust me, but last time I checked there wasn't a long line of people waiting to take on the Death Mob."

"Why are you willing to help me? You said it yourself—whoever's in charge is willing to kill anyone who gets in their way."

"Because I have access to something your dad didn't." She smirks, pausing longer than she needs to, and I wonder whether she's trying to be dramatic or if it's just become innate. "A world audience."

I scoff. "So this is about boosting your ratings."

"It's about being smart. Where else are you going to go with everything you know? I assume you were the anonymous call to the CPD. They didn't exactly help, did they? The state attorney's office is corrupt, same with the FBI, and at least half the networks that refuse to cover this. Your dad's case stopped getting the coverage he wanted right before he died. Whatever we find out, we go through my contacts, and we report it to the world. That's our best protection."

I glare at her, wanting to find fault in what she's proposing, but she makes more sense than I want to give her credit for. More importantly, she's offering the one thing I could never envision—an exit plan. I have an incoherent string of facts that I can continue to collect, but I have nowhere to go with them. Detective Irving hasn't exactly been reliable. And the more I collect, the more danger I'm in.

"How did you know about the attack?" Emi presses.

For several seconds, I say nothing. I've spent the last two years loathing this woman I'm about to trust. "Twitter. They used numbers: latitude, longitude, day, and time. They hashtag the number of the attack." Trusting Emi tastes bitter in my mouth.

Her face scrunches in disbelief. "Death Mob kids understand latitude and longitude?"

"Type in coordinates to any search engine and you get the location."

Emi stares off into the distance and nods.

"Any idea who sent the tweet?"

I shake my head. "Whoever set up the account did it at the Harold Washington. I figured out which computer they used, but there isn't much I can do with that."

Emi nods again as if agreeing it's a dead end.

"What did the attackers look like? Hispanic? Latino?"

I shake my head again, slower. "Definitely not all of them."

Emi puts her hands on her hips and looks to the sky.

"I'll say it on camera. You can ask me what I saw. I'll say it publicly."

"I appreciate what you're trying to do, but we need to protect you right now too."

"My dad was in the process of linking all the deaths to people in Chicago." I blurt it out like it makes up for my silence and everything I'm not telling the press. I hate giving it to her, but without protected Internet access, I can't keep researching it anyway. "Jeremiah Dopney has to be connected to someone in this city."

"We've already tried."

"He is—I know he is." My eyebrows pinch together, frustrated she isn't taking me seriously. "Search harder."

She nods. "I'll look into it and get back to you."

"The attack—it's somehow tied to the Lakefront Project." The words fall out of my mouth before I consciously decide to tell her.

Emi claps her hands and spins around, once again staring off into the distance. "I knew it!" When she turns back, her eyes are ignited. "Can you prove it?"

"I'm working on it." The picture of Ryan's dad with Bill Morrell and the others is folded in the front pocket of my backpack. Even though I'm sure one of them heads the Death Mob, showing her would incriminate Ryan. I'm not sure if she realizes he's part of the Swarm or not, but I need to find out more before I hand over this piece of information.

Emi purses her lips together as if she's about to protest. Instead she nods her head. "Let me know what you find out."

With so much laid out in front of us, I start to second-guess myself. Maybe it's a trap. Maybe she's a part of the Death Mob. She wants to see what I know. Why didn't I consider this before I so willingly shared everything with the first person who showed interest?

"Okay then," Emi says. She starts walking down my porch stairs, her head bent in concentration.

Anxiety stirs in my chest, tightening it. She hasn't shared anything with me. I swing my bag around and begin rummaging for my inhaler.

"Lia . . ." Emi stops and turns. "I know you're stubborn, but lay low." There's sincerity in her voice. When I glance up, she's looking at me like she cares about what might happen. "Let me do the digging. I'll come back to share it with you. I promise."

She straightens her shirt and follows our stone path toward my back gate, her ridiculously high heels causing her ankles to wobble.

I want to believe her. But she is, after all, Emi Vega.

CHAPTER 20

Sitting on my mom's white linen couch, I pick at a spot on the arm of the sofa where the fabric has pilled. Lip Spikes or Copperhead or Spider Tattoo may or may not be outside watching me. Stalking me. Waiting to kill me. And I'm starting not to care.

Meanwhile, I've aligned myself with a guy from the Swarm, the mayor's self-absorbed son, and a reporter. Not just any reporter—Emi Vega. I can't help but wonder if I'm caught in some sick and twisted *Alice in Wonderland* dream where my world has turned upside down and nothing is as it seems.

Upstairs, the floorboards creak with each step my mom takes. Her walk is methodic as she follows her nighttime routine. Work clothes off. Loungewear on. It never wavers.

I twist the threads between my thumb and index finger, listening for any sign she's coming back downstairs, even though I know she won't. Dinner was uncomfortable. We sat on opposite ends of the table in awkward silence, acting as if my dad's murderers hadn't resurfaced and neither of us was struggling to cope.

At one point I said, "The TV cabinet looks nice." The doors had been fixed some time during the day.

She responded with, "Stay away from Cullen Henking." The tiny flick of her eyes signaled it was not up for discussion. That was the only eye contact we had all evening.

The faucet runs upstairs. She's washing her face, brushing her teeth—the last of her ritual before climbing in bed and reading until she passes out well before nine o'clock.

Grabbing the printouts from my bag, I sneak into my dad's office, thankful the floorboards downstairs don't make a sound. I pull the picture of old Chicago off the wall and flip it around. Leaning it against the wall, I sit cross-legged on the oriental rug in the middle of the room. Even though I've reviewed my crime collage hundreds of times, I scan it for any connection to Daniel London or Harry Hewitt I somehow missed.

If Bill Morrell was a fall guy like Emi said, which of the men from the picture are in charge? And why are London's and Hewitt's kids a part of the Swarm even though they don't seem to want to be in it?

I pick up the Hewitt family photo, taken a few years back. Ryan's face is rounder, young—not so hard and angular. His gray eyes are captivating. Maybe it's the way the sunlight hits them, but they look warmer—not so metallic. His smile lights up his face in a way that makes him seem like the kid everyone always wants to be around. It's weird seeing him this way. I wonder what it would've been like to meet the kid in this picture. Would I have liked him? Had a crush on him? Would I have felt that jittery rush of nerves and excitement every time we talked? This kid is nothing like the guy who threw me off Navy Pier. Something happened after this picture that turned him into a cold, distant killer.

I tape the printouts of Ryan's family photo and the Lakefront Project men in the upper corner and rehang the picture on the wall.

Other than the whirling hum coming from the vents, our house is still, filling me with unease, activating every nerve in my body. My mom must be reading or already asleep. Either way, the silence is suffocating—especially in the office, where my dad's ghost lingers.

I grab my ratty slippers from the hall closet. Pushing aside the curtains on our French doors, I scan the blackened space for any sign of a scum reporter trying to snap a shot or a disguised teenager waiting to murder me. When I see nothing, I crack the door and peer into the night. Sconces shine over the scattered garage doors, filling the alley with cones of light. I flip on our floodlights, illuminating the square patch of land constituting our backyard. Our Japanese maple shivers in the breeze. Its leaves have turned bright red—a sign that fall has set in.

A car drives along the side street a few houses down. Its tires roll across the gravel. Other than that, nothing. Everything looks quiet. Safe.

Back inside, I grab a quilt from the couch. My cell sits on the coffee table. A few days ago, I never went anywhere without it. Now, the threat of anyone hacking into my phone and stalking my activity makes it a liability. If checked tonight, someone would find hits on Dopney's condition, local news reporting about Cullen and me, and my social media sites, which I hadn't touched since I set them up years ago. But tonight, I added my first post to each—a picture of Cullen and me from today's interview. Within a couple hours, I had six hundred and eighty-two new followers on one account, three hundred and eighty friend requests on another, and just like that, I have an audience. Of course, the fact that anyone in Chicago cares about me or my love life with everything else going on is disturbing. Though not as disturbing as Dopney still in the ICU. He isn't improving.

Refusing to be a caged rat in my own house, I leave the phone and head up to our rooftop deck.

My dad used to say the view from our roof was the reason he bought the house. At night, the city's skyline towers over our home, sparkling like Emerald City and shrouding me in commotion. A CTA rattles as it slides around the elevated tracks. A city bus squeaks and hisses as it stops to pick up passengers. A siren wails as a fire truck pulls out of its station a few blocks away. The city never sleeps, which is reassuring. Out here, I'm never alone. I wrap the quilt around my shoulders and fall into a swivel chair at our outdoor table, letting the tension melt away as I watch the city's shifting lights.

I'm twisting my necklace around my index finger until the blood drains from it when something scrapes the concrete next to me. I inhale a sharp, raspy breath, trapping the scream in my throat as Ryan pulls a chair away from the table and sits down like he's having lunch with a friend.

Somehow, he crossed our gravel-strewn alley, walked through the gate of our back fence, and climbed three flights of metal stairs without making a sound. His ability to sneak up on me makes me shudder. Even Charlie is quiet.

Ryan wears workout pants and a hooded sweatshirt—different from the one he wore at Navy Pier. Once again, he looks massive. Tonight, he *looks* like part of the Swarm.

He watches the skyline. "You've been busy."

Somewhere on the street below a car door slams. I twist my necklace another turn and bite the inside of my cheek. I hear a car door slam a block away just fine, but I can't hear a hundred-and-seventy-pound guy walk up three flights of metal stairs?

"I don't trust him." Ryan's reference to Cullen Henking is clear.

I shrug. "I thought it might distract from Emi Vega calling me a Death Mob stalker." I lean my head back against the chair.

"You could just leave the Swarm alone."

"Before I find out how your dad's involved?" It has more bite than I intend.

Ryan snorts. Several minutes pass before he says, "You just don't quit, do you?" Standing, he tucks his hands into the front pouch of his sweatshirt. I'm sure he's leaving, but instead he walks to the porch's brick ledge that faces the city.

I tighten the quilt around my shoulders.

The side door of a van rolls before snapping shut on the street below. My head swivels toward the front of our house. If news crews are down there, they could see Ryan.

I shuffle to the ledge. Somehow, he's standing in the perfect spot—the only spot on our roof blocked by a corner where the bricks stack a little higher than the rest. I lean back and forth, gauging whether someone might glimpse his hand on the ledge from the street below, but he's concealed. I wonder if he knows that.

Three floors down, a narrow space of grass squeezes between our house and the neighbor's. Flashes of water crashing against the cement wall at Navy Pier reel through my head. The way Ryan held me against the railing before throwing me in. I step back.

"Your dad was the one who found me."

I turn toward him, tensing, anticipating what he's about to tell me. Several wisps of hair fallen from my ponytail whip across my face.

Ryan clears his throat. "I was in a pretty bad place when I met him. A good friend of mine had died. Suicide."

The newspaper article I read earlier today mentioned Jamie Cunnings, his suicide. Jamie's father was part of the Lakefront Project too. It can't be coincidental.

Ryan stares at the city like he's talking to himself. "Every night, I'd pass him while walking my dog. No matter which way I'd walk, he always seemed to take the path that crossed mine. He'd nod, and that was it."

"You live by me," I whisper.

Ryan shrugs his left shoulder, not confirming or denying it.

"One night, we ended up at a light, waiting for it to change. Without looking at me, he told me where I could find him if I ever wanted to 'do something about it.' He wasn't specific, but he didn't need to be. I knew exactly what he was talking about."

Ryan turns toward me. The city lights catch his eyes, turning them silver beneath the lip of his cap. "He risked his life by approaching me. For all he knew, I could've turned him over to the Swarm and had him killed the next day. I never figured out why he trusted me or how he knew who I was."

His gaze holds such intensity. I lean in like some magnetic pull is drawing me toward him. The air buzzes with it, like yesterday, when he held my ankle, pulled the glass out of my foot.

My dad had razor-sharp instincts. I trusted his decisions, relied on them. And for whatever reason, he believed in Ryan.

"How long have you been following me?"

It's a silly question. Still, I watch his eyes like his response matters.

"I check in on you."

The wind picks up, blowing more strands of hair across my face. Ryan stares at a wisp caught on my lip. Pinned beneath his gaze, I do nothing to move it.

"Two years," he says.

A few days ago, that might have scared me. But seeing how far the Swarm goes to cover themselves complicates things. If my dad meant as much to him as he claims—I would have done the same had I been in his place.

"How is your dad involved?" I ask.

Ryan's quiet. Minutes pass, and I wonder if he's stopped talking. Or maybe he's searching for the best way to tell me his dad runs the whole thing.

"My dad did something illegal," he says at last.

Adrenaline pumps in through my veins, making me alert, desperate.

"The Swarm used it as blackmail. Either my parents would go to jail or end up dead, or I'd participate."

My shoulders drop as I slowly accept what that means. If he's telling the truth, if he *knows* the truth, his dad isn't in charge. "And your parents were okay with that?"

"They don't know."

I think of everything my mom doesn't know and the rift that's caused between us. I wonder if he feels as alone as I do sometimes.

"They blackmail others?" Amy London. It has to be the same for her too.

Ryan nods. "Not all of us, but a lot of us. They make it sound simple at first, like we just stand there while other people do the hitting, but it's horrible watching people beaten to death. So the Swarm set up a system. Punch the victim, and it shortens your indentured servitude. Deliver the final blow and you're out—no strings attached."

Ryan talks in an emotionless voice like he's detached from what he's saying. The look behind his eyes as he stares at my lips turns blank. "The Swarm becomes rabid after those first few hits. There's this crazed shift. People lose their inhibitions."

Mob mentality. I think of Bird Man from the library. His creepy books.

"My friend couldn't take it anymore," Ryan continues. "He hit a victim. He didn't mean to, but his hit was the final blow. The Swarm released him. Three months later, he took his own life—couldn't live with what he'd done."

"Jamie Cunnings."

As if snapping out of it, his eyes meet mine. "The Swarm takes a toll on all of us."

"How do you do it?"

He leans toward me, narrowing the space between us. "I've grown numb to it all. The attacks. The nightmares. I don't have another option." His sweatshirt brushes against the blanket I have around my shoulders, prickling my skin beneath it, and I wonder if he's haunted during the daytime as well. Like me. "Too many people I've cared about have died. I guess at some point you're willing to risk everything to protect the ones left, regardless of the cost."

"Your brother and your friend," I whisper.

"Your dad."

The guilt and the constant drive to make up for the fact he's still here—it controls him and every decision he makes. He doesn't need to say it for me to understand it well.

I inch closer, like we're trading secrets. "It's connected to the Lakefront Project, isn't it?"

The light catches his eyes again. Deep silver. Ryan brushes away the strand of hair still caught against my bottom lip with his index finger. "I don't think it's a coincidence that Save the Parks protesters have been getting a lot of press lately."

The world spins. Flips upside down. My head grows light, and I think of Alice tumbling down the rabbit hole, sure that this is the moment everything changes.

"I think your dad knew that," Ryan says, pain etched across his face. I can't tell who it's for—me, my dad, himself? He looks like the boy in the picture—a guy who plays soccer, a guy I can trust.

"I think he was pretty close to figuring out who ran the Swarm when they killed him."

He talks so softly. The space between us grows smaller.

"Lia, your dad—" he starts, but he's interrupted.

Someone is coming up the stairs leading to the rooftop.

Ryan's head snaps. He jumps in front of me, shielding me from the stairs.

"Get out," my mom growls.

Ryan's back turns rigid.

I step out from behind him. "Mom, it's fine. He's—"

She cuts me off, ignoring the fact I'm talking. "Stay away from her."

My mom's voice is strong, threatening. Her hair dances frenetically around her head in the wind, but her eyes are narrow and forceful. I doubt Ryan even notices the way she grasps either side of our rooftop ledge like she might blow over if she doesn't hold on.

Ryan's hands dangle at his sides. I consider grabbing one and telling my mom who he is, but I don't know how to describe him.

Her voice drops. "Don't think I don't know who you are and what you did."

Ryan jams his hands into his hoodie, drops his head, and heads down our back stairs.

My mom leans over the rooftop ledge to make sure he's gone, clutching the metal rail for support.

I step forward, squeezing the blanket around my shoulders. "I know him, he's . . ."

Her head snaps in my direction. Her eyes flash. "He's the reason your father's dead."

CHAPTER 21

I walk into class well after the bell has rung and throw my bag down on my desk in the back row. Mr. Mater's showing everyone how to balance equations on the SmartBoard. He doesn't acknowledge my tardy arrival.

Adam looks up from his iPad, where he's pretending to take notes. "No sign of your stalker last night, I take it?"

I cock my head and give him the best pissed-off face I'm able to muster at eight thirty in the morning. "Did someone leave his clothes in the dryer too long?"

Adam's white long-sleeve shirt and leather pants are so tight, I'm surprised he hasn't lost circulation. He rounds it off with combat boots and a tiny smirk, indicating he knows he can pull it off. And he can. For as skinny as he is, he's fairly defined, which is beside the point.

Adam shakes his head. "You're dodging the question."

I rifle through my bag for my science binder so I can at least pretend to participate. "It was a stupid question."

"Why are you so overly sensitive?"

A girl a couple rows in front of us turns around and gives us an irritated look. She sports a ponytail too high on her head for a high schooler.

I'm tempted to point this out to her when Mr. Mater stops his lesson to look our way. Of course, when he sees that it's me disrupting his class, his glance skims past me. He continues his lesson as if nothing happened.

Katie sits with perfect posture on the other side of the room, doodling in her sketchbook. Whatever she's drawing, I'm sure I'm a part of it, and I wonder how she's depicting me. Every time I've texted her, she's taken a while to respond, and I'm not sure why. Or when it began. Is it because of the whole Cullen Henking charade? Is she still upset I left her with him when I ditched lunch a few weeks ago? Does she regret helping me find Amy London? Or has she simply started realizing my friendship isn't worth it? One look at that illustrated diary of hers would either confirm or deny my speculations. I'm kind of glad I can't see it.

Mr. Mater returns the pen to the SmartBoard tray, marking the end of his lecture. "I posted a handout online." Students begin rumbling before he finishes speaking. "Whatever you don't get done in class, complete for homework. Make sure you submit your answers by eight o'clock tomorrow morning." Mr. Mater shuffles papers on his desk, officially dismissing us to work for the rest of the period.

I take out my iPad and access Mr. Mater's home page. I'd be fine working by myself today, but Adam, without invitation, swings his desk around to face mine.

"A delinquent not stalking you anymore is a good thing." He straightens his cuff, aligning it with the leather band around his wrist. "Even if he is incredibly attractive."

I glance at Katie, hoping she'll join us. Instead, she scoots her desk to work with the girl next to her without looking our way. Adam doesn't address it, almost like he expects it.

"I'm doing number one without you," I say, like Adam cares that I don't wait for him. He could balance these equations while writing his research paper for English and get an A on both.

Adam leans over his desk. "It's not like we haven't all been guilty of letting a hot guy cloud our judgment."

"Why are we still talking about this?" I snap, burying myself in the first problem on Mater's stupid assignment. I pretend to care about something that will never serve a real purpose in my life in order to ignore the throbbing nerve Adam just hit.

After my mom kicked Ryan out, I thought he'd show up the next night, at least give an explanation for my mom's accusation. But he didn't. For several days, I watched for signs of him following me, but he wasn't around. And the longer he stayed away, the more I realized how easy I made it for him to lie about everything. What's sad is that I'd considered him an ally in a world where people want to use me or kill me instead of realizing the alternative: Ryan's involvement with my dad got him killed.

"If you'd rather talk chemical equations, we can, but then you'll never find out what I've discovered while doing a little of my own research."

I look up from my iPad. My heart skips. Adam stares at his own tablet with a little grin.

"Shall I go on then?"

I should chastise him for putting himself at risk and refuse to talk about any leads with him. Even I've laid off researching anything these last few weeks. Aside from checking my follower status a few times, which continues to grow without me doing anything to encourage it, I've stayed off the Internet entirely. I open my mouth to protest, but Adam holds up his index finger, cutting me off.

"Before you pretend to prioritize my safety, let me remind you the Benny the Bull hacker has yet to be caught."

Freshman year, Adam hacked the United Center's scoreboard. Every time George Hutchinson went to a Bulls game with his family, the scoreboard displayed a series of anti-bullying messages to George from Benny the Bull among the happy birthday shout-outs. Adam hacked it at least a dozen times—George's family had season tickets. It was well deserved. George threw Asian slurs at Katie for months. Benny the Bull insured that George left Katie alone.

My entire body thrums with anticipation. "That's hardly the same thing."

"Sure it is. Everything I do is impressively rerouted through so many encrypted layers, it's exciting."

"That means nothing to me."

Adam smirks. "My digital tracks are indecipherable. That's all you need to know. Keep in mind I found that Twitter IP address for you. These people aren't that good."

A tiny, nagging voice of reason warns me not to encourage him. He shouldn't be investigating the Swarm. It's too dangerous. But I'm already hanging on his every word. And he knows it.

"As I was saying," Adam continues, "I looked into who's made the most profit from the Lakefront Project. Wasn't easy."

I grab my pendant and twist it around my finger.

"Interestingly enough, your stalker friend's dad made several million along with all the other men in that photo. Just Phase One of the project brought in close to five hundred million in revenue."

I'm taken aback by how much is being made from selling off

property along Lake Michigan that used to be owned and protected by the city.

Adam leans in. "Five hundred million, Lia. That's apparently the price it takes to create and run an organized mob that kills people. And there's money being hidden—real estate records, property taxes, zoning, city budget. None of it matches up."

He's going too slow. "Who's profiting the most?" It's going to be Harry Hewitt. Ryan was wrong, or lied—doesn't matter. His dad heads it.

"That's the thing—the money's spread out. Plenty of contractors and real estate agents have made a quick dime off selling the property or the construction. Most of them have teenage kids."

"Who are forced into the Swarm." My head feels light and dizzy. Adam has done it. He's figured out the key players, how they're all connected, which sounds bigger than even I'd assumed. But all that matters to me right now is the person who heads it all.

Adam picks at the corner of his iPad case and stares off toward the front of class. Anyone watching him might think he's studying Mater's handwritten scrawl on the SmartBoard, but I've seen that look hundreds of times. He's piecing something together.

"Here's what I don't get. The city makes money by selling off property to people who want to live in Chicago, which means they want the city to be desirable. And tourism would only increase the money coming in on top of whatever they're making off this Lakefront thing."

Every inch of me tightens. "Who is it?"

"So then why scare everyone off with the Swarm? Why make everyone want to get away from the city?" His eyes narrow and focus on one spot across the room, but I don't care about the opposing objectives of the Swarm and the Lakefront Project.

"Adam!" I practically scream, shaking him from his daydream. "Who's in charge?"

He shrugs. "The mayor."

Like it's the only logical answer, and I should've realized that several minutes ago. The classroom chaos recedes into distant background noise, and I become acutely aware of my breathing, the tiny little wheeze that underlies every breath I take.

After Dopney's attack, the mayor, with his slicked-back hair and his thousand-dollar suit, stood behind a podium and promised to pursue Dopney's attackers. He sat at my dining room table, brought me coffee drinks, claimed we were on the same side, fighting the same battle. He praised my father's work after he had my father murdered. My face grows hot as I think of how close I came to telling him everything I knew.

A familiar laugh draws me back to the present.

Cullen Henking cackles on the other side of the room. Some girl sits in his lap with her arm around his neck. He's holding a pencil out of her reach in some stupid, flirtatious middle school game of keep-away.

I glare at him.

The girl presses her chest against his and reaches for the pencil in his outstretched hand, extending well beyond his back.

Cullen's eyes catch mine. His smile widens. He shrugs as if I'm glaring at him because I'm some brainless, jealous schoolgirl, and he hands over the pencil. Mr. Mater walks over to them. He says something that makes her sit in an actual chair next to Cullen instead of on top of him.

Adam notices me clenching my iPad. "If you want to bash that thing over his head, I won't stop you." He turns to the spectacle Cullen has created. "In fact, I'll take down anyone who tries to get in your way."

The girl unleashes a high-pitched giggle, and I'm forced to look away before I hurl myself toward Cullen and gouge out his eyes.

Adam lowers his voice. "Mob attacks started eleven years ago. About two years before Henking ran for office. His entire campaign revolved around destroying the Swarm and rebuilding tourism in our city through the Lakefront Project."

"His house was the first to be built, wasn't it?" I ask in a voice that doesn't feel like my own. I hate Cullen Henking. Now more than ever.

Like Adam can read my mind, he says, "Whether he knows his dad is a murderous tyrant or not, Cullen's still a douchebag."

The blonde next to him leans over her desk and puts one hand on Cullen's forearm. His behavior has always been disgusting and self-indulgent. Helping his face appear in every Chicago newspaper and news program made it worse.

My mom dismissed the mayor when he left our house. Ryan told me he didn't like me hanging out with Cullen Henking, which I mistook as a jealous thing. Stupid. Foolish. How did I not figure this out? How did I not see this coming? Instead, I helped Cullen and his dad look like city heroes saving a distressed little girl.

"Don't look now, but Douchebag Boy is headed our way."

Cullen saunters over, a smug, condescending smile on his face. He heads straight for me without breaking eye contact.

I grit my teeth, keeping my hands locked on my iPad. I don't trust them and what they might do if Cullen pushes me over the edge.

Cullen crouches down at my desk. He brushes a chunk of my hair behind my shoulder. "It might be hard—seeing me with someone else." He stares at my hair and tucks another lock behind my ear.

I grip the iPad tighter. It takes everything I have not to reach out and choke him.

"Don't get me wrong, I appreciate you."

The tendons in my arms are on the verge of snapping. He makes it sound like we slept together. I focus on his mouth. Not his eyes. Still want to gouge those.

He puts his hand on his chest—a mock heartfelt gesture. "Do you know how many sites have verified me because of you?"

"It's almost charming how much you think she actually cares about you," Adam says. "Although intelligence has never really been your strong suit."

Cullen stands. "Straight people have never really been yours. Don't pretend to understand."

"The only thing I don't understand in this scenario is why you continue wearing that shirt knowing you pit out every time you wear it."

Cullen glances at the armpits of his collared shirt. Adam snickers.

Hundreds of things run through my mind as I scramble for something to say. Something to put him in his place. Shame him. Before I decide on anything cohesive, the words squeeze out between my clenched teeth. "Your father..."

Cullen tugs at his collar, straightening his shirt. "What about him?"

"He won't get away with any of it," I say under my breath.

Cullen smiles. It's arrogant, dimpled. "I don't mean to hurt you, Lia." He leans over and kisses my head. "I know you sometimes confuse fantasy and reality." He chuckles under his breath, walking back to his circle of groupies on the other side of the room.

"I'm all for making him feel inferior, but if Cullen is in on the whole Death Mob thing, that might have been taking it a little too far," Adam says.

His phone chimes. "From here on out, we leave the comebacks to me."

I should regret what I've said, that I've tipped my hand. I spent the last few weeks acting like I didn't care about the Death Mob. But as Cullen takes a seat across the room, all I can think about is how I will not let any of them get away with what they've done.

A cluster of students in the far-right corner of the room all turn at once. They stare at me. One girl reads to the rest of them—something from her tablet. For whatever reason, I'm sure it has nothing to do with Cullen.

Even Katie is holding her phone and staring at me from across the room with disbelief.

Something's going on.

Adam pulls his phone out of his pocket to read the incoming texts. His face grows serious. He looks up. I shrink beneath everyone's gaze as I wait for him to spill it.

"Jeremiah Dopney," Adam says. "He's dead."

CHAPTER 22

ook at us. It's almost like we're real people living in a fun city again," Adam says.

I twist my Thai noodles around my chopsticks and shovel the mini beehive into my mouth. Green onions, cilantro, and lime assault me all at once.

I should be at home, curled up on my couch, watching some mindless show that doesn't require participation. Mourning. Trying to forget the echoes of Dopney's screams as the Swarm closed in on him. The noises are what haunt me the most—the waves crashing, the crowd shuffling and jeering, the dull smack of each hit as they beat him in the center of their pit. I don't think I heard the actual blows during the attack, but now they rattle around my head, following me wherever I go.

The sounds become more visceral at night. More than once, I've woken drenched in sweat, having dreamt that I was the victim. The Swarm surrounds me, tightening their circle. Lip Spikes throws the first punch, knocking me sideways, and they devour me like piranhas. I'll writhe in pain in my bed, unable to breathe, until I force my eyes open and concentrate on the photos of Hana taped to my bedroom walls. By focusing on the pictures surrounding me, I avoid succumbing to the nightmares like I did after my dad's death.

I overheard my mom on the phone with Dr. What's-His-Name, telling him about the prints, that I'd enlarged them and hung them like posters around my room—something I had to do when the black rock beach became too hard to visualize. Whatever his reaction—concerned, impressed—no one made me take them down.

I look at Adam, whose face is relaxed as he says, "I can't even remember the last time we came."

I nod. Force a smile. If it weren't Adam's birthday, I wouldn't be here. Pretending.

Adam and I sit in a red vinyl booth pushed against the back corner, next to the kitchen's constant noise and commotion. A stark contrast to our usual spot against the front windows, where we sat almost once a week this past summer. We called it our weekly Thai fix. That feels like forever ago. Another lifetime.

Outside, commuters shuffle past one another on their way home from work. Heads down, arms tucked against their bodies. They walk at a brisk pace. One man wearing a peacoat and stocking cap hugs the window. His arm scrapes against it as he passes. His head darts around like it's tinged with panic. It's as if the city has suddenly realized that flash attacks are a real and present threat. All it took was Dopney's death nine days ago for people to finally pay attention. I wonder if his parents resent that. Like I do.

"Before the attack . . ."

Adam shakes his head. "Nope—that's against the rules."

I force another beehive of noodles into my mouth. "You nixed so many things we could talk about at dinner, the only things left are weather, religion, and politics," I say, unable to swallow the food in my mouth. My mom would be appalled.

"My birthday, my rules. Though now that you mention it, the weather has been odd this year. Eerily and preemptively cold, don't you think?"

Adam leans to one side and pulls his phone from his burnt orange corduroy pants. Once again, they're so tight, I'm shocked he can fit his phone in his pocket. He wears a black turtleneck and matching leather jacket, which he hasn't taken off. His black eyeliner is a bit thicker and his black nails look freshly painted, making him look more dressed up than usual—something I'm sure he's going for.

Adam flips through his phone.

"Anything from Katie?"

He shakes his head and glances at me. "Something must have come up." I can tell by the way he avoids eye contact that Katie doesn't want to be around me—not that I blame her. I'm a ticking time bomb. Destined to explode. Or implode. It's only a matter of time.

At least Katie would have been the better dinner date. I have no idea why he chose to spend the night with me instead.

Adam sets his phone on the diner-style table and rubs his earlobe between his thumb and forefinger before leaning back against the red vinyl.

Someone opens the door, ringing the bell attached to it. My attention snaps to a couple wearing matching Burberry scarves. I know before they do they are in the wrong restaurant. The guy leans over the counter and the hostess points to something across the street.

I twist another pile of noodles around my chopsticks. Once upon a time, this used to be my favorite dish.

"Seriously," Adam says. "This is supposed to cheer you up, but it's only bringing me down." He rolls his eyes. "All right, Debbie Downer—all topics of conversation are fair play. What are you thinking about?"

I snort, staring at the Thai noodles I can't manage to eat. Like I have to say it.

"Dopney." He leans across the table. "Just in case that twisted little brain of yours is deluding you—it wasn't your fault. You know that, right?"

Of course it was. I know it. He knows it. Eventually, the entire world will realize it. My eyes begin to water.

"Lia." He waits until I look up. His deep-set eyes hold my gaze. "You'll never save the city with all that guilt weighing you down."

My eyes drop to avoid crying. Adam's always been the one who knows me better than anyone. I should tell him that. That he's my best friend. That I couldn't survive this, or even high school, without him. When I look back up to say it, Adam's moved on. He's tugging on his earlobe again, mesmerized by the clownfish swimming around the fish tank near the kitchen entrance. "Knowing everything you know now, what would you do if you had the date of the next attack?"

Save the victim. Make Detective Irving listen. Make him promise to rescue the target once the attack starts. No one else can die. Then, I'd go to the location and hide there. When the Initiators delivered the first hit, I'd record it. I would stream it live to every social media site I have so no one could delete my pictures or videos. All my new followers would watch and be disgusted by it. The video would go viral, forcing the FBI to get involved. To take down the mayor, I'd incriminate as many perpetrators as I could, knowing one of them would rat him out—even if that meant exposing Amy London and Ryan. It would force us all to accept the consequences of our actions.

Of course, admitting all of this would only indicate how much time I've spent planning this what-if scenario.

I shrug my left shoulder.

"Calling the cops was useless," Adam says.

I nod, recalling the receptionist's condescending voice, assuring she'd pass along my message. Whether she did or not, CPD is so corrupt that I wonder if Irving is too. Nothing came of my dad's attack. He never responded to any of the messages I left for him. My mom likes him. Seems to trust him, but what if he's one of the bad guys and I'm a bigger fool than I thought?

"You've considerately demonstrated the idiocy behind going down there yourself."

I scrutinize Adam's expression. He's never been one for hypothetical talk. He looks perfectly at ease, as if we're talking about how ridiculous our math teacher looks with her failed attempt at pink-tipped hair. "Where are you going with this?"

Adam sips his Diet Coke. "Nowhere." He takes another drink. "Just wondering. You ready?" Adam throws money on our bill before I can reach my bag and dig for my wallet.

"You can't pay for dinner on your birthday." I didn't get him a gift. The least I could do is pick up the tab.

He stands, pulling the collar of his designer leather jacket tight against his neck and accentuating how attractive he really is. "Get me next time." Adam walks off, indicating it's not up for discussion.

I grab my bag, fling it around my torso, and pull my hat low across my brow. Ducking my head, I follow Adam as he meanders through the packed tables.

Adam holds the door for me, and we step onto the sidewalk.

"C'mere," he says, holding out his arms. An unprecedented gesture.

"What are you doing? You hate hugs."

"As of today, I'm officially more mature. And you look like you need one."

I wrap my arms around him and try not to get snot on his shirt—he'd never hug me again. Adam pats me on the back several times, indicating his discomfort. He releases before I do.

The corners of my mouth flinch. It's my best attempt at smiling. "I'll call an Uber," I say.

"Don't be silly. You're tough, but you still have scary people out there who want you dead. And your stalker boy seems to have abandoned you. Arguing will only delay the inevitable, and I'm dying to get home."

"Birthday cake?"

Adam winks. "Hackers forum."

We turn down the street and walk toward Adam's car a block away.

"I also have a little something for you."

"This isn't the way it's supposed to work on your birthday."

"Don't worry. I didn't expect much from you tonight."

I'm not sure whether to be grateful or saddened by his perception. I cross my arms against my chest—the night is colder than I thought—and wait for Adam to hand over my fortune cookie. I must have left it.

He knows I love those stupid stale desserts. But Adam keeps his hands in his jacket pocket, drawing out the anticipation in true Adam fashion, as we walk down the middle of the sidewalk.

I grow jittery, being so exposed.

He raises his eyebrows. "October twentieth."

Adam wears a mischievous smile I can't quite place. I stop dead in my tracks. He turns to face me in front of the alley and smirks. "If you can't be the city's vigilante, someone has to be."

The date of the next attack. A month and a half after the last one. I try to remember the last time the attacks were so close together, like there's something to it. My hands, hanging at my sides, sweat and tingle. Just as I'm about to ask how he found out, a voice calls out, "Adam?"

Our heads turn toward the alley. Aside from two metal trash bins wrapped with chains, the alley looks empty.

My body tenses.

A guy in a heavy down coat steps out from behind the rusted blue bin. "Today's your birthday, isn't it?"

I squint to make out the details of his face, concealed in shadows cast by the surrounding buildings. His eyes are large and dark. There's something coaxing about the way he looks at Adam.

Adam doesn't move. He offers no sign of recognition.

The air picks up, brushing against the back of my neck. This is wrong. Everything about it. This guy isn't Lip Spikes or Spider Tattoo, but he's one of them. I'm sure of it.

I snatch Adam's arm, to drag him past the alley, make a run for it.

Someone grabs me from behind and picks me up. A greasy hand reeking of nicotine covers my mouth.

A third guy dressed in heavy black clothes shoves Adam into the alleyway.

Adam braces himself as he sprawls onto broken brick pavers.

I'm carried deep into the darkness. Past trash bins. Around a bend. I thrash against my attacker, knocking my hat off my head. But his grip is tight.

I hear a shove or a hit, I can't tell. Adam grunts behind me. I'm whipped around, hair smacking my face. The alley spins as I try to make sense of it.

Adam struggles to stand. He regains balance only to be pushed toward me. His head snaps back as his body heaves.

I scream, but the noise is muffled under the greasy hand smothering half my face. I buck and kick, desperate to get away, to help Adam as they close in on him.

The guy chuckles in my ear. "I like a girl with fight in her." The words ooze out of his mouth, filling me with a horrific sense of dread.

One attacker winds his arm back, punches Adam in the gut, lifting him off the ground. Adam collapses. He wraps his arms around his knees as the other guy kicks him in the side. Once. Twice. Adam groans and grunts. I imagine his internal organs bursting.

Panic explodes in my chest. I scream and writhe, clawing at the wrist smothering my mouth.

Adam crawls to his hands and knees. His back is curled as he tries to stand. One of them kicks Adam in the face. It pops, like bones shattering. Blood pours from his mouth.

I thrash harder against the arms gripping me and shriek into the palm pinching my face. My lungs pump beyond their limits as I gasp for breath.

"No, no. It's not your turn yet." He presses his cheek to mine and slides his oily skin against me as he turns his head. His nose. His chin.

Adam slumps on the ground. Another kick lands on his chest. Bile climbs up my throat. *He's dying.* And I'm helpless to do anything except watch it happen.

Something metal scrapes my jaw. It's pointed, like a pen or a nail. And then a second one. Two spikes drag upward to my ear, and everything inside of me liquefies.

Lip Spikes.

My lungs constrict and shrink. They refuse to expand, to take in air. My legs buckle, forcing Lip Spikes to loosen his grip as my body goes limp, a dead weight in his arms. He struggles to hold me upright. I jerk my shoulders, a sad attempt to break free, but darkness encircles my vision as my body shuts down.

A thick, bulky shadow barrels into the alley—so fast, I'm sure it's another hallucination. I hear a thud. A crack. Adam's attacker is launched into the alley wall. His head smashes against the brick, and he collapses.

Lip Spikes tenses. His grip tightens around my waist.

I try to focus. Adam's other attacker springs back to a defensive pose, lifting his fists to his chin.

I blink. Squint. I can barely make out silhouettes except for Adam, who lies on the ground, lifeless.

Adam's attacker throws a punch into the night. A fist shoots out of nowhere and slams into his face. Two forms tangle with each other, wrestling in the alley. A resounding blow pierces the darkness. Another crack. Adam's attacker rolls out of the shadows clutching his stomach.

I can't make my legs work. Can't figure out what's happening. I inhale through my nose, try to pump my diaphragm, but it's not enough. The air squeezing into my chest is too shallow. Too slow.

A hulking form emerges, stomping toward me. Tight fists ball at his sides.

Lip Spikes shuffles backward, dragging me with him, jerking me back and forth as I fight to steady myself.

Two gleaming gray eyes glare beneath a dark hood. *Ryan.* The look in his eyes is frightening. He wants to hurt Lip Spikes, who must see it too, because he shoves me.

I pitch forward, stumbling into Ryan's chest. He grabs me, steadies me, his body rigid, pulse racing. Ryan motions to leave, to chase Lip Spikes down, but I cling to his shirt and gasp. Choking turns to coughing. I can't control it. Can't get relief. I ball his shirt in my fists. My legs buckle, and once again my entire body fails me.

Ryan snaps from the frenzy possessing him. He holds me up, while clawing at my purse slung around my body. My inhaler finds my lips. Mist shoots in, and I breathe. I gulp the oxygen, relieved to feel my chest expand. I inhale. Exhale. Over and over again, until my vision returns, and I'm able to lock my legs in place.

Ryan wraps his arms around me. He presses his lips to the top of my head. "It's okay. You're okay."

Every muscle in my body burns. He searches my back, my head, my hair like he's looking for bullet holes or knife wounds. "You're okay," he says again, and I'm not sure if it's for my benefit or his.

Scraping and shuffling fill the alley behind me.

Ryan spins around, shielding me as Adam's attackers scramble to stand and take off down the alley. Away from us. In the opposite direction Lip Spikes escaped.

Ryan holds out my inhaler. "Another breath."

But I shake my head. Pull away. "Adam," I whisper.

Adam lies motionless on his back in the middle of the alley. His arms are outstretched, limp like they've been drained of energy and life.

A sharp pain rips through my chest.

He can't be dead.

I run to him. Collapse next to him.

Don't die.

Adam's eyes are closed. His face glistens with a mess of sweat and blood. It pools around his nose. Gushes from a cut on his chin where the skin's busted open. His eyes and cheeks are swollen and tender. I trace my fingers along his neck, feeling anxiously for a pulse, but I have no idea where his pulse should be.

Ryan kneels beside me. He brushes my shaking hand away and checks for Adam's pulse while pulling his cell out to dial 911.

"He's still alive," he whispers.

I break. Tears pour down my cheeks. I want to hug Adam, hold him, tell him everything's going to be okay, but he's so broken. He *looks* dead.

"There's been an attack. One guy beaten unconscious," Ryan says into his phone. "We're in an alley one block north of Diversey and Sheffield. Behind Penny's. There's a girl with him. She has asthma. She's breathing heavily."

I don't notice the whistles and crackles in each breath, the deep pressure in my lungs until Ryan says it. He mutters off a series of yeah and no that only half register. I stare at Adam's bloody, broken face and pray he's going to be fine. *He has to be fine.* Adam is too charismatic, too genuine, too beautiful and smart for this world to exist without him.

I can't exist without him.

At some point Ryan tells them to hurry and hangs up the phone.

"They guarded the alley." His voice is cold, detached, filled with torment.

Eyeliner smears across Adam's temples. I want to wipe it clean—Adam would want it wiped, but he looks too fragile to touch.

"I ran after you as soon as I saw it, but . . ." Ryan shakes my inhaler, hands it to me. "I should've been faster."

I struggle to hold it steady as I inhale and release. Ryan's words suggest that he's been following me, that he didn't completely abandon me. Beneath his hood, his eyes look weak and anguished. He rolls his hands and squeezes them together.

I want to ask him where he's been. Why didn't he try to explain himself after my mom's accusations? Did he have anything to do with my father's death? Because his disappearance seemed to confirm that he did. But all of it seems futile with Adam clinging to life, bleeding in the middle of a dark, dingy alley. This can't be the way Adam dies. Adam would be appalled by this alley. The way his hair is caked with red and matted to his head. On his birthday.

"This is my fault." I choke on the words. All the things Adam did to help me: the search aggregator, the pictures we found on his account, the digging around.

Ryan grabs the inhaler dangling from my hand and puts it in my bag. "Don't."

"If he dies…"

"He won't." It's an empty promise. There's doubt in his voice. Both of us know Adam won't survive.

Sirens howl in the distance.

"I'm sorry, Lia." The apology is halting. I look at him, wondering what he's apologizing for, exactly—Adam, my dad, leaving me, knowing me. Either way, he's about to disappear again. And as much as I've wanted him around, right now, I don't care.

I brush away a chunk of hair stuck to Adam's forehead. He doesn't move. His stillness is terrifying.

Red lights flash against the brick alleyway. Somewhere near the street, car doors open. Footsteps rush into the alley. A radio dispatch muffles something as two guys with a gurney hurry our way.

One paramedic, the younger of the two, makes eye contact with Ryan as he steps back. The EMT pauses a fraction of a second before kneeling down next to Adam. His partner checks Adam's vitals. I'm brushed aside while they strap a neck brace around him. They roll Adam's limp body onto the gurney.

"Are you hurt?" the younger EMT asks, shining a light into my eyes.

I shake my head. "Just him. He …" My voice catches. I stare at Adam's face. I don't even recognize him.

"She has asthma. She needs oxygen," Ryan says, sounding cold, sterile. I swear I detect a trace of underlying desperation.

The EMT glances at Ryan. They seem to have an exchange in the few seconds they look at each other before the EMT turns back to me. A muffled voice says something on the dispatch attached to the EMT's shoulder.

The EMT puts his hand on my arm. "We're going to take you and your friend to a hospital." He has a black circular tattoo on his forearm. "The police will be here in less than thirty seconds," he adds.

It's an awkward thing for him to say. The EMT's eyes once again flicker to Ryan.

"You're going to be okay," Ryan says as the EMT grabs me by the elbow and leads me toward the ambulance. Another EMT joins the group. Two of them wheel Adam away.

"I'm going with him." Panic claws at my chest as Adam is pulled from me. I turn to find Ryan backing into the shadows.

More lights—red and blue reflect off the brick. The police have arrived.

"You'll need to come in the ambulance with us," says the EMT. "We'll check you out. Get you oxygen. Then I'm sure the police will want to speak with you. You're the only witness to what happened tonight."

The EMT must realize Ryan witnessed part of it too. I glance back at Ryan, who backpedals a few more steps. His eyes flash. My heart skips a beat. Then he turns and runs the other way.

The EMT stops me, squeezes my elbow. I focus on the tattoo on his forearm—up close, it's a thick black circle with angular bars and swirls patterned inside it like a kids' maze. "My reports will state we found two people in the alley—you and your friend, who was unconscious." The EMT's expression is serious, concentrated, stressing the importance of what he's saying. "That gives you about twenty minutes to get your story straight."

"He made the call," I say about Ryan.

"That's part of what you need to figure out." After a prolonged pause he asks, "You ready?"

I nod my head. His message is clear. For whatever reason, I need to pretend Ryan wasn't here tonight. With that in mind, I let the EMT lead me toward the ambulance and Adam. Right now, he's the only person in the world who matters.

CHAPTER 23

Wasps. Hundreds of them. Millions. Their buzzing is deafening. They swarm my walls, cramming the corners, crawling over each other in angry hoards. They tear the drywall, hungry to destroy. Devour. Attack. I need to run. But my body is on fire. Flames scorch my throat. My chest. And I can't escape. The fire. The insects.

My jaw falls open. Someone pours dry ice into my mouth. It's toxic and smells like plastic. My hands swing, punching, flailing, reaching for someone to help me. But instead of choking me, the vapor slows to a trickle, sliding down my insides and extinguishing the flames. My insides singe, turn to ash, and I sink back into my bed, where I hope to sleep forever.

The noise cuts. The insects stop all at once, and someone is lifting my head. I wake with a gasp, my eyes wrenching open to pitch black except for the little blue orb around my clock. My room. My bed.

A hand brushes my arm. "Lia."

Ryan. I struggle to make out the hard lines of his silhouette.

"You're okay." His voice is thick, muffled.

I blink, my eyes adjusting. There are no wasps. Just Ryan tucking my neb mask beside the machine. The clock reads 2:22 a.m. I don't know what day it is. My head is heavy, muddled, and my eyes are crusted with a mucus-y discharge. I rub them with my palms.

Adam.

The memory impales me, and I shoot up in bed. "Where's Adam?"

Ryan presses my shoulders. "Adam's at the hospital. He's banged up, but the doctors are good. They're . . ." Ryan pauses long enough for me to know he's lying. "They're going to help him."

I squeeze my eyes. Fall back on the stack of pillows. Pain wrings my insides with its giant fists and shreds me with its nails.

In the ambulance, paramedics checked his vitals, decided whether his life was salvageable. My tears and pleas meant nothing.

Adam's blood was dried, caked on his skin like scales, a desert dryland. It worsened beneath the harsh emergency room lighting where they pulled us apart. I screamed and thrashed until they strapped me to a bed with Velcro and inserted plastic tubing to pump oxygen into my veins. A guy in scrubs, with cold hands and a baby face, pushed something into my IV. "To help you rest," he said in a voice that was calm and irritating. My fingers stiffened into claws, but I was trapped, tied down like a lunatic and pulled away from the only good thing in my life.

Ryan eases off my bed and sits in a chair in the corner of my room. He leans over his knees, clasps his hands together. The blue glow makes his skin look ghostly.

"How did I get here?"

"You came home a couple hours ago. Your mom carried you inside."

I glance at the door, surprised she had the strength to bring me upstairs. Her thin arms. My dead weight. Especially after spending the last twenty-four hours with me at the hospital, where doctors insisted on near-constant monitoring. I slept through most of it, but she didn't. My eyes flash to the door. If she heard us talking, my machine buzzing…

Ryan picks up on what I'm thinking. "She took something to help her sleep. I don't think she rested much in the ICU."

"How did you get here?" We speak in hushed, emotionless tones. Like we know we've been defeated.

The corner of his mouth lifts. Not quite a smile. "Through the basement. I still have a key." Ryan's face bends in anguish. Guilt. He rubs his forehead. "I'm sorry I left. I couldn't… with the ambulance and the cops…"

Dark purple shadows fan out beneath his eyes like brushstrokes. His hands wring together. He shakes his head as part of some conversation he's having with himself. "I'll talk. I'll share everything I know about the Swarm. What I told your dad. And everything I've learned since." His jaw clenches. His eyes flash in the light.

I should feel something. A tiny spark should ignite inside me, eager for this moment. What he's offering to do is better than any lead I've tried to pursue. It beats any tangible evidence I could have conjured. At the very least I should be scared for what it means for him and his family. If he does this, he and his parents will wind up dead like my dad, framed like Morrell, or imprisoned, which is what he tried to prevent by joining the Swarm in the first place.

But I feel nothing.

"I should have done it earlier," he whispers.

"No." No matter what I've tried, the Swarm has always been a step ahead. Whoever's running it is smart, not likely to give up. "They silence people too easily. They'll find a way to discredit you and sweep it under the rug."

Ryan peers up at me. His hands clench together, flexing every muscle in his arms.

"We need others." My voice is raspy. I fight to sound assertive. "You're not the only one being forced into it. We need to get others to come forward. The more people we have, the harder it is to eliminate us."

Ryan's hands twist. "I'll find them." We sit in silence, traced by the light thrum of the air conditioning. Ryan understands the position this puts him in. He knows the implications of what he's committing to, probably better than I do. It's nothing I could ever ask of him, of anyone really, knowing what the Swarm is capable of. After what they did to Adam, what they wanted to do to me. But I can't sit back and let them keep getting away with any of it.

Neither can he.

"Get some sleep," he says, leaning back in the chair where the light no longer hits his face.

"What are you going to do?" I ask.

"I won't leave you again." His voice is low, aching. "I'll be here."

I want to smile, but my lips won't move that way. Not with Adam's life hanging in the balance. Instead, I sink into the down engulfing me. I can feel the sedatives overpowering me.

"Ryan," I say. His face is like the kid in his family picture, vulnerable, hopeful. I glance at my walls plastered with pictures of Hana, checking one more time for insects. "Start with Amy London."

He nods.

The heaviness wins, and I give into it.

CHAPTER 24

Ryan pulls over in front of Northwestern Memorial Hospital, steps away from the revolving door. Light bursts from the lobby. "When you're done, don't come outside. Wait for me. I'll see you."

Shouldn't be hard. The entire first floor is made of glass. A shot cracks as a bullet pierces the wall. Veiny cracks shoot through the panel like lightning, shattering the structure, until it bursts and a thick avalanche of diamond shards crashes to the pavement. The clinking is deafening. Suffocating. It reverberates inside my chest.

I squeeze my eyes, pinch the bridge of my nose, and focus on the hum of Ryan's car, the heat from his air vents skimming my neck, and I remind myself it isn't real.

Ryan wraps his hand around my wrist. "I can take you home."

His grip steadies me. It slows my racing heart. "I'll be fine," I say, trying to convince us both.

I step out of the car, sprint across the ten feet of empty sidewalk, and slam into the spinning door. I don't breathe until I'm inside.

Hurrying through the halls of Northwestern leading to the ICU, my boots *click-clack* on the linoleum floor. Everything reeks of bleach, as though trying to mask the underlying odor of people suffering, dying. The putrid florescent lighting tints everything and everyone pale green.

I clutch the foil base of the plant I bought at the gift shop and the name tag I refuse to put on. Because it's 8:15—fifteen minutes before visiting hours end—the hall is near empty. I pass a man consoling his wife, who wipes at her red-rimmed eyes. A doctor buried in his phone. I keep my head down, hoping no one recognizes me.

My chest is compressed, like I'm wearing a corset crushing my ribs. I hate hospitals. This hospital especially. My sister died here. My dad. Dopney. And even though Adam is still alive, I don't trust it. Everything bad in my life happens here. There must be hundreds of hospitals in Chicago, hospitals much closer to Adam's attack. But like Fate mocking me or torturing me, they brought him here.

I turn the corner to the nurses' station that guards the ICU like a fortress. I'm ready to argue that Adam is practically family, that I must see him.

Instead I find Katie in the waiting room, a stack of sketchbooks open on her lap, a row of colored pencils—definitely not the Crayola kind—fanned across the table beside her. Her dark hair frames her face like curtains. My steps hitch when she doesn't see me right away.

Katie's thin brows are knit as I sit next to her and stare at her drawings. They're of Adam. Each one captures a different side of him—his deviant smirk, his softer, genuine smile, the intensity in his eyes and his brow when he's unlocking something the rest of us wouldn't understand. One sketch depicts him that day in the lunchroom just after the

Navy Pier attack. He's throwing his hand out and saying, "Your pettiness never fails to disappoint." That one's too painful, and I avert my eyes.

When Katie looks up, her concentrated expression doesn't change. She scans my face, the red-flowered plant in my lap. She cradles a sketchbook against her chest and leans back in her chair. She doesn't ask me how I am. If I was hurt. She doesn't throw her arms around me and commiserate with how awful the last forty-eight hours have been.

"How is he?"

Katie's face is deadpan when she answers. "Not good."

My chest squeezes tighter until I'm sure my lungs will collapse. I nod my head and grit my teeth, trying to hold it in. "Has he woken up?"

Katie shakes her head. The movement is tiny. Controlled. "He made it through surgery. He has stitches on his face and head. Fractured ribs, cheekbone. Broken leg. But it's the internal bleeding they're worried about."

The near-empty waiting room feels claustrophobic. Sweat breaks out along my forehead.

When I came here with my mom after my dad's attack, the press wanted a statement from us. They wouldn't leave us alone. The hospital staff had to set up blockades in the hallways. They hid us in a room in the ICU, where we waited to hear whether my dad would win his fight. Doctors operated for so many hours I lost track. My mom fielded calls from our relatives as the afternoon turned into night, and the outcome became grimmer. When the doctor came to tell us my dad was dead, his scrubs were speckled with my father's blood.

I put the plant on the table beside me and pull off the bag slung across my body, as if that will help. "Why did it have to be this hospital?"

Katie slams the sketchbook against the stack in her lap, rattling the colored pencils beside her. "Because his dad works here." Her voice shakes. "His dad is the plastic surgeon who's been piecing Adam back together."

I look toward the rooms like his dad is about to walk out of one of them. I don't remember if I knew his dad worked here. My eyes flicker back to Katie.

"You didn't think about that, did you?"

"It hasn't been easy..." I begin, but Katie silences me.

"You've been so wrapped up in your own world and your mission to do whatever it is you're trying to do that you haven't really thought about anything or anyone else."

I've never seen Katie angry before. I can't swallow. Or talk. Or think about Adam lying in his hospital bed, clinging to life because of me. I squeeze my gut. I'm probably the last person anyone wants to see around here. "Will you text me when there's an update?"

She blames me for everything. And she should.

I indicate the flowers I picked up from the gift shop. "And give him those?"

Katie looks from the plant to me. "It's a poinsettia," she says, like there's something obvious I'm missing. "He's Jewish."

I fight to hold back the tears pooling along my lids. I get it, I should have thought of that. I should've known not to get involved, let my friends get involved. A gnawing ache in the pit of my stomach threatens to chew me from the inside out. I nod. "Please text me as soon as you hear anything new." I'm desperate for this, to stay connected. I have to know how he's doing—good or bad.

Looking down, Katie smooths the crumbled pages of her

sketchbook, where she's captured each detail of Adam's face. He would love these sketches, the sheer number of them.

Katie squares the stack on her lap. "I will."

"Thank you," I whisper, knowing I don't deserve it.

I turn away, ready to run down the halls, out the exit.

"Lia," Katie says. I look over my shoulder as she tucks hair behind her ear. "Be safe."

I grip the straps of my bag and scurry off.

Everything bad in my life happens here.

Rounding the corner, I'm about to run when I see two men, down the intersecting corridor, standing outside an open door. Dr. Marshall—I will not call him Steve—nods as Mayor Henking talks.

I duck behind the wall and press myself against it like I might collapse without its support. Why is he here? How is this possible? Has he come to kill Adam himself? I curse the quivering in my knees. My legs need to stay strong so I can run to the ICU. Throw my body over Adam's if I have to.

I force myself to peek around the corner. The back of Mayor Henking's dark head doesn't move. He wears an expensive suit, tailored, likely afforded by murdering people throughout the city. "It's a strong proposal, Steve."

Dr. Marshall tucks his hands into his white coat, which he wears over a white shirt, blue tie. "I hope you seriously consider it. The NICU expansion would do a lot of good."

Mayor Henking flips through a portfolio and drops his voice. "For the black and Mexican crack babies who will end up in my jails in fifteen years?" He tucks the leather folder beneath his arm.

At first, I'm not sure I heard him right, his tone so low and smooth, but Dr. Marshall doesn't respond right away, like he's been caught off guard. It's his hesitation that confirms I heard the mayor's racist comment correctly. A wave of anger rolls through me. As if I need another reason to hate this man.

"We're a Level Three NICU. Preemies are flown in from all over the Midwest," Dr. Marshall says. "The Jim Henking NICU would expand our capacity, so we wouldn't have to turn away any babies who need the treatment."

"The Jim Henking NICU. That does have a nice ring to it." The mayor extends his hand. They shake. "I'll discuss it with my team." The mayor turns, takes a step in my direction.

I shrink behind the wall until I can't see them. I pray they didn't see me.

"It'll be hard to compete with the Henking Hotel," the mayor says. "Have you seen the plans for it? Taller than the Trump building. Right on Lake Michigan. Just stunning. It would change our whole skyline."

I can't tell if the mayor is getting louder or if they're walking toward me. I scan the hallway, looking for a room to hide in, a stairway to duck into.

"And that fountain," says Dr. Marshall, his voice flattened.

There are no restrooms, no doorways. Just a long, empty corridor of eggshell white. Not even a plant to hide behind.

Mayor Henking laughs. "If you want to add a fountain featuring a thirty-foot statue of me to your NICU project, give me a call."

"Henking Hotel would be quite a legacy," Dr. Marshall says.

They're closing in.

"Chicago was headed toward bankruptcy before I turned it around. Now I'm funding projects like these. I've done a great deal for this city, and I want that remembered. I think I've earned that."

A *great deal*? Like creating the Swarm? Using it to murder people? Blackmailing kids to participate? He can't be serious.

There's clapping on the back and chuckling, the mayor saying, "By the time we're through with our improvement plans, no one will be calling us the Second City anymore," in his schmaltzy way, but I'm only half listening. My shoulder blades press against the wall, like I can knock a hole into it and escape, when suddenly their noise cuts.

They see me before I see them.

My blood drains, leaving in its place a dizzying rush.

"Lia," Dr. Marshall says. "Everything okay?"

They must notice the alarm scrawled across my face. I nod. "I'm visiting a friend."

Both men stare at me, tower over me. I can't look at the mayor. Dr. Marshall pulls his hand out of his white coat and gestures toward me. "Lia is one of our NICU success stories."

The movement makes me flinch, and Dr. Marshall drops his hand.

The mayor nods. "That's right. You had a twin who didn't make it, right?"

He might as well pull out a knife and stab me in the lungs. At least air would be able to get to them. They look at me expectantly, waiting for me to say something. Instead I picture a stupid, gaudy fountain featuring a thirty-foot statue of the mayor and wonder whether they're joking. It didn't sound like it.

"It's an unfortunate but common story," Dr. Marshall says to the mayor. He turns to me. "I got to know your parents very well during the months you were here." His face scrunches as he talks, taking on a concerned expression like he's noticing I'm not registering what's happening—the spastic, PTSD girl.

"Can I help you get somewhere?" he asks.

"I heard you were involved in another incident," the mayor interrupts. There's a slight change in his voice. No longer cordial. It's fake. Empty. Hypocritical. Politician. "I'm very sorry to hear it, Lia."

His polished smile. His gleaming, white teeth. His groomed eyebrows, which look like they've been tweezed and combed. He ordered the hit on Adam and me.

"The commissioner said your attackers just ran off." There is something deliberate and taunting about the way he is looking at me. "I've read many police reports. That almost never happens. What a lucky girl you are." The crow's-feet in the corners of his eyes make him look congenial despite his dark undertone. "That must be some guardian angel looking after you."

My eyes flit to his. He's referencing Ryan. I know he is. He's challenging my account of what happened. Because he knows Ryan was there. Lip Spikes and his friends were supposed to kill Adam and me. Someone told the mayor what happened, had to explain why I wasn't dead.

The blood coursing through my veins turns to lava. I glare at the mayor with more hatred than I've ever felt. This is the man responsible for the horror controlling the city. He ordered my dad's murder. Adam's attack. Meanwhile he's deciding on how to commemorate his *legacy*?

I want to say something that will hurt him. Something that will reduce him to shreds. Something that will make him feel an ounce of the loss and guilt and pain I have felt for the last two years.

The hallway lights flicker and dim. My knees flinch, anticipating an ambush, while no one else seems concerned.

Dr. Marshall points to the ceiling. "Visiting hours are over." He must sense the tension. He claps the mayor's back and steers him away from me. "Never underestimate a survivor, Jim." He winks at me. "Have a good night, Lia."

The mayor nods. "Take care of yourself."

As Dr. Marshall and the man who ruined my life walk away, my fists clench until my nails crease my palms. I turn toward the exit, where Ryan waits to drive me home, when something catches my eye.

Katie. She staggers toward me down the long corridor, bracing herself against the wall like she might fall over. Her silky hair sways with each jerky step.

My legs twitch. Their first instinct is to turn. Run.

Katie's crying and her lips are parted, and I know down to my core I don't want to hear whatever she's coming to say. I want to escape and hide and curl into a ball in some deep, dark corner where nothing is changed.

But my limbs are confiscated. They're not my own. They grow light and hollow and empty. And by the time Katie reaches me and hugs me, she's the one holding me up.

She sobs into my ear.

I cling to the uncertainty of what she's come to tell me. Hold on to a few more seconds in a world where Adam still exists.

We clutch each other. Her nails dig into my back.

By the time she says it, I've already conceded.

Adam is dead.

CHAPTER 25

No matter how many hours I sleep, it's not enough. Heaviness seeps into my veins, saturating me, dragging me down to the murky bottom of Lake Michigan.

It's insatiable.

I lie in bed wrapped in my comforter like a corpse beneath the sheets, drifting in and out of wakefulness, only half aware of fleeting moments as days pass.

Detective Irving stops by. I drift off to the muffled back and forth between his gruff rumbling and my mom's steady replies, unsure whether he came to talk to me or my mom. Either way, he's two deaths too late.

We get a new security system. Drills rizz and alarms screech as they install it. Somehow, Ryan still sneaks in every night. He refills my water glass and whispers I'm sorrys when he thinks I'm sleeping.

But it's not his fault.

I should've stopped Adam. Never involved him. Adam would be alive, on the other side of Chicago, hacking Internet trolls and exposing their hypocrisy if it weren't for me.

My mom doesn't force me out of bed. She doesn't urge me to see

Dr. What's-His-Name. She brings my meals and lets me grieve. She wipes my arms and legs with a washcloth and talks about the sponge baths she gave me in the NICU. After Annie died. After Annie's lungs collapsed and doctors couldn't revive her. It only reminds me of what I've always suspected: somehow I killed her too.

With every sleep, nightmares haunt me. The attacks on Dopney. My dad. Adam. I smell their blood. Hear their bones crack. The Swarm closes in while I stand too paralyzed to save them.

One morning, I'm dreaming of something pleasant—Adam's laugh, his wit, his perfect face. We're sitting together on the CTA, watching something on Adam's phone when he leans over and whispers in my ear, *"You'll never save the city with all that guilt weighing you down."*

I jerk up, flinging the blankets, sure I heard him. His voice is too real, too lifelike. I scrutinize each corner and hiding place, searching for him. He's here. Hiding from me. Teasing me. My ear still prickles with the sound of his voice, and for several minutes, I'm insistent it wasn't a dream. But no matter how hard I try to convince myself, my room is empty except for my bag, my hat, my scarf, and my phone, beckoning me. Screaming at me to get up.

I grab my cell. October 10. The next attack is ten days away.

As usual, Adam's right.

I access my social media sites and post three pictures on each—one of my dad, one of Dopney, and one of Adam—to ensure they aren't forgotten. People should see them, remember them, be haunted by them if that's what it takes to demand justice. I shouldn't be the only one.

Forcing myself out of bed, I shower. Dress. I follow a checklist of daily routines until I've built enough momentum to open the front door and leave my house with a relentless determination to finish what I started. The only difference is that it's no longer about saving the city. This is about destroying the people who robbed me of my dad and my best friend.

I board the city bus and get off at Navy Pier. I pass the Dock Street entrance and pace the walkway, stalking tourists, until I find one I'm looking for.

Sitting on a wooden bench across from the giant Ferris wheel, I pull the sleeves of my sweater over my palms before tucking them beneath my thighs. I watch the ride, studying its mechanics. Each blue gondola takes thirteen minutes to complete one trip, three rotations around the wheel. Thirteen minutes should be all the time I need.

The wheel stops. Double doors open on the bottom six gondolas. A family of four enters one of the cars and begins their trip around. Evil Twin Family.

I pull the rim of my knit hat lower over my brow.

The kids—twins from the look of it—had been screaming and crying over who stood in front while waiting in line. Their parents, tourists, didn't know what to do. They looked exhausted and, more importantly, distracted.

The high-pitched screech of iron twisting and bending worms its way into my consciousness and yanks my attention upward. A surge of wind rocks the gondola at the wheel's peak. It's reckless and fast. Brackets pop. Hinges snap. The gondola plunges downward, ricocheting off metal spokes like a Ping-Pong ball in an arcade game. The wind smacks it, vaulting it in an arc through the air until it crashes against the cement, smattering into millions of pieces.

I squeeze my eyes. *Not real.*

I tick off each sense as I focus on it—a breeze brushing against my face, the smell of lake water and funnel cake, the carousel's muffled recording of an organ playing carnival music.

When I look again, Evil Twin Family is ascending the Chicago skyline, the Ferris wheel completely unharmed.

I push my aviators tight against my face and walk toward stroller parking.

The key is to keep moving. Look like I belong. Thirty-eight paces to the stroller, I grab the woman's cell from the cup holder and make my way to the line for the Ferris wheel. I don't look around. I don't speed up. My heartbeat rings in my ears as I slide the phone inside my bag. I glance up, pretending to be awed by the Ferris wheel's height. Evil Twin Family, in car eleven, has completed their first rotation.

It's ten o'clock on a weekday. The line is short. I wave off the camera guy taking commemorative pictures. He nods without protest. It's weird I'm here by myself. If he doesn't take a picture of me standing in front of the green screen alone, he doesn't have to feel sorry for me.

I snake my way through the ropes. The attendant points to a number. I walk across the aluminum platform and wait, trying to ignore the restless energy flowing through my arms.

When the doors open, I freeze. Evil Twin Family sits in the gondola I'm about to climb into. The kids scream—they don't want to get off. Sweat dampens my forehead beneath my hat, matting my hair against my head. My aviators slide down my nose, but I refuse to push them back.

An attendant wearing a fleece jacket directs me in. Evil Twin

Family still hasn't exited. The dad scoops his daughter, who dangles boneless in his arms. The mom tugs on the son's arm. He pulls back, trying to stay seated. The mom, with fiery-red hair and a Louis Vuitton tote sliding down her arm, looks at the attendant as if to ask if they can just stay.

I swallow hard. What if her phone rings? What if she has a distinct ringtone? She'll hear. She'll know I stole it.

"You need to exit, ma'am," Gray Fleece Attendant says with a drawn-out Wisconsin accent.

I could kiss him.

The parents drag their kids out of the car just as the exit door closes. I rush to sit as Gray Fleece Attendant waves the couple behind me into the same car. The paunchy pair waddles in. My shoulders stiffen. The automated doors close. The air conditioning whirls on, and the wheel carries us upward.

"Oh, that was fast," the woman says in a slow, shrill voice. She fans herself as if she's overexerted herself.

I glance at Evil Twin Family below. They drop the girl, kicking her legs in circular motions, into the stroller and hurry away. They don't seem to notice the missing cell.

Shoving my hat inside my bag, I grab the phone, plastered with the twins' pictures on the case. They'd snapped so many shots along the pier, I was able to glimpse her password—a phishing technique I learned from Adam.

I picture his smile, the way he lifted his left eyebrow every time he said something clever and wanted me to praise him for it. If he were here, he would chastise me for the risks I'm taking, while crouching in the seat beside me, directing me on what to do next. Thinking about him is enough to drain me. I clench every muscle to keep from slumping against the plastic and giving in to my grief.

"Is that your brother and sister?" I look up to see the woman smiling at me, waiting for my response. A limp felt hat dips awkwardly in front of her face.

I shift in my seat and fan my hands over the case, concealing the pictures, wondering if she realizes this phone isn't mine. But her eyebrows lift in curiosity. Her face is all lit up like her intrusive chitchat is interesting.

"No." I turn sideways to face the window. I type in the code, *102877*, and set the alarm for eleven minutes. For the first time in weeks, I access the Internet without worrying about who might be monitoring my activity.

Adam discovered the date of the next flash attack, but if I'm going to record it, if I'm going to expose Lip Spikes and make him pay for everything he's stolen from me, I need the time and location.

"Look at this view," the man says to his wife. They point out buildings like they've never seen skyscrapers before.

Tourists.

I access Twitter, wondering if the Swarm is stupid enough to use it again. It takes twenty-six seconds to find what Adam found. *#14.10.20.1930.*

My breath hitches. It's missing numbers. It has the time, 7:30, but latitude and longitude aren't there. I fumble through my bag for a pen and write it down in the corner of my book. Flipping to the back, I record the tweet's time stamp and username—a random series of numbers and letters.

The car releases a tiny whine as it glides across the wheel's climax. I throw my book back into my bag and lean my head against the gondola's glass encasement. How will the Swarm know where to attack without a location? More importantly, how will I record it?

"Maybe she knows." The woman speaks up. "Where can we find the best deep-dish pizza? We want something authentic," she says in her cheery voice, overarticulating her words.

"I hate deep-dish," I say, trying to shut her up.

"Really? I thought all Chicagoans—"

"Gluten allergy." I have no such thing.

"Oh, bless your heart." She isn't deterred. "Which one do city people like the most?"

We begin our second rotation—seven minutes left. I bend over the phone, deepening my concentration. "They all taste the same."

Without pausing, she turns to her husband. "I wouldn't have thought that. How about that one place we passed in the cab . . ."

I don't listen to the rest. I scour Twitter for any hint of the location. I search every social media site I can think of. Drowning out the ridiculousness of their conversation, I scan through pictures, posts, gifs, videos, but before I know it, the seven minutes have passed and the alarm is going off and I haven't found the slightest hint of where the attack will take place.

I erase my search history and set the phone on the corner of the bench, careful not to let the couple see what I've done. As we near the platform, they scoot to the edge of their seats. The doors open. The attendant with bushy sideburns and a Blackhawks hat holds his hand out for them. I make sure the phone is tucked into the corner before stepping off, but the attendant blocks my path, signaling for me to stop. He smiles. "I thought I recognized you," he says. The doors close.

I bang on the glass. "Open up."

I turn to exit out the other side, but Gray Fleece Attendant leans in. "Your next ride's been taken care of."

I don't want another ride. I want off. I'm about to shove my way past him when Cullen Henking steps inside. My eyes dart to the phone lying on the bench. Instead of barreling out, I back into the corner seat, concealing the phone behind my leg, and pray it doesn't ring.

Cullen enters carrying a large bouquet of flowers wrapped in patterned tissue. If I weren't trying to avoid a panic attack, I'd be disgusted by how much he spent on them.

Gray Fleece Attendant holds out his cell. "Can I snap a quick pic of you guys?"

Cullen puts his arm around me. Before I know it, Gray Fleece Attendant's taken a picture of Cullen smiling, me gaping. The doors close, the air kicks in, and the car begins to move.

I'm wondering how long I have before Gray Fleece Attendant posts the picture online when a tiny flat screen flickers on, talking about Navy Pier attractions.

Cullen flashes a sympathetic smile and holds out the bouquet. "Hydrangeas and orchids—they're my mother's favorites." He wears a button-down shirt, a sweater, dress pants.

Cullen never talks about his mom, which makes the whole scenario even stranger. From what I hear, she spends half her year in Arizona—without the mayor.

I refuse the flowers. Cullen sets them on the seat.

The back of my throat burns. I reach into my bag for my inhaler. Cullen looks away like I'm doing something obscene as I shake it and take in a blast of medicine. I hold the breath in my mouth until I cough.

"Why are you here?" I ask between coughs. He must have skipped school to follow me here. What exactly did he see me do? I shift my purse so it covers my lap.

"I'm sorry. About Adam."

A burning sensation ignites behind my nose. I look away. He doesn't get to be sorry about Adam. He hated Adam. His father murdered him.

I slide my right hand down the side of my leg and tuck the phone beneath my thigh. "I bet you are."

"We might not have gotten along, but I wouldn't exactly wish death by hate crime on anyone."

"Hate crime?" My voice shakes. "Who's calling it that?" I didn't even think of how authorities would brush this aside. Dismiss it like typical city violence.

Cullen props his elbows on the blue ledge of the car and looks south along Lake Shore Drive. His house stands out like a gaudy beacon. He shrugs as he says, "Everyone," like my question is ludicrous. "For the record, I don't have anything against gay people." He rakes a hand through his hair. "My dad's left-wing on all LGBTQ issues. Gender-neutral public restrooms are his latest crusade."

"It had nothing to do with Adam's sexuality," I say through clenched teeth. The shaking spreads throughout my body. "The Swarm murdered him."

Our car whines again as it nears the top of the Ferris wheel. Cullen looks down over his shoulder at something below. A nervous, surreptitious glance.

"Who's down there?" I squint at the pier and am hit with a wave of nausea as I realize how high we are.

Cullen clears his throat. "The Save the Parks Gala is next week. I'd like you to be my date."

At first, I'm sure I've misheard him. My neck bends forward, waiting for him to clarify.

When he doesn't, I snort. "You can't be serious."

Cullen narrows his eyes toward Lake Michigan. "You've had a couple rough weeks—might be nice to go out." His voice is flat, irritated even.

"Your social media status needs another boost?"

Cullen lowers his voice, "Don't be difficult, Lia." He glances out the window as we make our first pass of the platform.

"Is your dad out there?" I grip the phone beneath my leg. I wiped the search history, but the mayor could still figure out what I'd been hunting for.

Looking at the courtyard below, I scan the carousel, the swings, the remote-control boats, the outdoor bar. People are gathering, milling. Dozens of them. I close my eyes, steady myself.

It's not the Swarm. There's no attack.

Sweat beads on my lip. I push my sunglasses back onto my face.

I take a deep breath, focus on the technicalities of breathing. Air in. Lungs expand. Air out. I force my eyes open. When I look again, I see families, not teenagers. And no sign of the mayor.

"Say yes."

"What?" I turn back, momentarily forgetting what he's talking about. Everything about Cullen—his expression, his posture, the way he rakes his hand through his hair—looks restrained.

"The gala—just say yes." He won't make eye contact. His chin points down. His nostrils flare. His lips press together to form a slight grimace.

The car whines again as we hit the crest and make the final turn approaching the platform.

"Find another date."

Cullen watches the city like his ego's been hurt.

I press the phone against the side of the car, hoping it will stay undetected when we get off—as long as it doesn't ring. Slinging the strap of my bag around my torso, I wipe my palms against my jeans.

Cullen scoots toward the door, ready to jump out. Thankfully, I don't need to worry about him acting chivalrous, insisting I get off first, and finding the phone.

We near the platform where Richard stands next to Bushy Sideburns. His hands are tucked into the pockets of his suit pants as if he's enjoying the blustery day.

The doors open, and Bushy Sideburns gives us a wry smile like we just spent the last thirteen minutes making out on the Ferris wheel.

Cullen steps out looking annoyed by Richard's presence.

I exit next, leaving the phone concealed from view. It will take another ride around the Ferris wheel until someone turns it in or steals it. Either way, it's not linked to me.

Richard wears designer aviators. Like he's trying too hard. "On behalf of the mayor and myself, I'd like to extend our condolences about the atrocity that happened to your friend."

During the few times Richard and I have interacted, he's seemed genuine in his concern. This time, there's no sincerity behind his words.

Chills zip down my arms and legs. Richard's hand grazes the small of my back, making me cringe as he escorts me off the platform. Cullen follows behind. He pulls out his phone and scrolls through it, the Ferris wheel turning in the background.

"We're all hoping you can join Cullen next week. The event is certain to alleviate the stress you've been under."

I look at Cullen absorbed in his cell and realize for the first time where this is coming from. This is the mayor's idea, not Cullen's.

I didn't expect this coming from Richard, though I'm not sure why. He is, after all, the mayor's henchman.

Anger begins to gurgle deep in the recesses of my gut. Is this the mayor's way of torturing me? "I'm surprised the mayor is going. I thought he was against the Save the Parks campaign."

Richard smiles. His tie flaps in the wind. He smooths it down with his lanky fingers. "You more than anyone else can probably understand and appreciate the need to unite our city right now. The mayor loves Chicago's parks as much as anyone else."

There's a smoothness to Richard I've never seen before.

"He bulldozes them to put up million-dollar mansions. Like his."

Richard's hand drops from my back. He stands in front of me. For once, he's not hunched over. He stands tall on his skinny frog legs, revealing his height. "Selling off a few lakefront properties created revenue for the city, which has allowed him to improve neighborhood parks. He created government-funded scholarships for kids to attend the Park District's summer camps for free. The mayor fully supports park preservation."

I straighten my shoulders, extending my small frame. "When it doesn't cost him millions preserving it."

Richard chuckles. His laugh slides under my skin.

"Your presence with Cullen could help revive this city. Our unified stand of support will show the city that we're all on the same team."

"And what team is that?" They can't actually expect me to stand beside the mayor after what he did to my father, to Adam. They're deranged.

Richard's phone buzzes. He checks the screen and tucks it back into his pocket. "We all want the same thing, Lia. To rally around our new Chicago. To watch our city thrive. The people of this city need something to rally around right now." He talks with such ease. It surprises me.

"Why are you doing this?"

"This city has taken a liking to you." Richard takes a step closer. I swear he does it to intimidate me. "They would love to stand behind you."

"Which is why you want me to stand next to the mayor." At an event that's controversial for him to attend.

Richard smiles. "We'll let you stand next to Cullen."

My fists ball at my sides. "You're going to have to find yourself someone else."

Richard checks his phone again. He dismisses it, puts it back into his pocket, regards the Chicago skyline. "As you already know, this city is dangerous, Lia. The mayor is willing to protect you in any way he can if you're willing to help him." Richard lowers his chin, creating thick folds in his puffy neck. "I would hate for you or your mom or anyone else you care about to find themselves in another unfortunate situation. They seem to happen so readily these days."

My head grows light. Black spots crowd my vision, and I blink them away. Richard's threat is clear. If I don't play along, they will continue to kill off the people I love. This is about tormenting me. Controlling me. Making me do their bidding.

"This is in the city's best interest, but it's also in your best interest. It's a good opportunity for everyone." Richard looks down at his phone. "I've got to take this one." He holds up his finger, signaling for me to wait.

I stand in a tiny courtyard at the bottom of the Ferris wheel, between groups of people milling about. Kids scream and laugh on the carousel and the swing ride as my thoughts whirl. As angry as I want to be at what he's forcing me to do, I keep getting hung up on the word *opportunity*. Hundreds of people who already hate the mayor will be at the gala. Cameras will be there. Could I somehow use this to my advantage? Make it my opportunity to expose him?

Richard puts his phone into his coat pocket. "We can arrange for you to have something to wear. We'll send it to your house."

"Something that will look good on camera," I say through clenched teeth, but my words are drowned out by someone shouting nearby. I don't realize the yelling is aimed at us until I catch my name.

"Wait! Lia Finch!" Bushy Sideburns repeats as he runs up with the flowers I left in the car. He has a big, goofy smile on his face like he's being helpful as he holds out the bouquet. "You almost forgot these."

I'm about to tell him he can keep them when Richard reaches out and grabs them instead. "Thanks."

"Your phone too." Bushy Sideburns holds out the cell with the twins' family pictures plastered all over the case for me to grab.

"That's not mine." My face flushes as I try to sound convincing, like I've never seen it before and have no idea where it came from.

Richard stares at me. He's reading my face. I can feel it. I lift my chin while Bushy Sideburns stands there, holding the stupid phone out for me to take, refusing to turn around and leave with it already.

Richard grabs the phone from the attendant, watching me the entire time. "This phone isn't yours?" He glances down at the pictures on the case.

I shake my head.

"Isn't that odd," Richard says, like he's piecing it together.

He taps the screen and stares at the number pad as if trying to decipher the right key code to unlock it. Richard looks back at me, doing my best not to appear guilty.

"There it is!" A woman leaves the stroller with two screaming children behind with her husband. She runs up to us with Bushy Sideburns still standing there. "That's mine." I try to look clueless as Evil Twins' mom reclaims the phone. "I must have left it on the Ferris wheel."

Her red hair blows around her head as she grabs it from Richard, giving him a distrustful look.

Richard watches me as he lets her take it. Bushy Sideburns and Evil Twins' mom walk away in separate directions, while Richard tucks his hands into his pockets and flashes a wicked smile. "Next Saturday then. Cullen will pick you up. Seven o'clock. Sharp." He takes a step back, tapping Cullen on the shoulder like it's time to go.

Cullen looks up at me. His face unreadable, or maybe I'm too freaked out about what just happened to read anything right now.

And then it hits me. I pull out my own phone and call up the calendar.

Next Saturday. October 20.

The date of the next attack.

CHAPTER 26

What brings you in today?" an overly eager Apple sales associate asks. She stands across a blond wooden table covered with laptops on display. I scrutinize her expression, her body language, gauging whether there's more to her interest in me than selling me a computer. Maybe a desire to snap my picture. Or maul me.

"Just looking." I turn away, hoping to shoo her along. I fidget with my purse straps slung across my chest. But I sense her presence, lingering like some rancid odor that won't disperse.

"You looking for something to use for school? Entertainment? Graphic design?" Overeager Girl circles around, trying to reestablish eye contact. I pretend I can't hear her.

I duck beneath my new wool hat and bury my chin into the folds of my scarf. I take a circuitous path away from the laptops in the front of the store toward the desktops shoved to the back corner like an unwanted afterthought.

Despite it being Friday, I'd hoped the store would be crowded, so I could come in, get what I needed, and leave without anyone bothering me. My fallback is to play the icy, rude girl, so that anyone tempted to solicit me leaves me alone—at least long enough to look up a few things and get out before I'm noticed.

Overeager Girl doesn't follow me. I hear her attack her next victim with the same horrid line she used on me. Same cheery intonation. "What brings you in today?"

I scan the store, avoiding eye contact. Sales associates harp on that kind of thing as an invitation to chat. Luckily, every associate is preoccupied, dishing out rehearsed lines and cheesy smiles to customers about devices more current and expensive than the desktops in front of me.

I loosen my scarf. My hands hover over the keyboard, hesitant at first. One more glance to ensure no one is coming, and I fire up the Internet.

I don't know whether Ryan has found anyone to come forward, but he needs as many names of kids forced to participate as he can get. The more people willing to talk, the safer they'll all be. Even though I'm trying not to speculate what the mayor has planned for the gala next week, I have to do this now. Just in case.

Knowing time is limited, I focus on the men in the photo that Adam and I found in the library. Harry Hewitt and Daniel London both have kids in high school. Edward Cunnings *had* a son, who committed suicide. That leaves four other men, all affiliated with the Lakefront Project.

I type *Bill Morrell* and hit enter. His face pops up on the screen, taking me back to the anguish, confusion, and resentment I felt after my dad died.

A man screams. It's terror-ridden, and a shudder ripples through my body. I clench my gut and try to ground myself. But my nerves are too heightened, making any kind of self-monitoring or mindfulness unreliable. Another scream slices through the night, coming from just outside the store. I watch the store's patrons. None of them so much as flinch. I inhale slowly, dismissing the sounds and my body's visceral response to them. With my heart jackhammering in my chest, I push past it, unsure whether the cries in my head were Dopney's or my dad's. Either way, they aren't real.

I skim through the hits, trying to ignore *Steven Finch* every time I see the name, and find Morrell's obituary, featuring a black-and-white picture of him in tweed. Beneath it, a paragraph about how he was this admirable, upstanding citizen, which I still find hard to believe. I scan it, searching for names of the people who survived him. Sure enough, Morrell had two daughters. At the time of his death, one was twenty-two. The other was seventeen. They lived in Kenilworth, attended New Trier High School.

I google Kellee Morrell, the seventeen-year-old. She would have been the one the Swarm targeted. When I can't find anything fast enough, I move on to social network sites. Every ten seconds or so, I scan the store, checking to make sure no one is coming. Six minutes pass. Another three. Until finally I find a Kellee Morrell who went to New Trier, now attends Yale, and is apparently on their diving team.

I scroll through her pictures. She's won all kinds of awards for diving. Spends a lot of time with her mom and her sister. In every picture, she has this strained, haunted expression. Her lips have a slight curve to them—a sad attempt for a smile. And she wears pearls. A lot. Not exactly Swarm material.

The longer I stare at her picture, the more convinced I become of her story: the Swarm approached her, she refused to be blackmailed, and they framed and killed Morrell because of it. It's exactly what they threatened would happen to Ryan's parents if he didn't comply. My theory becomes so vibrant and plausible in my head, I grow giddy until I realize there's no way to prove it. Kellee is at Yale. I can't even count how many states away that is. Reaching out through social media is not an option. She's a dead end.

I roll my wrists and move on: Maximilian Horowitz, Clyde Jennings, and Frank Davies—the last three men from the picture. Sure enough, all three of them have a son or daughter in high school. The teens' online presence is more limited than Kellee's, but each of them looks pained in their pictures. Withdrawn. Because like Kellee, they've been blackmailed and forced to participate in murdering people?

I scratch their names down on a Post-it. Adam could produce their home addresses and the schools they attend within the hour. The second I think it, his familiar scent of cedar and grapefruit swirls around me. I think of the way Adam hugged me, the way his lean arms wrapped around me right before . . . I close my eyes and breathe. Deeply. Adam laughs in his self-assured, uninhibited way. The sound is so clear, like he's standing beside me, helping me. Still.

If anyone understood how badly I needed to take down the mayor and destroy the Swarm, it was Adam. He knew that my drive to hunt them, expose them, and watch them suffer the consequences—for murdering my father, ruining his reputation, robbing me of my sanity and any chance at a normal life—is the only thing that's kept my mind from collapsing. If I'd continued seeing Dr. What's-His-Name, he would have recognized it too. Only his take on it would have been much different from mine.

The ghost of Adam's laughter swirls around my head. And then I see him, standing behind a pinched-looking woman a couple tables over. He mocks her as she complains to a sales associate that Siri's voice is too robotic. She wants something that sounds more natural, more human. I can't help but snicker at the way he mimics her expression, her gestures so well. We laugh together. One last time. I hope I never forget that sound. As much as it pains me, I bury it, sending Adam and my memories of him down the dark, twisty tunnel.

If I survive this week, I'll start seeing Dr. What's-His-Name again. I'll go to his psychiatric care center if he thinks it will help. I will allow myself to give in, to break down, to accept help, and to heal the way I'm meant to. I *promise*—in exchange for strength, whatever I have left, to stay focused and clear-headed, at least until after the gala.

I check my watch. Fourteen minutes have passed. I study the sales associates, the customers in the store. No one looks interested in me. Like an addict, I type in one more name: Ryan Hewitt. For as much time as I've spent with him, I know very little.

Ryan Hewitt pops up on every site I search. None of them are the Ryan Hewitt I know. I add *Chicago* and even his dad's name to the search, but it doesn't help. The only other detail I know about him is the kind of car he drives, which won't do anything.

"What exactly do you want to know?"

I spin around to find Emi Vega smirking at me. She wears a black belted coat with the collar popped and red stilettos. Her caramel hair is tucked into a red knit hat. An oversized Prada bag hangs on her shoulder.

I close out my windows, wondering what she saw.

"Last time I fell for that, you disappeared."

Emi crosses her ankles, sticks her hands into her pockets. "These things take time."

Her ankle jeans look perfectly tailored, and it annoys me.

"You got what you needed from me and bolted. What is it you need now?"

"I have your answers." Emi lifts an eyebrow. She stares at me with a smug look on her face. "If you still want them."

My pulse quickens. I stand as still as possible, hoping she doesn't notice how desperate I am to know what she's uncovered. After weeks of nothing from Emi, I'd dismissed her as another person using me.

"It wasn't easy. Someone's put quite a bit of money into hiding this one." Emi shifts her purse straps as if we're talking about something futile. She then pulls her phone from her pocket and flips through it. "Jeremiah Dopney's parents, Alicia and Alex Dopney, are this quaint, wholesome couple from Brunswick, Ohio. Jeremiah is their only child. However . . ." Her eyes and thick lashes flash up at me, drawing out the reveal. "He was adopted—something that was not easy to find—and born here in Chicago, at Prentice. Again, not easy to uncover."

She pauses like I should hail her as some sort of god for figuring this all out—like she doesn't have a team of research assistants helping her. My hand slips from the desktop keyboard.

"His father's name isn't on his birth certificate. His mom is listed as Sydney Baker." She steps toward me, leans against the blond wood table.

"Am I supposed to know who that is?" I try to sound indifferent, but my head grows light anticipating the connection that made Dopney a target and got him killed.

"Less than a year after Sydney Baker gave her baby up for adoption, she married Frank Cornell."

"Get to the point." My mind reels. Sydney Cornell sounds familiar—she's someone I should recognize.

Emi's eyes go flat. She breathes through her nose as if I'm the one annoying her. "Let's not forget I did this for you."

Emi Vega doesn't do anything without something in it for her. But I'm too eager to hear the rest to get into it.

She straightens her posture. Crosses her arms. "Sydney Cornell is an infamous Lake Forest socialite who just happens to be the chairperson for the Save the Parks Gala." She raises both of her eyebrows and presses her dark-red lips together.

"The gala raising money to shut down the next phase of the Lakefront Project."

Emi smirks. Her eyes ignite. "Exactly."

I'm caught in a moment of sheer disbelief. She did it. What she found links the attacks to the Lakefront Project. It's the connection my dad needed. Authorities can use this to incriminate Mayor Henking and anyone else involved. "They need to reopen my dad's case," I whisper.

The excitement drops from her face. Emi shakes her head. "Easy, there. You won't find a prosecutor who'll touch this. Not unless you have something else to offer."

Like a handful of teenagers willing to come forward to share intimate details of how the Swarm operates. A rush of adrenaline quivers through me. I'm about to tell her when I realize what she wants to do, what she might have already done. "You want to write a story about this."

"It's the only way to get people to open their eyes."

This was always about getting the story for her, boosting her fame. And if she does that, she ruins everything.

I turn to the Apple desktop, clear the search history. I exit out of each window, find the database file in the hard drive, and delete that too. I need to get out of this store. Away from her.

Emi reaches into her bag and grabs something from it. Before I realize what she's doing, she sticks a flash drive into the desktop.

Is she trying to retrieve everything I just searched for? So she can use that too? "What are you doing?"

Emi takes the mouse and begins clicking. "There's a high school kid over there who hasn't stopped staring at you since you entered the store."

I search for who she's talking about, half expecting to see Lip Spikes glaring at me, but I don't see anyone.

"Either he's checking you out in a very creepy way, or he's been sent to follow you. If it's the latter, I'm guessing he's going to be all about this computer once you leave. And simply clearing the search history and trashing a file isn't going to cut it." Emi is deep into the Internet database when she pulls a folder from her flash drive and dumps it into the browser archives. She closes each window, pulls her device out, and drops it into her purse.

Emi crosses her arms and leans her hip against the table. "It's a sub program." She nods toward the desktop. "Scrambles the history. You're covered." She says it with confidence. It's clear she's done this before.

"The article's already written," Emi continues. "I don't mention you. But I bring up your dad's death and pose the question that his attack might not have been the only targeted one."

I grab the straps of my bag and step away from the desktop. This could give the mayor time to circumvent any real accusations. And from the sound of it, it does nothing to clear my dad's name. I push my shoulders back. She wouldn't have this article if it weren't for me.

Emi's expression softens. "It's the only way, Lia," she says. The diamond studs in her ears the size of my thumbnail flash as she tilts her head.

She's going to make a fortune off this article.

"What if people blame Sydney Cornell and boycott the gala?"

"I'm releasing it after the gala."

"Will it vindicate Rafael Nuñez?"

"CPD dropped that lead weeks ago."

I open my mouth for another retort, but I have nothing to say. Nothing to argue. I can't exactly tell her I have people—one person, actually—willing to talk.

"I'm hoping to get a few shots of Sydney Cornell with people from the Lakefront Project at the gala. All of them are so narcissistic, at least some of them are bound to be there, even if it blatantly contradicts their objectives."

Something inside me crumbles. "I'm going," I whisper.

Emi's eyes become squinty. "I get that you want to do something, but this really isn't the place for you to—"

"With Cullen Henking," I cut in. "The mayor wants me near him. He's making me go."

Recognition clicks on Emi's face. She rests her fingers on her lip. "For a photo op. Of course he would."

I don't know if I should say it or not. It comes out before I decide. "The mayor heads the Death Mob."

"We still can't prove it. And until then, you should—"

"The next attack is the night of the gala."

For once, Emi is silent. She stares at me for several prolonged seconds. "Where is it?"

"Didn't say."

More silence hangs between us as Emi seems to consider what it may mean.

"Remind me not to underestimate you." She glances at the computer. "Though you suck at covering your tracks."

She pulls out a cell from her Prada bag. "This is for you." She hands over a phone. The plastic covering is still on the screen. "If you think of anything, or"—she stares at the phone—"if you need help, my number is programmed in there. The password is zero, nine, two, eight, one, five." She smiles wryly, indicating there's something to the numbers I'm missing.

"Am I supposed to recognize that?"

"The last two are Hewitt boy's address." She looks at her nails. "I pinned it on Maps, if you're interested."

I stare at the phone, wondering what else she put in there.

Her eyebrows pinch. She holds eye contact. "Whoever's running the Death Mob . . ." Emi drops her voice to a whisper. "Especially if it's the mayor—just be careful."

"Are you ladies interested in phones today?" a sales associate in blue-rimmed glasses asks as he rubs his hands together.

Emi doesn't look his way. "We're on our way out."

"Alrightee then. I'll just be over here if you need me."

Emi grabs my wrist. "Don't go to the gala." Her concern catches me off guard.

A stinging sensation starts beneath the bridge of my nose. "I have to."

"I can find you a way out."

"They threatened my mom." My voice is small, desperate.

Emi drops my wrist. Nods. She smooths out the front of her coat as if regaining her composure. "Well—my wife, Olivia, is notorious for being on time, and I'll be late on our anniversary if I don't leave now. But you know how to reach me. Keep that phone with you at all times." She nods again. "Good luck, Lia." Without waiting for a response, she heads out the glass doors and into the night.

The back of my throat burns like I've swallowed ash. I pull out my inhaler and take in a deep, medicated puff.

On my way out the door, I pass a guy staring at me. At first, I don't recognize him, but when I take a closer look, I see the creepy spider tattoo crawling up his neck, behind his ear.

Spider Tattoo.

My throat clenches, trapping my breath inside me. I dart through the glass doors, glancing back to see if he's following me. Instead, he heads over to the desktop I was using and starts punching at it with tight concentration.

I don't dare wait to see if Emi's program works. Without a second thought, I turn away from the Apple Store and take off running.

CHAPTER 27

I kick my covers and flip away from the clock on my nightstand. It's past midnight. My mind won't stop racing.

If my sister Annie were around, would any of this be different? Would Adam still be alive? Would she and I find a way to take down the mayor before the gala? Before Emi's article? Something that ensures he rots in prison instead of spending the city's blood money on flashy hotels with gaudy fountains.

I flop to my back, tangling my leg in the sheets.

That's what this is about for him: His image. His legacy. He's murdering people so he can splash his name all over city buildings. I should've recognized it the first time I met him. His artfully grayed hair. His perfect teeth. He's a narcissist—the dangerous kind. And the whole Lakefront Project reflects it. For the last ten years, the project's platform has been all about bringing in revenue, generating tourism, and saving this city. But those promises are all secondary to the real reason behind it all: the mayor's ego.

I'm not sure whether to laugh or simply despise the irony behind it all. This city turned their backs on my dad's entire career when he was pegged as a narcissist. And yet everyone, including the media, seems to give the mayor a pass? Unless the mayor found a way to control the media too.

My right eye twitches, and I massage the dull ache pulsing inside my head.

I need to go back. Reanalyze my crime wall. Every Death Mob victim must be linked to someone tied to the Lakefront Project. It's how the mayor gets people to agree to his plans. And he's controlling those already involved with the project too, like the men in that picture. The Swarm can't exactly attack everyone. My eyes dart around the ceiling, connecting invisible dots like a constellation that's always been there but is finally crystalizing. That's what the blackmail is for.

Ryan said his dad did something illegal. Maybe they all did. Bribery? Extortion? Embezzlement? One of a million other possible scenarios I can't even imagine? Maybe they were coerced into it. Maybe they were already corrupt. Either way, every single one of them had a kid in high school. That's more than coincidence. The mayor must have chosen those men so he could force their kids into the Swarm.

I rub both eyes with the palms of my hands. I'm so close to figuring it out. I know I am. And still, so many unanswered questions spin through my head in dizzying circles with two more nagging than the rest. Why didn't the tweet about the next attack include the location? And how will I catch the Swarm on video if I don't know where it is?

Unless the attack is meant for me.

I inhale. Air crackles against the back of my throat like vinyl record static. Whatever the mayor is planning for the night of the gala, I'm running out of time. The day I cut my foot, Ryan asked me if I'd responded to the tweet about the Navy Pier attack, if I'd signed in. There has to be something to that.

I jump out of bed. The sheets, still twisted around my ankle, tumble to the floor. I kick them away and scurry to my bag. Squinting in the dark, I rummage through it for the phone Emi gave me, the one I've been avoiding for the last three days. I tap Google Maps. Like Emi promised, Ryan's house is pinned. And it's only a few blocks away. I still find it hard to imagine him living so close.

I throw on an oversized pair of sweats, wrap my scarf around my neck, and pull my wool hat low over my eyes. I'll need to skirt the Escalade camped out front, which shouldn't be too hard. The bigger challenge is getting to Ryan's without a hallucination overpowering me.

Dr. What's-His-Name would bank on me failing. Which is all the motivation I need.

Just before I walk out of my room, I listen for movement coming from my mom's room.

Nothing.

Grabbing my keys off the desk, I slink down the stairs and head for the back door. My palms sweat as I punch in the alarm code, deactivating it, praying the staccato beeps don't wake my mom.

I tiptoe down the porch stairs like I might disturb someone hiding in the bushes waiting to kill me. Careful not to activate our floodlights, I hug the house, tracing the perimeter of our yard, while watching the night for any sign of movement.

The leaves on our Japanese maple flutter all at once. For a split second my heart leaps as I think it's a person hiding among the dead blooms of our hydrangea bushes. Not exactly a hallucination, but still too neurotic if I'm going to make it four blocks.

I sidle up against the fence and inch around the garage. My hand grazes the brick as I round the corner and pass the side door. I'm about to clear it when the door jerks open. A thick hand grabs my wrist and yanks me inside my garage. Before I can make a run for it, the door slams shut, trapping me inside.

A burst of adrenaline ignites every nerve in my body. I spin, looking for my attacker, ready to punch or kick, whichever I can get in first.

Someone grabs my shoulders to steady me—and I'm looking into Ryan's eyes.

I shake him off, gulp for air. "What are you trying to do to me?"

Ryan's hands slide down my arms, lingering at my wrists.

I bend over. Visions of Adam's silhouette cowering in the alley flash like a strobe light inside my head. Blood leaks from his face. I shut my eyes. Squeeze the images out. "Don't do that. I can't…"

Ryan bends low, until his face is near mine. He clears a chunk of hair from my cheek and tucks it behind my ear. "You okay?"

I step back and inhale, burying the images of Adam. They threaten to slice me open as I shove them deep into my gut and work to regain my courage, release the pressure in my chest.

Ryan stands, leans against the hood of my mom's SUV, and waits for me to finish my mental breakdown.

I shuffle, searching for space, but my elbow hits the mountain bike propped against the wall. The front wheel turns, scraping the concrete. The back wheel clashes against a metal shelving unit littered with tools we haven't used since my dad's death. I think of the blogger, sideswiped by an Escalade, and I inch away from the bike like it's a dark omen. I can't move far; there's barely enough room for Ryan and me to stand across from each other without touching.

He tucks his hands into the pockets of a zip-up hooded sweatshirt. "Where were you going?"

Short huffs burst from my lips, echoing through the dark. They're too loud. Too weak. I grab my sides, keeping my arms close to my body as my crap lungs take their time steadying themselves. "To find you."

Ryan stares at me through the shadows with an unbearable intensity.

"I need to talk to you. You're not exactly easy to get ahold of," I whisper.

"And you thought sneaking around in the middle of the night would be a good idea?" Ryan searches my face before taking off his Blackhawks hat and dropping it on the hood of my mom's car. He rubs his forehead. "You have three Swarm members watching your house." He's quiet, but firm. "One out front. Two on either side of the alley."

My head turns on instinct, like I can see them through the cement walls.

"You wouldn't have made it a few steps past your gate," he says.

I'd only considered the Escalade out front. Three is more than I expected. I imagine light snaking through the darkness and glinting off the metal in Lip Spikes' mouth. The garage shrinks. The air becomes thick, musty, claustrophobic. I unwind my scarf, slide my hat off, and drop them on the ground.

"They announced the next attack."

Ryan's eyes soften like he knows no matter how many people we find to come forward, there's not enough time to prevent it.

I stretch my torso, expanding my lungs, trying to release the unwanted pressure burning in my chest. "There's no location."

Ryan nods. "They've never done that before."

I figured as much. The whole thing is a setup—without any key information, I'll be walking into a trap, one I might not escape.

"But they'll tweet it out, won't they? The night of the attack."

"I think so."

"That's how you know who to hit. The victim is identified just before the Initiators start."

Ryan dips his chin. The movement is controlled, slight. "They send a pic."

I envision Navy Pier. Dozens of blue orbs filled the gray, misty day as phones went off just before the attack. I shake away the idea that on Saturday night, it could be my photo on everyone's screen.

"That's why you sign in through Twitter. To give whoever's in charge a list of everyone at each attack."

Ryan's eyes narrow. "Where are you going with this?"

Ryan said earlier that not everyone's forced into the Swarm. "The Initiators aren't blackmailed. They must volunteer."

"Initiators are idolized. They're well taken care of—money, gifts." His voice is low and contemptuous. "Some kids join for their chance at that."

"So the tweet is an all-call. They need the attacks to be big." It's how the mayor invites more people, which means anyone can join. I can't imagine what kind of person signs up to savagely murder someone else, but that's not the point. "If I tweet back, then Saturday night when the location goes out—"

"No," Ryan snaps. His jaw ripples beneath the skin. The muscles in his arms and chest tense. "Why would you do that?"

"The mayor wants me to go to the Save the Parks Gala with Cullen." I glance at him. "He says it's for the press, to have me standing next to him…"

Ryan's shoulders stiffen. "The same night."

"They're picking me up thirty minutes before the attack starts."

I search his face for a sign—any indication that there's no correlation. That my worst fears are outrageous and illogical. But Ryan's square jawline is sharp, his expression hard. "You can't go."

"They aren't exactly giving me a choice."

I've considered every angle—refusing, boycotting, running away. None of my options are good. These people killed my dad. Adam. Fourteen others. My mom would be next.

Ryan's expression turns worried or desperate—I can't tell. Either way, it stirs my anxiety, and for the first time since knowing him, I'd rather he bury his emotions like usual. "Tomorrow. I'll go to the CPD."

"Not without more people." I lift my chin to make up for my size. For my shoulders that come up to his chest. For how narrow and small I feel every time I stand next to him. "We can't afford that risk." I pull the Post-it from my pocket. As I do, the back of my hand knocks into his stomach, which is solid and strong. Heat splashes across my neck, down my back, but Ryan doesn't flinch. Like he didn't feel it. Like it doesn't matter how close we're crammed together.

I rake my ratted hair. "It's a list of others forced into it. Their parents are tied to the Lakefront Project like your dad."

Ryan stares at the paper while I hold my breath, waiting for him to grab it. All it would take is one subtle shift for my hand to brush his hoodie. Goose pimples skip up my arms.

"If I take this, will you back off? Stick to our plan?"

I consider promising I'll wait for him to come forward, which would be a lie. Or arguing back that this is my fight just as much as it is his. Instead, I say nothing.

His fingers graze mine as he slips the sheet from my grip and tucks it away. The rest of his body remains perfectly still. Light from the alley comes in through the window, hitting his eyes in a way that makes them look almost silver like the sun touching the lake on a dreary day. "I get that you feel guilty." His lips form a slight grimace. "I do too. But you can't act reckless because you're alive and they aren't."

His words hit me like a punch in the lungs, stealing my breath.

Annie. My dad. Dopney. Adam.

A dull whir underlies the dark silence.

Ryan's eyes flit back and forth between mine. "I'll find a group to come forward because you asked me to. But you need to give me time."

"I'm out of time." My voice shrinks. "We both know the attack's meant for me."

For the second time tonight, I want him to tell me I'm paranoid, to deny it as a possibility. But his silence confirms what I know is true. Ryan looks at me with that expression of his, when his edge is gone and his guard is down and his face is full of depth and emotion. Like he doesn't know what to say. Like there's nothing to say.

I cross my arms, pressing them tight against my ribs to ease the sharp ache inside me.

He takes a half step toward me, so our toes touch. "I won't let that happen." His voice is low and coarse.

His gaze flickers across my face.

My stomach flips.

Ryan grabs my arms, and every muscle I have turns taut. His thumb brushes against my bicep as he pulls me in, closing the last inches between us. My face flushes, and I'm thankful it's too dark to see the red blotches I know are spreading up my neck.

His eyes search mine as he lowers his face. He looks uncertain, like he's waiting for me to stop him or slap him or give any indication that I want to kiss him back, but my thoughts are empty, wiped away. I stare at the straight line of his lips as they near mine before uncrossing my arms and letting them fall against his. A wave of heat rushes through me. His lips brush mine, and he kisses me. The kiss is gentle and short and nothing like I'd imagined.

He pulls away like he changed his mind, like he realizes I'm not worth the risk, or the kiss itself was terrible. But instead of stepping back, he holds his face inches away from mine, searching for a reaction. He looks so vulnerable that my heart flutters, and my lips flicker upward at the irony of it.

Ryan flashes back the tiniest of smiles before he leans in and kisses me again. This time he doesn't pull away. He presses my back so I move closer, forcing my arms to encircle his neck. His other hand slides up my neck and weaves its way into my hair. His tongue sweeps against my bottom lip, and my heart thrashes. I'm sure he can feel it, and I don't care.

His arms tighten around me, drawing me into him. Like doing so will help us escape everything. And for several moments, it works. He isn't the Swarm. People aren't staking out my house. No one wants to kill me. No one else even exists except Ryan and me, kissing each other in the crammed corner of our detached garage.

When he pulls away again, I can't help from biting my lip, suppressing my smile.

Ryan smiles back, and I realize it's the first time I've seen him smile without restraint. His whole face bends in a way that fills my body with warmth, especially as he tucks a strand of hair behind my ear. "We'll figure this out. You've gotta trust me."

I want to believe him. Just like I want to believe two broken and flawed people like us could like each other and maybe even—one day—date like normal teenagers. I don't know what's better: believing there's a chance everything will work out or admitting that no matter how well prepared either of us is going into Saturday night, everything will most likely spin out of control.

Ryan's lips brush against my ear as he kisses the side of my head. "Sooner or later they'll announce the location." His voice is rugged. "And when they do, we'll make sure you're nowhere near the next attack."

He wraps his arms around me. "You're not in this alone," he says.

I lean into his shoulder, the strength of his arms.

I almost tell him my plan. How earlier this evening, I set up a live-streaming feed on the phone Emi gave me that's automatically synced to whatever I record. How I linked the feed to a dozen social media sites, which have been joined by over seven thousand followers in the last few weeks, ensuring someone will see it before the mayor can take it down. I have my audience, which I fully intend to exploit. Like my dad did.

I open my mouth to say it, but I can't. I can't risk him trying to talk me out of it.

Instead we stand in the corner, saying nothing to each other, as I try to block the visions spinning through my head, the images of the Swarm closing in on us both.

By the time I slink into my house, it's after 2:00 in the morning. My room is quiet and undisturbed. I peek through the blinds without rustling the wooden slats. From what I can tell, there are no reporters in front of my house.

The Escalade, however, is parked on the side of the street a few houses down.

I jerk back, putting distance between myself and the window.

My hands shake as I grab Emi's phone from my nightstand.

I toss the covers over my head, concealing the phone's light, as if whoever's in the car below can figure out what I'm doing.

I access Twitter, find the tweet about the attack.

My eye begins to twitch. Rubbing the space between my brows, I push past my indecision.

I sign in using my fake username and press *reply*. Hoping I know what I'm doing, I type, "I'm in," and hit *send* before I can change my mind about delivering a direct message to whoever sent the tweet announcing the attack.

keep my hair in a low ponytail. It brushes against my back every time I turn my head, sending shivers down my spine. I blame the black cocktail dress the mayor's office sent for me to wear, with its open back and tight bodice. The skirt has four slits, leaving panels that barely cover my legs when I walk. Not exactly modest, but also too sophisticated for a sixteen-year-old, which I'm guessing is the point. Whatever role I'll be playing tonight, they want me to look older than I am.

I tap the burner phone to wake it, like I've somehow missed the notification giving the location of the attack. Aside from the time, 6:53, the screen is blank, which doesn't feel right. Maybe I messed up the sign-in, because the coordinates should have come by now. With the attack at seven thirty, the organizer would have to give everyone in the Swarm a chance to get there. Not that I can't figure out where it is on my own. Seven thirty is about the time I'll be arriving at Museum Campus.

I grab the picture on my dresser of me and my parents on the blackrock beach—the only one not hanging on my walls. We huddle in our raincoats as it drizzles. The sun rises behind us, turning the sky purple. It's from the trip we took to Maui, just the three of us. The happiest moment I remember. I tuck it into the thin designer clutch that was delivered with the dress so I can keep the memory close. For when I need it.

I'm clasping a rhinestone into my ear when my mom walks past my room wearing something silver and swirling, instead of the loungewear I expect from her at this time of night. Collecting my purse and my two phones, I head downstairs after her, where she's rolling the kitchen cabinets open and shut.

I find her rummaging around the cabinet where we keep the medicines, dressed in a satin gown with a light, billowy skirt floating gracefully around her legs. Her hair is swept up on top of her head. Her makeup is flawless, making me wish I'd spent just a bit more time touching up my own eye makeup—even if Cullen is my date. My mom looks beautiful in a way I could never replicate.

"What are you doing?"

My mom pulls out a bottle of aspirin and drops it into her purse. When she looks up, I'm amazed by how green her eyes appear.

"I'm going to the gala," she says.

I figured my mom supported the Save the Parks initiative, but she's not one for public appearances when they aren't required.

"Why?"

Her eyes glisten. There's sadness behind them, or maybe it's the makeup deceiving me. "To watch over you."

I fidget with the clasp on my clutch. "What exactly do you think I'm going to do?"

My mom takes a step toward me. "I think you're going to be strong and brave like you always are. But I don't trust the mayor or his son."

"You can't—"

"You're my daughter," she says in a raised voice, talking over me. "And when you decide you're done with whatever it is they're making you do tonight, I'll be there to bring you home." My mom holds out her hand, which has something grasped inside of it.

When I extend my own hand in response, she drops the inhaler into my palm. She reaches for my face and cups my chin while brushing her thumb against my cheek.

"You look like him."

I bury a sob that's threatening to erupt. *Please don't cry.* If she cries, I'll lose the composure I'm fighting to maintain.

"You're stunning," she whispers. "Smart, stubborn, strong, and stunning. Like him." Her hand falls. Her eyes bend. "You don't have to do this."

"Yes, I do," I whisper back, trying not to choke on the lump thickening in my throat.

She touches my shoulder and kisses my forehead. "Then I'll see you in an hour," she says before disappearing up the stairs.

The doorbell rings, but I can't move. I consider running upstairs to say goodbye. One last word. A wave. A hug. As I grab my long coat and head for the door, a nagging feeling pulls my heart—not saying goodbye to her is a mistake.

But if I do, she'll catch on. She won't let me leave.

"Good evening, Miss Finch." The driver waits at the bottom of our stairs when I answer the door. He nods his head before turning toward the black town car idling in the street.

I squeeze my gut, take a deep breath, and follow him down our walkway. The chilled air glides around my neck, tossing my ponytail sideways. The town car is too small for the mayor's entire entourage. I pull the coat tight across my shoulders and pray it's empty.

When the driver opens the door, Cullen, dressed in a tuxedo, stares out the opposite window. He doesn't look my way as I step in.

We continue ignoring each other as the driver climbs in and pulls away toward the Shedd Aquarium. For several minutes, no one speaks, which is fine by me. The less expected of me, the better. Then, out of nowhere, Cullen claps his hands and rubs them together. "You're really going to hate this," he says, flashing a dimpled smile.

If I didn't detest him so much, I'd find him attractive in a way totally different from Ryan. Cullen's light brown hair is brushed to one side. He's clean-cut and polished, like he was made to wear tuxedos. "This is right at the top of things you despise most."

"How would you know?"

Cullen snorts. "Oh, come on." He drums his hands on his legs like he has pent-up energy he doesn't know what to do with. "You're not that complicated."

I tug at my coat, to cover my legs, and turn to look out the window. Cullen Henking is the son of the man who killed my father. He's part of whatever the mayor has planned for me tonight, making him just as dangerous and untrustworthy.

"The easiest way to get through it is to pretend you're someone else—like you're playing a role." His voice trails. "After that, it's easy to figure out how you're supposed to act, what you should say."

Sounds like a coping mechanism for aiding and abetting murder. "Is that what you do?"

Cullen's brown eyes glint. "We're talking about you—not me." He winks. "You look very pretty tonight."

I hold his stare, letting him know his flattery will not intimidate me. "Is that what you feel you should say?"

Cullen chuckles. "Oh, come on, Lia. Insecurity doesn't suit you. You know you're pretty."

My face flushes, and the heat travels down my neck. I change the subject. "What should I expect tonight?"

I watch for Cullen to flinch or wince or hesitate. But the only movement comes from his legs bouncing up and down in a skittish way I don't expect of him. I can't tell if it's related to what will come of me.

"A lot of rich, drunk, insincere people pretending to care about something they don't. Yourself included. They're going to be all about you and your Lifetime story." Cullen pulls out his phone and flips through it. "Good thing you don't buy into that crap."

I lay both hands on the purse in my lap, gently feeling the outline of the two phones and my inhaler crammed inside.

We turn down State Street, which seems more crowded than usual, even for a Saturday night. Two couples hail a cab at Oak Street. The men wear tuxes. The women wear long earrings and evening gowns. Black and purple skirts twist in the wind beneath their coats.

Across the city, I imagine the mayor and his entourage arriving in their limo. They snake their way around the white stone octagon, admiring the panoramic view of the city. The mayor, his wife—flown in for the occasion—and their party climb the formal staircase, beneath a white awning descending like a tongue from the aquarium's front entrance. Photographers and news crews crowd around the Greek columns, I'm sure, snapping shots of local celebrities like it matters.

My phone chimes. For a moment I think it's the burner phone, the Death Mob sending the tweet. But that phone's on vibrate.

Cullen glances my way as I stare at my lap.

I open the clutch and peek inside. Detective Irving's name lights up my screen.

My back tenses. After debating for several days, I called him last night. Left him a message. Gave him details of what I know about the attack with the hope that whatever's about to happen, he's ready to make arrests when it's over.

I imagine answering it, explaining in some coded way what I'm being forced to do. Would he care? Would he try to help? By calling him, I might have alerted the mayor that I'm onto him, giving him the greater advantage. My mom trusts Irving. I hope I can too. Either way, I can't talk to him with Cullen in the car. I silence the ringer, resigned to stick to my plan.

As we head south toward Museum Campus, the traffic thickens until we are inching along one block at a time.

Cullen rolls down his window. A muffled roar of shouting pours into the town car. "What's going on?" he asks the driver.

"Protestors rioting on Michigan." The driver looks at us through his rearview mirror.

I strain my ears. Chanting—I can just make it out. I'm not sure what they're saying. Looking toward the downtown chaos, I notice white flakes swirling in the air. It must have just started. The season's first sign of snow.

"It's all over the news," the driver says.

A mini flat-screen on the back of the passenger's seat clicks on in front of me. A WGN reporter—someone other than Emi—stands in front of a packed Michigan Avenue.

"... calling it a peaceful protest. Of the hundreds of protestors here, some of them are blocking storefronts, preventing customers from entering or leaving. Most of the protestors, however, seem to be gathering around the Water Tower. As you can see behind me, there are so many of them, it's difficult to move. The police currently are not intervening. While authorities have declined to give us their official stance on what's happening, they seem to be standing by in case protestors get out of control. Officers are forming a perimeter around the Magnificent Mile ..."

I lean forward, trying to make out what I can on the tiny flat-screen in front of me. Behind the reporter, protestors hold up "Save the Parks" signs. One sign reads, "Kill Phase Two, Not Our Parks."

"According to Mayor Henking's office, Phase One of the Lakefront Project produced nearly five thousand jobs and had an economic impact of over a billion dollars. Phase Two is projected to bring in twice that much, but the protestors here believe that profit isn't worth giving up more protected lakefront property." The camera switches to a black woman in a thick tan coat and knit hat. She defames the project in a deep, throaty voice.

Cullen rolls up the window, drawing my attention away from the screen. He looks annoyed. "Turn around. Take Lake Shore."

The street is gridlocked in both directions.

"They've shut down Michigan and are redirecting traffic," the driver says dryly. "All the roads are like this right now."

Cullen scowls. He grabs a bottled water from the center console. "Idiots."

"Why? Because they aren't supporting your dad?"

"You'd think people in this city would avoid crowds. You of all people should know that."

A cold sweat breaks out along my hairline. Footage on the flat-screen switches to a bird's-eye view from the WGN helicopter. Hundreds of people cram around the Water Tower. The police perimeter is too far from the protestors. If there were to be an attack there, anywhere near the center, it would be impossible to rescue the victim in time. The Swarm's attacks have never been this public. The outcome could be catastrophic. And the victim would be someone else. Not me.

My purse buzzes with a notification. The burner phone from Emi.

Every muscle in my body is fraught with tension as I reach in and pull it out.

A tweet from an unknown account.

41.897255-87.62448971

The coordinates. My hands shake as I google them. Zoom in on the location. Michigan Avenue. The Water Tower.

It's not what I expected, and I have trouble wrapping my brain around it. I should be relieved. The mayor isn't going after me after all. But instead, I'm panicked. Someone's about to die. Again. Like Dopney.

My entire body trembling, I text Emi: Next attack—Water Tower—protestors

I send the same message to Irving.

The car's dashboard reads 7:10. The attack is in twenty minutes. How will anyone get there in time, including the Swarm?

"When we get to the Shedd," Cullen says, "Richard will have a stock response for us to parrot all night. The guy's a control freak, but he's good with stuff like this."

Cullen swigs his water as the world begins spinning in slow motion. The car is stuck in a complete standstill. In the rearview mirror, the driver's face glows red from the brake lights in front of him. My heart beats so forcefully, it's the only sound I hear. I need to get there, record it, catch Lip Spikes' steely face and plaster it all over the Internet so everyone knows exactly who he is and what he's done. But as I open the door of the town car and jump out, the driving force is the overwhelming urge to warn them—to save them all.

Both lanes on State Street are gridlocked. Clutching my purse, I run around the back of the car. Squeeze between it and the taxi close behind. I cross the northbound lane and start running. The wind bites at my face. Flurries thicken. They smack my eyes. In the distance, protestors shout. I listen for screams of alarm, but the booming noise sounds angry, not fearful.

As I round the corner to Pearson, my foot gets stuck, yanking me back. I fall against the sidewalk, scraping my knee, my palms. Before I can look, someone jerks my heel out from between the metal slats of a city grate.

Cullen looks down at me with near abhorrence. "What are you doing?" He flips the collar of his tuxedo up around his neck, rubs his hands together. Small puffs of steam circle his nose.

I scramble to my feet. "Those people . . ." I try to breathe, but the pressure squeezing my chest is torturous. "They're in danger." I start jogging in heels toward the Water Tower, dodging people on the sidewalk as I go.

Cullen catches up to me. He grabs my wrist and begins dragging me the other way, back toward the car. "Don't be stupid."

I pull against him, but Cullen tightens his grip until he's pinching my skin. I try to shake him off. "We have to warn them."

"About what?" He stops and shouts at me. "What aren't you telling me?"

I have no idea what Cullen knows or how involved he is in his dad's Death Mob ring. It's only a matter of time before the Initiators throw the first punch, and they swarm their victim.

"The next attack," I say. My breath scrapes against the back of my throat—the first sign my lungs are giving out on me. "The Swarm is going to attack the protestors."

Cullen stares at me as if considering whether I've lost my mind.

"I have to at least warn them," I plead.

He lets go of my wrist, and I take off toward the Water Tower.

Behind me, Cullen's shoes click against the pavement as he follows me into the riot.

When we get to the edge of the plaza, the noise is deafening. Hundreds of protestors crowd around the limestone tower. Some of them hoist picket signs in the air while others mosh and chant with no aim or purpose.

Police officers form a broken perimeter on the streets. Some of them wait on horseback, watching the commotion unfold.

I point to them. "Tell the police."

Cullen rubs his hands together for heat. "No!" He leans in, screaming in my ear above the noise. "We're getting out of here as soon as you realize how idiotic this is."

The officers are relaxed, like they're hanging out on the street corner, eating hot dogs before a Cubs game. Some of them are laughing, joking. Didn't Irving get my text? Or maybe he doesn't care. Either way, they're useless.

I turn to the crowd. Everyone wears hats, scarves, and winter coats. But I see Swarm. Already. They are hard to spot. But they're in there. A short guy stands a few people in. His body is stiff. His hands are jammed into his pockets. He's wearing sunglasses. Another bulky kid stands on the stairs of the Water Tower wearing a stocking hat, wool scarf. A protest sign dangles from his fingertips as if it's a prop. The closer I look at the crowd, the more I see them. Teenagers, concealed identities, standing amid the crowd. They're waiting—not participating in the protest. How did they all beat me here? And then I see a thin girl dressed in black: North Face coat, stocking cap, sunglasses, and a bright, coppery ponytail running down her spine. Copperhead. She disappears into the crowd, slinking behind a woman wearing a puffy down coat and carrying a baby strapped to her torso. The woman raises a sign high above her head as her baby clutches the carrier.

I run into the heavy mass, shoving people out of my way. Half the crowd chants, "Save the Parks." Others slander the Lakefront Project, and the mayor for backing it.

The protest is utter chaos—the perfect storm for a massive attack.

I plunge forward, cursing my heels for slowing me down. The

clenching in my stomach scrabbles its way up to my chest, my lungs, my throat until I feel like I'm being strangled.

Forgetting Copperhead and whoever else might be in there, I tunnel in on the woman with the baby. I shove my way into the inner circle. Grab her elbow. She turns and glares like I'm arresting her.

"The Swarm's about to attack!" I scream like my lungs are strong and not in the process of shutting down.

But the woman just stares. The baby sucks his pacifier, his eyes wide at the surrounding pandemonium.

I tug her, pulling her away from the center. "Death Mob."

A man with patchy gray scruff jumps between us. "Here?" His face turns ashen. He must be the father.

I nod. "Run!"

He steers her away, shielding the baby as they push their way through the crowd.

A small sense of victory fills me as they make their escape.

I spin, arms and elbows butting into me. Identifying the victim is impossible. Someone's about to die and there's no way of knowing who I'm here to save.

Clenching my teeth, I grab a weedy guy with short buzzed hair, glasses. He screams "Save the Parks" like he wants to be the loudest rioter.

"Swarm attack," I yell. "Run!" I turn to the next person. Scream it again. Neither of them seems to care, but I refuse to quit.

Remembering my plan, I snatch the burner phone from my purse. I hit record and stick it in the air, as high as I can with no idea what I'm catching. Copperhead's pointy chin? Spider Tattoo's neck? The crowd jostles me. I can barely hold on. And then a blur of silky black catches my eye. It swings back and forth against a backpack with a trio of buttons.

I shove my way past protestors, crashing against them until I reach her. I spin Katie around.

"Why did you come?" I scream.

Katie's face radiates with passion and righteousness. But her eyes widen as she looks me up and down, taking in my coat, cocktail dress, heels, until her expression becomes horrified. Her picket sign droops. "Where are you supposed to be?"

There's no time to explain. I grab her wrist. We're too far in, too close to the center. Protestors jostle us as I search for the edge of the mob to make our escape. After two steps, we're pitched sideways. The crowd is growing rowdier. Someone slams into me, knocking me over. I brace myself against the cement. A shoe crushes my fingers. Another guy trips over my back, burying me beneath bodies. I scream. I can't save Katie if I'm trampled to death.

But the weight is lifted. A hand grabs my arm, heaving me upward, and I collide into Ryan, his Chicago hoodie. A baseball cap shields his eyes. A dark gray neck gaiter conceals his face to his nose. He yanks it down.

He looks panicked—more than he's ever shown. "What are you doing here?"

"How did you get here so fast?"

Confusion flickers in his eyes. "They sent coordinates an hour ago."

My stomach drops as the realization that I've been set up clicks. The mayor knew it was me. He baited me here, and I fell for it.

Before I can tell Ryan, he drags me behind him. His grip is tight. He's too fast. I can't keep up.

I turn for Katie. Scream her name. She runs after me, until she's next to me, clutching my bicep as we weave through people.

I grasp the phone and hold it up. I can't tell what I'm recording, if anything at all. The chanting and shouting are too intense to concentrate. But if these are my final moments, I'm taking out as many Swarm as I can.

Cullen pushes past a man in the crowd. "Lia!" He looks from me to Katie, trying to read the situation, before glaring at Ryan with mistrust. Ryan looks more like the Swarm than anyone else here.

I grab Cullen's hand. "We have to leave."

Ryan pauses long enough to scowl at my hand in Cullen's. Then he takes the lead, guiding me, Cullen, and Katie away from the center of the protest. And that's when my phone vibrates.

Before I can even blink, Ryan grabs his cell from his hoodie. Buzzing and chiming go off around us. Blue orbs light up the riot. Everyone around us seems to check their phones.

The Swarm is identifying the victim.

In the milliseconds it takes for Ryan to check the message and look at me, the uprising around us hushes, blurs, and disappears. I stop breathing.

It's me. I'm the victim. I walked right into their trap.

Ryan's unreadable gray eyes soften at first, then harden just as quickly.

He looks past me to Cullen. "Run." His voice is severe. "Get her out of here," he screams. "Run." Anger. Panic.

The noise and pandemonium return like an explosion, overwhelming my senses, my ability to think. Ryan turns and charges into the center of the riot. Cullen yanks on my arm and takes off with Katie matching our pace. I stumble behind, turning one last time to see Ryan charging the five Initiators parting through the crowd in my direction. Lip Spikes leads it. Hood, glasses, and the rest of his arrogant face exposed.

I lift my phone. Aim it.

All around us, people start screaming as they realize what's happening.

My legs buckle and flounder. The shaking in my chest overtakes my body. I stretch my arm higher, but my lungs are dying out.

Cullen catches me as I fall. He hoists my body over his shoulder and runs.

Katie's bag thumps against her back.

Bodies collide as people fight to escape. Someone crashes into us. Cullen careens, but he doesn't stop. He keeps running. The shrieks, wails, hysteria blend together, like one frenzied siren piercing the night.

I gasp for air, clutching my purse, the phone, and Cullen's tuxedo jacket, as he dodges fleeing people.

The searing in my chest is agonizing, like shards of glass slicing my insides. Still, I lift my head and the phone together. Past hundreds of people scattering in every direction, I zero in on Ryan. The Initiators. They collide. I can't tell who throws the first punch, but they all fall. All six of them. Another attacker jumps on top.

I hit Cullen's back. "Let me go!"

They're going to kill him. They're going to kill Ryan for protecting me. I thrash against Cullen's grip, crying and coughing and choking while somewhere Ryan is getting pummeled to his death.

People scream, run, bump into each other, trip over one another. I can't see Ryan. I'm losing him.

I pound Cullen's back until he throws me down against the outer Plexiglas frame of a bus stop harder than is necessary. "What are you doing?"

"Where's Katie?" The breaths are shorter. My lungs are burning. We're fifty yards from where Ryan is dying.

Cullen grabs my coat, shakes me. "Shut up and run!"

He stands, motions to grab me.

I smack his hands away and fumble for my purse, my inhaler. It bobbles as I force it into my mouth. I jab at the canister, unable to concentrate. Cool mist shoots in my throat. I swallow it. Hold it.

I crane my neck until I see Katie's backpack fleeing with the crowd. It bounces against her shoulders as she runs away toward safety, escaping the attack.

I have to go back.

I throw my inhaler and the burner phone and all it captured into my purse. As I do, the picture text lights up my screen.

It's Ryan. In his baseball cap, his gray gaiter, his hoodie.

Ryan was the intended victim.

I look at Cullen, breathe, try to get my lungs functioning. I stand, begging my legs to steady themselves. I grip the outer post. Force myself to turn around. I have to help Ryan. I can't let the Swarm kill him.

But Cullen catches me. "Dammit, Lia." He hoists me on my shoulder again. My body's shaking too hard to resist. Tears flood my face as I picture Ryan at the bottom of the Swarm. Dying.

People are screaming, running for cover all around us.

I look up to find the Swarm surrounding the Water Tower—the attack is full blown.

And that's when I hear the gunshot from somewhere in the middle.

The sound pierces my insides as if I know by instinct he's gone.

Like Dopney. Adam. My dad.

The Swarm scatters. Cullen takes off running.

Through the jostling and the chaos, I strain to find him, knowing it's the last time. Amidst the crowd, the silhouette of Ryan's lifeless body is collapsed against the sidewalk.

CHAPTER 29

Cullen fumbles with his house keys while I glare at the security camera filming us from the corner of his front porch, imagining who might be watching, waiting for us to enter. The lock clicks, and Cullen pushes the heavy door open. I follow behind, scanning his house for the mayor. An electric current pulses through me. It's the only thing keeping me from falling apart right in front of the ostentatious sculpture in their foyer.

I picture Ryan's face, his last hard look as he turned to meet the Initiators. The Swarm closing in on him like rabid wolves tearing apart their prey. This attack was quicker, more sudden, more intense, and then there was the gunshot.

My entire body aches to crash, but I refuse to let that happen. Not yet. I clench every muscle and tendon I have, hellbent on finding the mayor, exposing him, destroying him the way he's destroyed the lives of so many people in this city.

Cullen walks across the open space from the foyer to the living room and turns the television on. He flips to live footage of the scene. The words "Teen Dies in Death Mob Attack" stream across the bottom. Behind the reporter, lights highlight the Water Tower as dusk sinks in. Yellow tape frames the square littered with protestors' signs.

I turn away, close my eyes, and concentrate on the charge surging inside.

"*What* just happened?" Cullen grabs the top of his head. He looks ghostly white. He turns on me, eyes full of disgust. "You knew about it."

Cullen takes a few steps, charging like he's going to hit me. Instead, he spins around and squeezes his head with his palms. "You stupid, psychopathic…" He rips off his tuxedo jacket and throws it across the room.

I'd assumed Cullen was in on it all: the setup, the attack. I thought he'd heard Richard threaten me on the pier—not that any of that matters anymore. "Where's your dad?"

Cullen's entire face cringes. "How should I know?"

The driver was instructed to bring us here—a place we'd be safe. I didn't object. I welcomed it, expecting the mayor would be here too.

Cullen yanks at his bow tie and stares at his hands covered in grime. He holds out his cuff, which is speckled in red. "I have blood on me. Someone's blood," he says like it's my fault. "I know a lot of screwed-up people. But you're more screwed up than all of them." He shakes his hands like he's ridding himself of the night and stomps up the staircase, leaving me alone.

I yank off my coat and pull out the burner phone, scanning the room for the best place to prop it. The bookcases, the wet bar, the windowsill. My movements are spastic as I finally head toward the mantel. I set it between the iridescent vases, behind a heavy candle pillar so the camera lens peeks out. Stepping back, I survey the fireplace. The phone is concealed. I grab my other cell, call up the site where I'm streaming live. For several seconds, I watch myself in the low-back cocktail dress, standing in the mayor's living room staring at my cell. It's like I'm watching someone else, someone older, someone who hasn't lost everything.

I think of Ryan's lips on mine. Less than a week ago. The twinge in my chest threatens to infuse my entire body, incapacitating me. It should've been me. He was stronger. He could've taken down the mayor with everything he knew.

The lock on the front door jiggles.

My head snaps toward it. I tuck my cell into my purse and throw everything onto the couch.

Richard steps through the door looking disheveled. The second he sees me, he lets out a deep breath. His shoulders slump. He presses his palm against his chest. "Thank God. I came as soon as I found out. Where's Cullen?"

I freeze, thrown by his tone. His expression. "Upstairs."

"Are either of you hurt?"

"No," I whisper.

Richard crosses the room. He rubs the back of his neck and passes the TV, where paramedics hoist Ryan's white-sheet-covered body into the ambulance. Something about seeing it on the screen confirms it happened. It was real. Not a hallucination. The image sears me like a brand, leaving behind a fresh, new scar.

Ryan's hand grazes my shoulder. It slides down the bare skin of my arm. His lips brush the top of my ear as he says my name. "Lia." His voice is rough and coarse and close, like he's standing right behind me. And I wilt. It'd be so easy to give up, collapse on the couch, let the pain take over. I squeeze my eyes shut, pushing away the temptation, burying it deep, deep, deep inside.

"We're all so thankful Cullen was there to save you."

I ground myself in Richard's nasal words. There's something to the way he says it, like it's forced.

I open my eyes and narrow them. Richard walks toward the massive windows overlooking Lake Michigan, the night settling in. He makes a sharp turn and walks along the wall toward the mantle, pulling his cell from the inside pocket of his tux.

I realize what he's doing too late to do anything about it. Richard reaches around the vases. He taps my phone without detection and shuts down my live feed.

It hits me like a bullet, a very real and heavy blow.

Richard chuckles. He rolls his shoulders back and flips his cell around to show me his screen filled with muted gray. "This is your website." A smug grin spreads over his lips. His white teeth flash above his crooked bow tie. "Dead air," he says, drawing it out.

Richard slows his pace, his movements. He strolls to the wet bar on the side of the room and pours a drink from a crystal decanter. "You must have been so hopeful. Naïve. Delusional. But hopeful."

I glare at him. My chest heaves, and for once my lungs feel strong. My mind sharp.

Richard glances up at me. "I left the attack coordinates off the tweet knowing it would draw you in to respond."

I keep my face as stoic as possible, ignoring the throbbing in my temples. Of course. It was Richard. He's been one step ahead, not the mayor. The mayor's been too busy glorifying himself and his legacy.

"Can I get you a drink?" Richard looks around the room as if reassuring himself that we're alone. "Soda? Juice? Tea?"

I breathe deeply, like a bull before charging. Richard's been the mastermind, the one who orchestrated the attacks. Maybe I should be scared of him, of what he's capable of, but my father, my best friend, and Ryan are dead. Because of him. Richard and his puffy neck. His nasally voice. His crooked bow tie.

He grabs a bottled water from the minifridge and walks it over to me. Holds it out.

I continue to glare, refusing to move.

He sets the water down on the coffee table. "It took you longer to respond than I'd anticipated. I'll give you that. But once you did"—he chuckles—"it was easy to figure out everything you were trying to accomplish with your fake Twitter account, your new phone." He bites his lip, shakes his head, puts one hand on his hip beneath his tux. "Did you really think you'd outsmart me?"

I clench my teeth. "*You* killed them."

Richard snorts. "It's funny that you, of all people, would fall for a guy from the Swarm. That surprised me," he says in a patronizing tone. Richard stares at his drink as he swirls it. "Apparently it wasn't enough watching your dad or your best friend murdered. Those didn't slow you down. No—not you. You're resilient." His voice squeaks. He nods his head and sniffs his drink. "I like that about you." He then takes a sip, holding it in his mouth before swallowing. "But everyone has a button. It's just a matter of finding it, and once you do . . ." His laugh is shrill. Grating. "Well, you can get them to do anything. You—" He shakes his index finger at me. "You're interesting. Harder to control than anyone else in this city. I'll give you that. A lot like your dad. I just didn't expect it from a sixteen-year-old."

Adrenaline courses through my veins, making every extremity feel charged and twitchy. "I was going to your stupid gala like you wanted."

Richard snickers. He closes one eye. A prolonged wink. "You also impersonated the Swarm with your fake Twitter account." Richard tucks his hand into his pocket. "And what about the Apple Store? I'll admit, whatever program you installed on that computer, it took us a while. But I found what you'd been searching." Richard snorts again. "You led me right to him, you know. I knew someone from the inside was helping your dad, and Hewitt's boy might have gone undiscovered if it weren't for you."

I draw in a shaky breath. It takes everything in me to dismiss him. He's only trying to crack me. He wants me to crumble in front of him. But I refuse to give him that satisfaction.

"You run the attacks."

"I do a lot more than that."

His pride is disgusting. Infuriating. "You murder people."

"I keep people in line, Lia," Richard says with a calm demeanor. "The mayor has revitalized this city. I help ensure that vision by controlling what's broken."

"By forcing the city to sell lakefront property? Blackmailing teenagers?" I trip over my words. "Making them join your Swarm?"

He rocks from heel to toe. His grin widens like I've said something amusing. "You've only scratched the surface. I got a city ordinance from the early nineteen hundreds repealed. That takes politicking. Coercion. Control." He bites his bottom lip. Giddy, almost. "Let's not minimize what I had to do to make that happen."

Richard relishes it. He *wants* to brag about it. Celebrate it. Like he's dying to be recognized.

My voice shrinks as I begin to wonder if the mayor is involved at all. "It's all about control for you, isn't it? You use the Swarm to get what you want."

"It's not about what I want—it's about what this city needs." Richard's brow tightens. "You make it sound so simple, but I assure you, it's quite complicated." He smooths the hair sticking up on the crown of his head. "Do you understand how much debt this city was in before the mayor took office? Millions of people are collecting pensions for the first time in years. This city has been resurrected."

He pulls back his sleeve to check his watch before shaking his arms, straightening his jacket. Richard regards his drink. "I tried to give you a chance, Lia. But you're stubborn and, like everyone else, expendable."

"You're going to kill me."

He sets his drink on the table. "You've given me no other choice."

Richard takes a step closer to me as if he's considering murdering me with his bare hands here in the mayor's living room.

The doorbell rings.

Neither of us moves. We stare each other down. Before I have a chance to flinch, Cullen walks into the room wearing mesh shorts and a waffle-knit shirt. His hair is wet and combed to the side. His eyes are bloodshot. Cullen looks between us before settling on me with disregard. "Why is she still here?"

Richard holds his ground, blocking my path to the door and whoever's on the other side of it.

Heart pounding, I grab my purse and coat from the couch, hoping Cullen has created an opportunity. "I'm leaving." I have no idea whether Cullen has any allegiance to Richard.

Richard glares at me. "Not until I make the proper arrangements."

Even if I somehow escape this room, he'll have me killed. Stabbed. Dumped in the river. One way or another, my death is inevitable.

The doorbell rings again.

"You going to take care of that?" Cullen pours himself a drink at the wet bar from the same decanter.

Richard grabs the remote, switching the station to the grainy gray footage of a camera crew standing on the other side of the mayor's door.

It looks like Emi, dressed for the gala. She bangs on the door, demanding someone open it.

Richard stares me down like a snake about to strike. "Cullen," he says over his shoulder, "get rid of them. Tell them your dad will be releasing his statement within the hour."

Cullen throws back the brown liquid in his glass and coughs. "What if they're here for me? I was there tonight."

Richard raises his nasal voice. "Then decline to comment."

Cullen wipes his mouth with the back of his hand and heads for the door. Cullen mumbles something derogatory under his breath that I don't catch, and I don't care to either.

This is my chance. The second Cullen answers the door, I need to run toward it. Make my escape. Richard knows this too. It's why he's lined himself up to cut me off. Just in case I try.

Cullen opens the door, and light floods the house. Emi throws her shoulder into the heavy wood and shoves a microphone into Cullen's face. "Cullen Henking, how hard was it for you to witness tonight's attack?" Cullen tries pushing her out, closing the door, but Emi wedges herself against it, blocking it.

Emi surveys the house. She grabs her cameraman, who turns the camera on me. "We're live here inside Mayor Henking's home, where we've just learned Cullen Henking and Lia Finch were witnesses to tonight's fatal attack."

Cullen strains to drive them out, but he can't close the door. Richard turns to intercept.

In a few moments, the door will be shut. Emi and the cameraman gone. I'll never make it out the front. They'll block me before I get there. Instead, I step backward, searching for an exit.

Cullen and Richard are distracted by Emi.

I step back again, testing their response. When neither of them glances my way, I spin and run. My feet smack the hardwood floors. I don't look back. I race. Faster. Past the windows, I turn left into a breakfast room. There are double doors along the far wall. I skirt the table and lunge for them. Jerk the handle. It doesn't open.

I fumble with the lock as footsteps thump behind me. Closing in.

The lock clicks. I wrench open the door and take off into the night.

Waves hiss and crash onto the shore. The noise is overwhelming. I jump off the mayor's porch, landing on my hip with a thud. Sprawled on their lawn, I gather myself, scramble to my feet, and take off. The cold assaults my lungs. Wind whips the panels of my dress around my legs as I sprint through wet grass.

Behind me, steps pound against the porch. Richard's or Cullen's, I can't tell. But he's after me. Not far.

I veer right. Around the house. Toward Emi. "Here," I scream, hoping I'm louder than the wind, the waves, the traffic on Lake Shore Drive.

Clearing the corner, my face smacks a tree branch. I slip and fall backward.

Scurrying, I flip to my hands and knees. As I do, someone grabs my ankle, yanking me back.

I scream, clawing at the grass and dirt. Richard's hands grab my leg like a rope, and he drags me away from Emi and any chance at rescue.

Twisting my body, I swing my other leg around, kicking Richard in the face with my heel. He jerks back, releasing me.

I struggle to my feet and start running again, but his recovery is quick. Richard lunges for me, tearing a panel of my dress as he misses.

I take another step. My heel sticks in the grass. The tiny hitch of movement is all he needs. Richard grabs my wrist. He pulls me, wrapping his arms around my waist, lifting me, hauling me back behind the house, to kill me—beat me, stab me, shoot me.

A light bounces through the dark. Emi and the cameraman charge us. "There's Lia Finch. Richard Stewart, is she being held here against her will?"

Richard spins toward the spotlight accosting us both. He drops me. Richard straightens his posture, tugs at his lapels.

At the top of the camera, a tiny red light indicates they're recording.

"Ms. Finch needs to be questioned for her role in tonight's attack." Richard's voice is high. Nervous.

I rush toward Emi, ducking behind her.

"Under whose jurisdiction?" Emi cocks her head. She doesn't wait for an answer. "I have footage of Ms. Finch trying to break up the riot before the attack and sources that confirm she's been working with authorities to uncover the people behind the Death Mob."

Emi makes a point to look from Richard to me. "Why is your lip bleeding? Did we just catch you assaulting her?"

I slide behind the cameraman, as if he can shield me.

Richard inhales through his nose, trying to remain composed. "She's linked to three Death Mob murders, and you're interfering with a national investigation. I will press charges and have you jailed."

Emi taps her cameraman, who kills the feed. She glares at Richard. "I bet you're linked to more than that." Emi flares her nostrils. For several seconds, there seems to be a silent standoff between them before Emi speaks. "My station has this feed. Wrestling with a teenage girl on the lawn of the mayor's house. Your bloody lip. Her torn dress, messy hair. Doesn't look good. Especially if something were to happen to her."

Richard's expression darkens. "You'll pay for this. I'll see to it." He leans toward her. "You're disposable too, you know that?" Richard combs back his hair as if taming the strays will preserve his dignity. "Your kind always is."

My hatred toward Richard surges inside me but Emi doesn't flinch. If anything, she seems ignited. A ruthless smile spreads across her face. "Oh, retribution will be paid. Don't you worry about that." Her voice is smooth, silky. Emi steps toward Richard as if to continue, but the cameraman grabs her bicep. He guides her back, leading us both across the mayor's manicured lawn.

I stumble over my own feet as I turn to see Richard disappear into the night. Once he does, we break into a run toward the news van parked out front. The van door slides open. Emi jumps in behind me. The cameraman hops into the driver's seat. The van revs to life, and we take off down the mayor's driveway back toward the city.

CHAPTER 30

I double over in the back of Emi's van, in a folding chair not even bolted to the floor. Emi's cameraman weaves in and out of traffic while I try not to collide with the panel of illuminated screens and switches covering the entire left side of the van.

I wrap my arms around my waist. How did this all go so horribly wrong? Ryan's dead. Richard's still out there, likely arranging my murder before I get back to my house. I need to preserve everything he confessed. Telling Emi's not good enough. He'll kill her too.

I need to call Detective Irving.

Tears stream down my face as I fumble for my bag. "Richard uses the Death Mob to force people into supporting the Lakefront Project. He admitted to it." My hands don't work, like they're swollen. My bag drops. Both phones skid across the van's metal floor. I'm lunging for them when Emi puts her hand on my knee. She sits in a folding chair behind the passenger's seat.

"We got it," she says, her voice low and even. "All of it."

I lift my head. I've misunderstood her. "What are you talking about?"

She picks up the burner phone. "It has a spyware program on it. As

310

long as your phone is on, I hear everything. We recorded what Richard said. All of it."

I stare at her. My lips suspended. "You recorded it?"

"Every word." City light pours in through the windshield. Having come from the gala, Emi's hair is curled and pinned in place so it won't move. Her lips are dark pink. I notice her black-and-white gown for the first time. It looks more subtle than what I imagined she might wear.

I try recounting what Richard disclosed. I can't remember his exact wording. "Then we can prosecute. This is what we needed. There has to be someone who will reopen my dad's case."

Did he mention the mayor's role in it? Richard made it sound like he controlled everything, but the mayor must be involved. My excitement builds, but Emi's eyes go flat.

"What am I missing?" And then it hits me. She wants it for her article. Her own fame. "If you write about this, we'll all be dead by the time it comes out."

"Which is why I have to go live. In one hour, I'll broadcast Richard's admission to the entire world. We're editing clips of your conversation now. I called a friend of mine at the FBI, who's waiting for us to air. Before my interview is over, Richard will be arrested."

"What about the mayor?" I protest. What if he heads it like Adam thought? My dad set out to take down the entire organization, not just its right-hand man. Everyone involved has to rot in prison for the rest of their lives so the Death Mob is over forever. My dad's death, Adam's death, Ryan's death, all our sacrifices—they have to mean something.

"We don't have anything on the mayor." The van lurches to the right. Emi's hand flies out against the side of the van, bracing her, while my shoulder crashes into it. I reposition my folding chair and rub the bruise already forming.

Emi continues. "Richard admitted to organizing the Death Mob and targeting victims. He didn't reveal anything about the mayor being connected."

"You can't." There must be a way to get them both. If someone brings Richard in for questioning, they could get it out of him. Good cop, bad cop, whatever. If someone reliable investigated this, they could bring everyone down. The mayor. Lip Spikes. All the Initiators directly responsible for fifteen deaths.

Emi doesn't break eye contact. "Time is already against us. This guy has a reach into all levels of law enforcement. He's been running this thing for over eight years and controls half the city. We need to force the hands of those who would protect him. It's the smart thing to do, Lia."

"The mayor's involved. I know he is."

"Probably. But right now, we can get Richard." Her expression is serious. "You're right. He will try to kill you. We need to cut him off before he does."

The world spins, dizzying my thoughts, but Emi remains composed. Articulate. "There will be a case against Richard. And you're going to need to testify. We need to protect you too."

I wish I had someone to talk to, to help me figure out whether this is the best way like she says. Instead, I picture the Swarm closing in on Ryan. I hear the gunshot, and a piercing pain fills every inch of my body. I double over again. The second I do, I feel Emi kneel beside me.

"I want these guys too."

I lean back against the chair, too drained to fight her. "You've been listening in on me for weeks, haven't you?" I think of the night I kissed Ryan. I had the phone with me then. I wonder how much she heard. It should have been private, a special moment between Ryan and me, and she ruined it, listening in like some voyeuristic peeping Tom.

She doesn't deny it. She looks at me, letting me connect the dots.

"You gave me the phone to spy on me."

Emi doesn't flinch. "That's not entirely true."

At least she doesn't lie.

"I also wanted to make sure you were safe and give you a way to get ahold of me if you needed it."

"You saw me make a Twitter account. Pretend to be part of the Swarm."

She stares at me in a way that looks apologetic. I never considered she'd have access to my Internet history when I looked up each of the men from the Lakefront Project and their kids, all of whom were in the Swarm. "Did you figure out how the kids are connected?" I think of Ryan. If he were alive, she could've incriminated him and every other kid forced to participate. Like Amy London.

Emi nods.

I couldn't handle Ryan being the center of a media frenzy, getting dissected. "If you expose them, I'll find a way to discredit you."

"I have no interest in revealing them."

Streetlights along Lake Shore Drive blur by. My head buzzes like the leftover high of sucking too much helium. My eyes burn. It's only a matter of time before my lungs start tightening and the rest of my body shuts down. Like it always does.

I sink farther into the chair. "Where are we going?"

Emi switches from serious mode to game plan mode. She grabs her purse from the front seat and takes her black diamond earrings off. "You and your mom will be staying at the Peninsula tonight."

"I want to go home—"

Emi interrupts. "It'll be safer until Richard is in custody, which should be after we go live." She drops her earrings into her purse. "You have a suite." She puts a pearl earring into each ear. "The suite will be blocked off from the rest of the hotel. You and your mom have a separate entrance with tight security."

Of course Emi would arrange for a separate entrance leading up to a prestigious hotel room. Everything she does is over the top.

"I have a friend there," she says, like she knows what I'm thinking.

"Must be some friend."

"You're about to be the girl who saved the city from the Death Mob's tyranny. There will be plenty of people willing to help you out."

"Is that why you want to be the reporter who breaks the story?"

She stops moving. "You have no idea what's happening right now, do you?"

I look away feeling tired, spent.

"Your video went viral. By now, the whole world has seen your footage from inside the Swarm. It's global news. Three of the five Initiators have already been identified."

Something flutters inside me. "The one with the spikes in his lip?"

Emi nods. "Dante Ipstein. Arrests will be made before the night is over." The van comes to a rolling stop beneath the Peninsula's brightly lit curbside drop-off. "You've done it, Lia. The Swarm is unraveling."

"Now you get to expose Richard and revel in your success."

Emi's face hardens. "I'll let that slide because you had a rough night." She pulls lipstick out of her purse. Puts it on. "I gave you a phone, Lia. You pieced this thing together. You got Richard Stewart to confess. *You* took down the Death Mob. The success is yours. I'm just the one reporting it."

My eyes well. I want to be happy. Maybe even appreciative. It's what I've spent the last two years trying to achieve. But I'm drained, and the victory's come at the expense of too many people I loved.

"Stay here," Emi says. She maneuvers into the passenger's seat, where a hotel doorman opens her door. She rushes toward the lobby, leaving me with her cameraman driving the car.

Every inch of my body feels dirty. I want to get out of this dress, scrub the makeup off my face, including the mascara smeared on my cheeks that makes me look like some psycho clown. I need it gone. All of it.

I hear the gunshot that killed Ryan, and I shudder. I picture the Swarm closing in on him until I couldn't see him anymore. They seemed to swallow him whole.

When I glance up, the cameraman's watching me through the rearview mirror. He looks away when we make eye contact, but not before I notice how bloodshot and glassy his eyes look. One hand rests on the steering wheel. I spot the tattoo on his forearm peeking out beneath the rolled ends of his jacket. Inside what looks to be a thick black circle are angular bars and swirls patterned like a kid's maze. Only the top is visible, but I immediately recognize it as the same tattoo the paramedic had on his forearm the night of Adam's attack. He catches me staring.

"What does it mean?" I ask, my throat dry and swollen.

"Strength and resilience." The cameraman watches me as if studying my reaction. Once again, I'm caught by how red and glassy his eyes look.

"I've seen one like it before." I look toward the Peninsula's front doors, trying to end the awkward small talk.

He twists his body around so he's facing me. The confrontation catches me by surprise. "You don't know what it is?" His voice is hoarse. A thin layer of blond scruff covers his cheeks, chin, and neck. He appears to be in his early twenties, a lot younger than I initially thought.

"I was forced into the Swarm for two years," he says.

I stop breathing. Silence fills the car.

"I haven't slept more than two hours at a time since." His bloodshot eyes stare into mine. Neither of us moves. I feel like I should say something. It's my turn to talk. But instead I picture Ryan's eyes, the torment they reflected.

"I'd do just about anything to prevent anyone else from living through that." His agony is palpable.

I nod because I understand and because I can't find words to convey it.

He turns around in the driver's seat, returning both hands to the wheel like there's nothing left to say.

Emi opens the door, startling me. "Your room's ready. Your mom's already here." She climbs in and slams the door behind her. She looks from her cameraman to me as if picking up on what just happened.

"This is going to be a big night for a lot of people in this city." She readjusts the skirt of her dress and faces forward. "Let's go."

I reach for the van's side door, but Emi cuts me off. "We're going in the back way. More discreet." Emi hits her cameraman's arm, signaling him to drive. "National feed starts in thirty."

I slump in the folding chair once again. "Where will you be?"

"Here. We're broadcasting from another suite."

"Good," I say, wrapping my coat around me. "If I don't like what I see, I'm busting in."

Emi laughs. "I don't doubt it."

CHAPTER 31

I inhale the Albuterol and Pulmicort mist and imagine it traveling down my throat into my damaged lungs—but not to heal them. My lungs are beyond repair. The meds are meant to sustain life, until my body decides the payoff isn't worth the effort.

I was told Annie had the stronger lungs when we were born. I'll never know why hers shut down while mine kept pumping in my weak, two-pound body.

"Looks like she's on NBC," my mom says, flipping through the stations. At one point, NBC cancelled an interview with my dad. Now *Dateline* gets to air Emi's interview like they care about condemning criminals, exposing corruption.

Apparently if it yields high-enough ratings.

My mom and I sit on the king-sized bed, propped by pillows that would be comfortable if I weren't so broken. Maybe I should be nervous about what Emi's going to say in her interview. But as I watch the Botoxed broadcaster talk about a pet food recall, like what he's saying is the most important thing anyone's ever heard, I feel numb. My head rolls toward the coffee table littered with complimentary snacks: popcorn, cookies, assorted mixes, bottled water.

"Do you want something?" my mom asks. She doesn't tell me I should eat or try to assess the damage. Beneath the eyeliner and mascara, her eyes are rimmed with red, making them look greener.

I shake my head. Mist from the nebulizer seeps from my mask and billows around my face. I should be hungry, but I can't bring myself to eat. My stomach, like everything else, is hollow. My arms hang like dead weights to my sides, and my hair, still damp from the shower, falls down my back like a thick, blonde, lifeless ribbon.

Emi takes a seat across from a woman interviewing her in a room similar to ours.

My mom turns up the volume.

Behind Emi, the same painting of blue and beige chrysanthemums hangs on the wall. A banner at the bottom of the screen proclaims "Death Mob in Chicago: Exclusive Breaking News."

Instead of giving a rhapsodic exposition on the Death Mob era, a woman with pale skin and dark features jumps right into tonight's attack. She warns viewers the footage they're about to show includes a fatality, the victim's final moments.

Ryan.

I brace myself, and my mom puts her hand on top of mine.

Rioting protestors fill the screen. Whoever filmed it had an elevated vantage point. I imagine someone standing on top of a van parked on Michigan Avenue. The camera is too far away to see faces, but it's easy to spot the Initiators. They part through the protestors with ease. One of them winds up to punch Ryan, who's already charging them.

I don't realize I'm crying until everything blurs. Ryan hits first, but then he's devoured. Within seconds, he completely disappears. A flash of light explodes from inside the Swarm as the gunshot fires. The camera begins shaking as people run away. The footage cuts.

Hot tears stream down my face and pool at the base of my neck. I'm shattered, too stunned to move. My mom doesn't move either. Other than the hand resting on mine, she makes no attempt to make me feel better. She knows as well as I do, I will never feel better. Even once Emi outs Richard, and Richard is locked away forever, I will celebrate the victory but I will not feel better. I will feel hollow and damaged, scarred by everything I've seen in the last few months, just like Dr. What's-His-Name always predicted.

Emi sits in a Peninsula armchair. She looks at ease as she talks about my father, how he'd always been out to prove that the Death Mob was organized, though not by gangs, and that the victims were targeted. I should be on edge, waiting for her to announce to the world my father was right, but my body is heavy, like I could sink into the feather pillows and drown in the down comforter.

"After his murder, his daughter continued his mission. Lia Finch discovered that the Death Mob communicated through Twitter."

Emi wears a navy suit with a navy crew-cut blouse beneath it. Once again, her makeup has been toned down for national news. Emi tells the *Dateline* anchor how I began to unravel its inner workings. As she speaks, she portrays me as a hero, giving me more credit than I deserve.

I couldn't have figured it all out without Adam. And Ryan.

My insides twist. Ryan was willing to come forward. To risk his life. I think of the severe look on his face when he saw his picture, demanded

Cullen and I escape, then turned to face his attackers. Anyone else would have run.

I would have run. Or collapsed.

The *Dateline* anchor cuts in. "Lia Finch confronted Richard Stewart, Mayor Henking's chief advisor, tonight at the mayor's home after suspecting his role in organizing the Death Mob."

Emi nods.

Their conversation seems planned even though they only had twenty minutes to set up for this interview.

"Lia feared for her life. I helped her install software that turned her phone into a listening device. We did this for her protection. After recording tonight's fatal attack and sharing it with the world, she cleverly used it to record Stewart's confession."

It's not true. My plan failed. Hers didn't. But I'm too empty to care.

The screen turns blue and begins transcribing the conversation I had with Richard just over an hour ago as it plays in the background. It feels like a lifetime ago.

I barely recognize my voice. *"You run the attacks."*

"I do a lot more than that."

"You murder people."

"I keep people in line . . ." Richard sounds condescending. Like he knows he's about to kill me.

"It's all about control for you . . ." My voice is assertive, strong. But I don't remember saying any of it.

"It's not about what I want—it's about what this city needs . . . You make it all sound so simple, but I assure you, it's a lot more complicated than that."

All I remember is how certain I was that I would die.

Emi begins breaking it all down, but I miss it. The nebulizer's high-pitched whistle, indicating I've emptied all the medicine from the tiny cylinder base, is all I hear. It's been making this noise for a while. I take the mask off and flip the switch on the neb. As I do, I glance at my mom. Her face is stoic. She's always been better at holding it in than I am.

By the time I turn back to the screen, they're showing FBI agents leading Richard out of the mayor's house in handcuffs. Behind them, Detective Irving pushes reporters away as agents put Richard in the back of a dark SUV.

"He called me," my mom says, like I should know what she's talking about. "Ted Irving."

Detective Irving wears a long tweed coat. His thick, dark mustache covers his lips, which appear to be smirking.

"He filed warrants earlier tonight for the arrest of five teenagers—Initiators, he called them. He thinks they were involved in your dad's attack too."

I fall back against the pillow and take in the gravity of what she's saying. This is what I've been wanting for so long.

"Ted told me he used your live stream from the attack to identify them."

I wonder if she saw the video, what she thought about it. I lace my fingers through hers and squeeze. Hard. My voice cracks, sounding thick and phlegmy. "Would Dad be happy?"

My mom pulls a tissue from the box near the bed. "Your father would be devastated knowing you've gone through any of this."

She stares at me. Her makeup is smeared like she cried when I wasn't looking. She doesn't dab her face. Instead, she offers me the tissue. I take it and crumble it in my other hand. Then I lean against her shoulder while I watch the TV, trying to take comfort in knowing Richard is somewhere in handcuffs, and Lip Spikes might be soon.

"Do you think it's over?" I ask.

She pauses before answering with conviction. "Yes."

"The mayor might get away."

"Doesn't matter."

I close my eyes.

The second I do, screaming accosts me. I'm flung over Cullen's shoulder, crashing into hundreds of people packed together, fighting to escape. Somewhere Ryan is fighting for his life, but I'm suffocating in a sea of bodies.

Claustrophobia claws at my throat. I wrench my eyes open and gasp. Like I'm drowning, dying.

My mom cradles my head. She rakes her fingers through my hair and stays calm. She doesn't freak out. Or ask me what's wrong. She holds me. Waiting for me to realize it's not real.

"I might not be able to fight it this time." The visions. Hallucinations. They will break me after tonight. I'll spend my days at Compass, surrounded by people faulty and wrecked like me. But even with their help, I don't know how I could ever recover.

"It'll be difficult, but no one fights as hard as you." My mom chokes. She pauses, strokes my hair. "When you and your sister were born, doctors warned us. Neither of you were expected to live. You especially. Both of your lungs were collapsed. Your sister made it a week in the NICU. She fought hard, but she was so tiny." Her voice breaks. She swallows. "You were even smaller. Barely bigger than my hand. But you were so strong. You had this fight inside you, this will to live. For three months, I watched you exceed the hospital's expectations. You hated the tube that helped you breathe. So you showed us you could breathe without it. You kicked out the IV in your foot when you didn't need it anymore." She laughs. "You ripped out your feeding tube and started eating on your own before any of us thought you were ready."

I sit back to look at her. My mom's face is red, puffy, and drenched. Somehow she's more beautiful when she cries.

"Your father and I were so amazed by you. We always have been. You have more strength, more will, and more fight than anyone I've ever known."

"What if that's not who I am anymore?"

She smiles. Her eyes bend. "Strength isn't defined by who can hit the hardest in a fight, but by who's still standing at the end."

Something resembling warmth fills the cracks inside me. I should hug her, tell her I love her, tell her how much I need her to help me survive all of this. And I will when my words and my body start working again. But for now, I lean on her shoulder as she strokes my wet hair.

Outside the windows in our room, the city buzzes with life like nothing has changed. The city pulsates even though Ryan is dead and Richard is no longer in control.

I take a deep breath. Close my eyes.

That's when someone knocks on the door of our hotel room.

CHAPTER 32

Both of us freeze.

My mom swings her legs down from the bed and stands before I can even blink. She tiptoes past the sliding wood doors and into the living room. Her eyes are focused, her expression tight. She looks courageous in a way I could never pull off. Then she slips around the corner and I can't see her anymore.

My stomach sinks.

I imagine her leaning against the door and pressing her eye against the peephole. I wait for her to come running around the corner toward me, so that we can find an escape or a place to hide from the hit man at the door. I should find my phone to call the police or live stream my murder. At least then whoever's here to kill me wouldn't get away with it.

I strain my ears. Nothing.

It can't be Emi. She's still on TV. It could be the concierge or room service bringing more food we won't eat. Maybe it's Chicago police to berate me with questions. But as the seconds drag on, I'm convinced it's a hit man and that this was always the way it was going to end.

The doorknob rattles as it turns. The door opens, scraping across the carpet. The trembling begins in my hands. It snakes through my nerves until my whole body is shaking. I hold my breath, wait for my mom to talk. Whoever knocked will say something. Just as I'm about to scream, to lose control of the shaking and slip into a full-out panic attack, my mom steps into view. Her face is white with shock.

The hit man must have stabbed her. I'm about to see her body fall.

But then the door clicks shut, and Ryan steps around the corner.

He stands in front of my mom in a white T-shirt soaked in blood.

I want to trust my eyes, and I'm not sure if I should.

He walks hesitantly. He has a cut on his cheekbone in the middle of a swollen, purplish bruise. His shoulders hunch, like he's sore, but he's moving and breathing and alive.

I throw my legs off the side of the bed. I don't feel the carpet beneath my feet. My body shakes and wobbles so badly I can barely walk. I cross the hotel living room, wondering if I've somehow lost my mind, and I'm only imagining him standing in front of me covered in blood.

He lifts his arms, like he's opening them for me.

My cheeks burn as I pick up speed. Instead of collapsing into him, I shove him in the chest. "What are you doing here?"

He winces. "Lia—"

Every muscle is taught, threatening to snap. "I watched you die." I motion to shove him again, but he catches my wrists.

"I know," he whispers. "I'm sorry."

I clench my teeth, trying to contain the shake in my voice. "You let me think—" *You were dead.* But I can't say it. Because I can't believe it. Dopney. My dad. Adam. Ryan. I watched them all die. I know I did.

Ryan pulls me in and wraps his arms around me. "I'm sorry." His voice is low and coarse, and it reminds me of the first time I met him, when he threw me off the pier. He presses his lips against the side of my head just like I'd imagined in the mayor's house. It's too much. I try to push him away, determined to resist him and everything happening, but my efforts are futile. And I break.

My hands claw the back of his shirt. I sob into his shoulder. Every tendon in his back is tight. I reach around his shoulders, pulling my face into his neck, squeezing the space between us so it's nonexistent. I can't get close enough.

He must feel it too, because his arms tighten around me. One hand slides up my neck, weaves into my wet hair.

My body is weak, emotionally exhausted. I cry into his neck for longer than I should until my legs grow tired of standing.

Ryan pulls me back. "Are you hurt?" He looks me up and down, takes in the T-shirt and pajamas that were sent to our room.

I shake my head, step back. It's hard to wrap my head around it. Part of me is reluctant to believe he's alive and touching me. Like my mind has officially snapped and this is all a cruel, sadistic hallucination. "I saw you . . ." I picture the Swarm engulfing him. "I watched you die." It's all I can think and say.

I cross my arms against my chest, trying to understand, trying to remember how it happened.

Ryan's gray eyes look glossy. Shadows float beneath them, in the hollows of his cheeks. He tilts his head. "I thought it was going to be you." His jaw ripples. "All week, I thought you were the next victim. So I reached out to the names you gave me, everyone I could think of who might be forced into it, until I found enough of us to fix the whole thing."

Behind Ryan, my mom takes a seat on the sofa. She sees me notice her and looks away at the flat-screen still playing Emi's live interview.

"We planned it so once your picture was sent, we'd get to you before the Initiators. I had enough people to surround you and keep you concealed. To make it look like you were being attacked."

I reach out. My fingers graze his shirt where the blood has dried. "You're bleeding."

He flattens my hand against his chest. "It's fake."

"The gunshot?"

"Blanks." Ryan smiles just a little. "We needed a way to make everyone think you were dead and scatter." The crease between his brow deepens, making him look more vulnerable than I've ever seen him before.

I slip my hand away.

"I had a paramedic ready to take you to Northwestern and a doctor who would proclaim you were in critical condition until we figured out what to do next."

"But it wasn't me."

"When I saw my picture…" Ryan shrugs his left shoulder. "I tried to get as far away from you as I could. After the Initiators' first few hits, the plan took over. Everyone did for me what I'd asked them to do for you."

"Why didn't you tell me?"

He steps closer again, tucks my hair behind my ear.

"I should've."

I stare at the straight line of his lips and think of the night in my garage when he kissed me. I'm about to lean into him when something catches his eye, and Ryan turns toward the TV.

Emi nods her head. She looks confident as she says, "I'd imagine their next step would be looking into whether or not he acted alone…"

"Do your parents know you're okay?" my mom asks.

Ryan turns and nods. "I called my parents after I left the hospital. They don't know anything about what happened. I'm a minor. Authorities can't legally release my name or details."

"And the hospital just let you go?" I ask, drawing his attention back.

Half of Ryan's mouth lifts into a smile. "I snuck out. The Initiators got in a couple good hits, but they didn't break anything."

Ten minutes ago, I watched Ryan murdered on TV. Every inch of me ached with grief, and now he's standing in my hotel room with his square jaw, his dark brows, his perfect eyes. He's barely even injured.

"How did you find us?" my mom asks. There's concern behind her question.

"A friend of mine works with Emi Vega."

"Her cameraman," I say.

"Yeah." Ryan's lips flicker, like I've impressed him. He addresses my mom. "You don't need to worry about him telling anyone else. There are quite a few people willing to protect Lia right now. He's one of them."

Ryan nods at the TV. "What's going on?"

My mom crosses her legs and straightens her back. "Lia's responsible for many arrests tonight. She got Richard Stewart to admit he organized the Death Mob murders. And she got it on tape."

"That's not exactly what happened," I say.

Ryan stares at me with something like disbelief. I can feel the red blotches crawling up my neck and my face, spreading warmth inside me. Maybe even pride. Ryan turns back toward footage of Richard being led away in handcuffs from the mayor's house.

"You might as well take a seat," my mom says. She gives Ryan a weak smile. The last time she saw him was when she kicked him off our roof and blamed him for my father's death. "We have more than enough food here, and I have a feeling this will be on all night."

Ryan nods in appreciation.

"I didn't know Emi installed the software on my phone," I say, before he thinks too highly of me, my role in the evening. "Emi's lying. She's acting like I cornered Richard on purpose, but I didn't."

I search his face, waiting for his expression to change. But it doesn't.

My mom nods. "Tonight, this city took a step in the right direction. That's all that matters right now. We should celebrate that."

My mom walks over and squeezes my shoulder. "I'm going to take a quick shower. Don't open the door for anyone." She kisses my temple before walking back through the sliding doors and shutting them.

As soon as she does, Ryan closes the space between us. Our mouths collide. He slides his hands into my hair and holds me as he kisses me like he almost never saw me again.

When he pulls back, his face breaks into a smile, a genuine one like the first time he kissed me in my garage, and I can't help but smile back.

Emi's words cut into our moment as she ends her interview. "Thank you for having me." Both of us turn toward the TV.

"What do we do now?" I ask.

Ryan traces my face with his fingertips. "We watch Emi Vega spin her story, and every Chicago news anchor proclaim they never believed gangs were behind the Swarm. And we celebrate the small step."

I smile because he's right. And because somewhere beneath the lies is a truth my dad fought hard to uncover. Tonight we took a step toward that. This fight is far from over, and I'm not sure the healing will ever be over. But maybe that doesn't matter. Maybe that was always the way it was going to happen.

The TV flashes to Mayor Henking standing with his wife and Cullen on his porch stairs. "We are as shocked as anyone about Richard's alleged involvement in the Death Mob's murders. I assure you, we will do everything we can to cooperate and uncover the truth behind what's been going on." Cullen looks off to the left, avoiding the cameras glaring at him, in a very anti-Cullen way. Is he struggling to cope with witnessing the attack? Sulking because he didn't know about it? Pissed Richard was caught and his dad's about to be under tight scrutiny?

Reporters shout at them until one reporter's voice rises above the rest. "What was Lia Finch doing in your house tonight?"

The mayor smiles. "Ms. Finch was our guest. She is always welcome in our home."

Ryan pulls me closer. "You're never going back there."

I lean into him, knowing in my gut I'll have to. The mayor doesn't strike me as someone who gives up easily.

But neither do I. And this is a fight I'm not willing to lose.

I rest my head against Ryan's chest until I can hear his heartbeat.

And I breathe.

ACKNOWLEDGMENTS

For as long as I've dreamt of publishing my book, I've also imagined writing the acknowledgments—my chance to thank everyone who has helped me and this story get to this point. I've lost track of how many revisions this book has had and how many years it took me to complete. But my journey toward publication and becoming a serious writer started with people who believed in my story and were willing to take a chance on me.

Neil Couturier, a beautiful, talented writer himself, has believed in this story since its inception. As my go-to critique partner, he's read almost as many revisions of this book as I have, including the early and sometimes scary drafts. He's shared in every high and low and sat down with me for countless brainstorming chats. Some of my favorite lines and scenes came from those discussions. I would not be an author without his continual support and creative genius pushing me throughout this entire process.

Dawn Ius took a chance on me when she chose to mentor my manuscript in Pitch Wars. At the time I submitted it to her in 2016, the manuscript was rough. But Dawn recognized its potential and worked with me to shape it into a book. With that perfect balance of cheering for me and kicking my ass, Dawn helped me and my book become a contender.

My agent, Jenny Herrera, took a chance on me when she pulled me out of the slush. Not only did she offer me representation, which caused several fits of grateful, happy, ugly-crying, she also gave me brilliant and spot-on editorial feedback before sending me off to my revision cave to revise yet again. Both fierce and wicked smart, Jenny is the ultimate warrior, the kind you want to fight alongside and hope to never come across in battle. I cannot thank her enough for her support, her encouragement, her counsel, and her witty sense of humor. That last part should not be underestimated—in this industry, being able to laugh as often and as loudly as possible is essential to surviving it.

My team at Blink took a chance on me when they acquired my book and offered me the dream I've coveted since I was nine. A big thank you, with all the virtual hugs attached, to Sara Bierling and Jacque Alberta; their sharp insight and careful attention to detail helped me polish this book into its presentable shape. Thank you to Jillian Manning for first showing interest, and to Jennifer Hoff, Hannah VanVels, and the entire team for their enthusiasm and support.

I'm so lucky for the game-changers, who created opportunities for me I might not otherwise have. But I'm equally thankful for and humbled by how many people have influenced me and my story along the way. Thank you to the very talented author Kurt Dinan for his unwavering support, his smart critical feedback, and his ability to find humor in any setback. Every writer needs a quick-witted friend like Kurt to keep them sane. Thank you to the lovely and talented Tamara Girardi for her friendship and her ah-ha commentary several times throughout this process. Thank you to all my early and late readers—Susan Meyer, Deb Bailey, Kara McDowell, Jennifer Camiccia, Tara Creel, Keena Roberts, and Sam Taylor—for their encouragement and feedback. A huge thank you to the entire Pitch Wars community. When I first started writing, I underestimated the importance of the writing community, and now I'm not sure where I would be without it. Thank you, thank you, thank you to Brenda Drake for her unselfish comradery and support of all writers, and for creating and facilitating the Pitch Wars community and contest.

In writing this book, I had to lean on experts in technology, realty, law, asthma, and psychology. Thank you to Randy Saeks, Walter Pituc, Mario Greco, Amy Gabriel, Randy Orr, and Amy Lewis for graciously answering my questions.

Thank you to every student I've ever had who has complimented something I've written. I still remember writing a short piece for a class activity during my first year of teaching and putting it on the overhead projector (yes, that long ago). After reading it out loud, I prompted my students with a question about voice, and a seventh grader named Morrison answered by telling me I should be an author one day. I'm grateful for that indelible moment, and every lovely, indelible moment since. I've shared my writing in one way or another with my students since I started teaching. The kind words and enthusiasm they've shown has encouraged me and given me the confidence to persevere through a very long and hard process.

Thank you to my mom, who has been proud of everything I've ever written, no matter how terrible it was. In fourth grade she helped me bind my poems with those plastic, sliding bar report covers that were really big in the eighties. That year, she encouraged me to give my "published" mini anthologies as gifts to everyone I knew. In doing so, she ignited this dream of publication. Love you, Mom. Thank you to my dad, who read an early draft of this book and compared me to his favorite writer, James Patterson. Regardless of how far-fetched the compliment, it meant the world to me. Thank you both for telling every single person you've ever known that they need to buy my book. I promise you are so much better parents than the parents in this story.

Thank you to my sisters, Jackie and Sarah, who have remained on call to help me with whatever designer, social media, or Chicago-related questions I had while writing this book. Thank you for celebrating alongside me during all the fun moments and holding my hand throughout the rougher moments of writing and of life in general.

To Avery, Jake, and Mason, my little preemie: having the three of you in my life has made me better in every way. Thank you for being my constant and endless source of love, inspiration, and laughter. And finally to Marc. Thank you for supporting me, always. Thank you for making my dreams your goals. Years ago, when I told you I wanted to run a marathon, you helped me train and ran alongside me. And when I told you I wanted to publish a book, you didn't flinch. You cooked more dinners and even did an occasional load of laundry to give me more writing time. You're my biggest champion and my best friend. I feel so lucky to be sharing the journey with you.

ABOUT THE AUTHOR

Kimberly Gabriel is an English teacher who writes every chance she gets and struggles with laundry avoidance issues. When she's not teaching or writing, she's enjoying life with her husband, her three beautiful children, and a seriously beautiful boxer in the northern suburbs of Chicago.